the

spiral

DOWN

ALY MARTINEZ

The Spiral Down
Copyright © 2016 Aly Martinez

The Spiral Down is a work of fiction. All names, characters, places, and occurrences are the product of the author's imagination. Any resemblance to any persons, living or dead, events, or locations is purely coincidental.

ISBN-13: 978-1533171801
ISBN-10: 1533171807

Editor: Mickey Reed and Erin Noelle
Cover Designer: Hang Le of By Hang Le
Interior design and formatting: Stacey Blake of Champagne Formats

the

spiral

DOWN

chapter one

Henry

Rain fell from the sky in sheets. It'd only been drizzling when
I'd boarded my private jet not even a half hour earlier. Now, I
could barely see the airport outside my window.

"No, babe, it's not a big deal. I just would have liked to see you
while I was in town. It's been a while. That's all," I said, shifting the
phone to my other hand.

Dipping my finger into the empty glass that had once been the
home of gin and tonic number three, I stared at the melting ice as I
stirred it in a circle.

Her raspy, sleep-filled voice no longer sounded anything like
that of the little girl I'd met when she was only five. But, after sixteen
years, Robin Clark no longer resembled that child, either.

"I swear I thought the shower was next weekend. I got my dates
mixed up. I'm so sorry," she lied. She did that a lot.

"Don't worry about it. It's cool," I said, pretending to believe her.
I did *that* a lot.

And it killed us both a little more every time I did.

"I love you, Cookie," she whispered.

I wasn't sure if that was a lie or not anymore.

But I knew one thing was true. "I love you too, kid."

We sat in silence for several seconds, neither of us willing to hang up. However, neither of us knew what else to say. A million words hung between us, but none of them would solve anything. God knows I'd said them all over the last five years. Still, she'd never heard any of them. Not really.

With my heart physically aching, I swallowed hard and bit the bullet. "Listen, I'm about to take off. I'll be in L.A. for a show next week. Why don't you come and we'll hang out for a few days?" It was an honest invitation.

I didn't receive an honest response.

"I'll be there!"

"I'll have Carter set it up. I'll come by tomorrow afternoon and give you the details. I can't stay long, but maybe a quick dinner or something."

"Perfect."

We didn't linger with drawn-out goodbyes. A few seconds later, my phone was off and I was once again gazing out at the pouring rain, wishing I were anywhere but on a plane.

Carter, my head of security, settled in the seat beside me and opened the latest issue of *Sports Illustrated* magazine.

My stomach clenched when the plane jerked as we backed away from the gate.

"Tell Levee I love her, okay?" I said to Carter without dragging my eyes off the terminal disappearing in the distance.

"Here we go," he mumbled, closing his magazine and turning his attention my way.

"Can you do me a huge favor? If I don't survive, make sure it's open casket and I'm wearing—"

"Blue. It makes your eyes pop," he finished for me.

"Right, but—"

"But your eyes will be closed, so you should wear green instead. It looks better with your complexion."

"Yes, but—"

"But your complexion will be ashy since you're dead and all. So let's just go with a sleek, black suit. It's timeless." He arched an incredulous eyebrow.

Lifting my glass in the air, I rattled the ice at Susan, my personal flight attendant. She was busy buckling herself in for takeoff, but she flashed me a warm, motherly smile in acknowledgement that she had seen me.

"So maybe we've had this conversation before," I told Carter.

He rolled his eyes. "Every time we fly."

I huffed but didn't bother explaining. He knew exactly how terrified of flying I was. He'd been there the day it'd all begun.

You would have thought that, after having traveled the globe for years, a simple two-hour flight wouldn't have been a problem. My racing heart and sweating palms argued otherwise.

In the eight years since my career had taken off, I'd gone from a somewhat-popular YouTube personality to the king of the music industry when Levee and I'd released our self-produced debut album, *Dichotomy*. Filled with half of her tracks and half of mine, it had soared to the top of the charts. There hadn't been a radio station in the country not playing our music. In a matter of weeks, our careers had exploded, which had forced the whole world to take notice.

The following years had been a whirlwind. Grammys, record deals, fame, fortune, *security*. I could have retired six months after I'd started and never wanted for anything again. Well, that's not totally true. The one thing I really wanted could never be bought.

I wasn't even sure it could be earned.

It was something so rare that I feared it didn't actually exist.

Love. Unconditional. Unwavering. Eternal. *Love.*

I'd given that to exactly two people in my life.

I'd only received it in return from one.

I'd been born a gay man. There had never been a moment in my life when I'd been remotely sexually attracted to women. If I had been, I would have married Levee Williams the second I'd laid eyes on her. Because I'd known, just that fast, that she was going to be the best thing that ever happened to me.

And she had been.

Riding the state's dime to college, I'd branched out on my own at eighteen, armed with nothing more than a guitar and a headful of mediocre lyrics.

In a lot of ways, alone felt better.

In most, it felt worse.

Luckily, within weeks of starting my new adventure, I'd met Levee at a local bar on amateur night. She wouldn't admit it, but she'd been attempting to hit on me when she'd first strutted over after her set. I understood how she'd misinterpreted my intense stare while she'd performed. But, when her kind, brown eyes lit as our gazes met, I knew, straight or gay, I needed to meet that woman. That night, over beers and more laughs than I had ever experienced, we bonded over music. Less than two weeks later, I moved in with her. Part of my heart bound to hers in a way I had never felt before. With no parents, no siblings, not even a foster mother who'd taken a liking to me, I'd spent most of my life searching for the sense of belonging she gave me only minutes after we'd met.

I fiercely loved that crazy woman. And it amplified as the years passed when I realized the feeling was mutual.

Levee was more than my best friend. Outside of Robin, she was the only family I'd ever had.

Which really meant she was the *only* true family I'd ever had.

I'd heard that God wasn't exactly stoked about homosexuality, but come on. What kind of a masochist sends a gay man his soul mate with boobs and a vagina?

Especially considering she was now married to Sam Rivers and six months pregnant with his baby girl.

I'd tried dating over the years, but the few men I'd found interesting had found me temporary. I was good for a night of fulfilling their secret fantasies. But that's where it ended. I guess that's what I got for having a thing for straight men. I couldn't stop myself though. It wasn't the sex. As a celebrity, I had plenty of men vying for my attention. Ass was easy to come by. But the high that came from being with a straight man, knowing he was going against his own genetic coding just for one night with me, made every minute of the pain worth it.

Those forbidden encounters were a drug.

And I was a junkie.

The hunt of finding that perfect blend of brute masculinity and subtle curiosity.

The chase of teasing and taunting, ramping them up until they were unable to get my clothes off fast enough.

The victory as they finally broke, giving in to the one desire they had never considered before they'd landed in my crosshairs.

That was the high.

But it was always followed by the crash.

Including the inevitable spiral down when they realized what they had done.

Some freaked, slinging insults and threats at me as if I had somehow magically cast a spell and charmed their dick into my mouth. Some wore their shame on their faces, gathering their clothes and rushing from the room without a backward glance. Some felt the high too and came back for seconds, desperate for more.

But they all left, one way or another.

Always.

Once I'd accepted that those encounters were nothing more than a fix, it'd stopped gutting me when they walked away.

While I'd had my fair share of partners, I was far from a whore. I didn't launch my expert skills of seduction on any straight man who crossed my path. That would have been a wasted effort. I was good; don't doubt that. But men didn't just fall naked into my bed, begging for me to take their bodies in ways they would never forget. At least, not the men I wanted. It took patience and dedication to achieve my high.

I spent two years working my way into a certain NFL quarterback's bedroom.

Worth every single second.

Or so I'd told myself as I'd felt another piece of my soul break away when he'd dismissed me from his life the very next day.

Maybe I was a whore after all.

But I'd tried the relationship thing and it just didn't work.

I'd given my heart to a man once. He'd given it back a month later.

I was devastated when he left. I was ruined when, two months later, I watched him marry a woman I knew he didn't love.

No. That's not true. It was me he didn't love.

That was a common theme in my life and exactly why I was so successful as a singer-songwriter. It was hard to be all "woe is me" with millions of adoring fans acting as if you were a god who'd returned to Earth.

While Levee struggled with the weight of her fame, I flourished under the spotlight. I was alive on stage. And, with no one waiting for me at home, I'd devoted years to touring. The roar of the crowd fueled my happiness to the point I feared the day when I would have to settle down.

And, right then, I was white-knuckle gripping the armrest as the jet accelerated down the runway before lifting into the sky.

"Shit. Shit. Shit," I mumbled as my stomach dropped when the landing gear loudly locked into place.

"You're fine," Carter said absently.

I was absolutely not fine.

"I'm gonna puke," I groaned.

His eyes never lifted from the pages of his magazine as he shook a vomit bag open and passed it my way.

"Thanks," I replied, disingenuous.

"No problem. Now, take a deep breath and try to relax. We'll be there in no time."

As the plane leveled out, so did my stomach.

Blowing out a loud breath, I dropped my head back against the headrest. "We should've taken the bus."

"There wasn't time for the bus. Your ass is supposed to be on stage in four hours. What we shouldn't have done is drive to San Francisco in the first place."

"We've been over this. I wasn't missing her baby shower."

He grumbled, adjusting in his seat. "I think Levee and Sam would've understood."

I narrowed my eyes and turned to glare at him. "Don't even start with me. They would have understood perfectly. But that doesn't change the fact that I *wanted* to be there."

My tour had been scheduled over a year in advance. Tickets had sold out in less than five minutes. But none of that had mattered when I'd found out that Sam's mom was planning a baby shower for Levee. I had very few priorities in life. However, being there for her was always one of them.

Susan approached my seat. "Can I get you another drink, Mr. Alexander?"

"Thank God. Yes!" I lifted my glass in her direction.

"No problem." Her eyes nervously shifted to Carter. "A word?"

Carter unbuckled his seat belt and moved past me. They huddled together behind the small bar in the front, but my focus was on the mini bottle of gin she was emptying in my glass. I was well aware that I needed to slow down. Drunk on stage wasn't exactly a novelty in my business, but slurring my words and stumbling over lyrics were a deal breaker for me.

Just as I was about to tell her to hold off on the drink, the plane suddenly jerked and my nerves skyrocketed all over again. I sucked in a sharp breath, and both sets of their concerned eyes jumped to mine.

Yep. I can sober up later.

Snapping my fingers, I ordered, "Drink."

Susan smiled compassionately before shooting an impatient glare at Carter. I would have cared what they were whispering about if I hadn't been about to pull an Incredible Hulk and peel out of my own skin.

"I'll tell him," Carter relented with a sigh, tagging the drink from her hand and then moving in my direction.

With shaking hands, I took the glass and tipped it back for a sip, relishing in the distracting burn in my chest.

"Tell me what?" I asked, settling the glass in a cup holder.

He motioned his chin at my drink. "Why don't you finish that first?"

The clear liquid sloshed as the plane suddenly banked to the left.

"Excellent idea," I said.

Carter's gaze once again lifted to Susan's in a silent conversation. Her lips thinned.

Throwing the rest of my drink back, I bounced my attention back and forth between the two of them. Susan looked downright nervous, and Carter appeared more than a little annoyed.

"Okay, what the hell is going on with you two?" I demanded.

"The pilot is having some chest pains," he announced.

Suddenly, there wasn't enough gin in the world.

Fighting to make my seat belt tighter, I gasped, "Did he pass out? Are we going down?"

Carter's expression remained impassive.

"Of course not!" Susan cut in.

Her reassurance did little to comfort me, because whatever magical mechanism kept the cabin pressurized suddenly failed. If the pain in my lungs was any indication, there was absolutely no oxygen left on that plane. We were all going to die.

Carter's heavy paw landed on my back, pushing my torso down so my head was between my knees.

"Calm down and breathe. We aren't going down. The copilot is taking us back to San Francisco. We'll be on the ground in no time."

The vise on my lungs didn't loosen.

Still hunched over, I nodded, having heard his words but finding no relief in them.

Susan kneeled beside me. "It's okay, Henry. Co-captain Baez is an amazing pilot. You won't even know the difference." She rubbed my back.

Embarrassment mingled with the worthlessness I felt in that moment. But I was helpless to reel it in. My body was out of control. I was left as nothing more than a marionette being held captive by my fear.

Reaching out, I gripped Carter's thigh desperately searching for a way to ground myself.

The man was a beast. At six-five and well over three hundred pounds, with short, black hair and nearly black eyes, he looked every bit of the scary bodyguard I'd hired him to be. There wasn't anything soft or gentle about him. However, he'd been with me for almost a decade. He knew how I worked, even if he didn't like it.

He patted my hand, and then I heard the crinkle of his magazine opening.

"You'll be fine," he said.

I wasn't sure he was right.

chapter two

Evan

"Stay." **I caught** her arm.

She sniffled, the unshed tears still lingering in her eyes. "I can't."

I stood, pushing off my couch, and followed her toward the door. "Nikki, please."

"I can't do this. I love you, Evan. *Love*," she stressed in case I'd missed it the last five times she'd said it. "I'm sorry if you don't feel the same way."

I closed my eyes and shook my head. I'd known it was coming. She'd been hinting at it for weeks—almost saying the words before chickening out when I'd abruptly change the subject. Today, she'd caught me though. And I'd had nothing to say in return. *I care about you* doesn't quite have the same ring to it as *I love you too*.

Nikki and I had been dating for six months. Sleeping together for seven. Unofficially living together for two. But, up until thirty seconds ago, we had never uttered those three magical words.

Actually, I had only used those words one other time in my life. And the scars from that mistake still covered my heart. Nikki didn't know they existed, but she was paying for them all the same. I wasn't going to lie to her just for the sake of sparing her feelings. The world was fake enough without artificial emotions being tossed around.

Darting in front of her, I blocked her path to the door. "Don't leave like this."

"Right. And what? You just want me to stay in *your* house knowing you'll never feel the same way I do."

"I didn't say I'd never feel the same." Deep down, I knew I wouldn't. But I figured that information wasn't going to help my case.

Nikki was an incredible woman. Beautiful. Sweet. Funny. Smart. I loved spending time with her. I loved coming home from a long flight and knowing she was at home waiting for me. I *loved* the way her body felt underneath mine.

I just didn't love *her*.

We had an undeniable connection, but it didn't overwhelm me. Thoughts of her didn't consume me. Nor did carnal need set me ablaze.

Nikki was the spark, but she wasn't the fire.

But maybe love didn't have to be a wildfire burning out of control, devouring you until there was nothing left of you for anyone else.

But that's all I'd ever known it to be.

Maybe the level of comfort I shared with Nikki was what true love really was. Maybe it was standing in front of me and I'd set my expectations too high. Maybe I was about to watch the best thing that had happened to me since college walk out of my life just because it didn't hurt enough to feel like love.

Maybe.

But the ice that encased my heart told me it wasn't.

I needed the flames. I needed the burn. I needed the undeniable explosion.

Her chin quivered as her lips tipped up in a half smile. "Can I move in with you then?"

I blinked in confusion. "Nik, you basically already live here."

She took a step toward me. "No. I mean…can I *move* in with you, Evan? No *basically*. No *practically*. Can I pay the electric bill and give up my apartment?"

My pulse spiked. I didn't realize I had taken a step away until she moved toward me.

"That's what I thought," she whispered, fighting back more tears. "Move, Evan. I need to go."

"Wait." I sidestepped to stop her. What the fuck was I doing? *Let her go, jackass.*

Guilt lodged in my gut as I stared into her red-rimmed eyes. Scanning through every possible excuse, I tried to find the right words that would keep her with me without having to lie to her face. I wanted nothing more than to return her feelings. I would have sold my soul just to feel the fire again.

But I'd never feel it with her.

I was only fighting the inevitable. "We at least need to talk. Are you coming back?"

She sucked in a shaky breath. "I don't know."

Raking a hand through my hair, I told her the most honest thing I had to offer. "I don't want you to leave."

She cupped my cheek and peered into my eyes. "I don't want to leave, either." The pain etched across her face told me it was the truth. The resolve in her stiff body told me it was going to happen anyway.

"Nik, come on," I said like a dumbass.

She wasn't being irrational. She had just realized she wasn't ever going to get what she wanted from me. And yet there I stood, asking her to stay anyway.

"Let me go, Evan," she breathed. The deeper meaning of her

statement wasn't lost on me.

Pain sliced through me, but short of lying and discrediting everything I had ever felt, I had no other choice.

My hand fell away, and seconds later, she was gone.

"Son of a bitch," I growled, banging the heel of my hand against my front door.

The sound of her car pulling out of my driveway rumbled in my ears—and my heart.

Nikki was the best thing I'd had in years. Yet it still hadn't been enough. Nothing was, and it was exhausting.

This was for the best.

It just didn't feel like the best though.

It fucking hurt.

After snatching my phone out of my pocket, I typed out a text letting her know I would be there when she was ready to talk. If she wanted to leave, I couldn't stop her. But I wasn't going to let things end like that, either. I owed that much to both of us.

Twenty minutes later, my eyes were aimed at the football game playing on TV, but my mind was elsewhere.

On Nikki.

On my past.

On my life.

On my future.

Lost.

I'd woken up that morning content. Not happy. But I'd had nothing to complain about.

Now, I felt nothing but unease.

My phone rang, and I immediately snatched it up off the table. "Nik?" I answered without looking at the caller ID.

"Roth? It's Jackson. I need you at the airport in twenty minutes."

"Sorry, sir. I'm off today."

"Not anymore. I've got a private jet, a rock star on a timeline, and no pilot."

Sitting up, I asked, "What happened to Craig? I thought that was his flight?"

He sighed. "It was. Chest pains. Baez turned it around. Listen, he's fine. But I need a captain in that cockpit in thirty minutes or Air Traffic Control can't fit us back in for hours. Now, get dressed and get your ass up here, or you're fired. I absolutely cannot afford to lose this guy. He owns his own plane and uses us exclusively. It's the closest thing to free money that exists. Oh, and this guy is terrified of flying, I need you smooth up there."

I rolled my eyes. It could have been raining bullets from the sky and I still could have landed that thing on a motherfucking postage stamp. I didn't need a reminder on how to fly.

"Right. Smooth."

"I'm serious, Roth. Jump your cocky ass off your pedestal and do me a solid here."

Weighing my decision, I glanced back at the door as if Nikki might barge through it at any minute. She wouldn't. She'd have to come back and get her stuff eventually, but it wasn't going to be today. No point in waiting. Flying was the only thing that could make me feel better.

Pushing off the couch, I started toward my bedroom. "I'll be there."

Hurry up and wait.

I'd made it to the airport in plenty of time, but due to the heavy rains in the area, all flights had been delayed. Air traffic was backed up for at least an hour.

I wished I'd stopped to grab some food on my way. I was starving, but the tiny, private airport wasn't exactly brimming with restaurants.

After dropping a few coins in the vending machine, I made my selection then once again checked my cell phone.

Nikki hadn't replied to my text. And the more time that passed, the more I worried she wasn't going to.

Not if she's smart.

"Shit," I mumbled to myself as my dinner became stuck behind the glass.

Suddenly, a man's yell snapped my attention from the snack machine. "No!"

A tall guy with messy, blond hair was staring at me from the other end of the hall. His hands were fisted at his sides, but his eyes were wide with absolute terror.

"No," he repeated on an eerie whisper.

I quirked an eyebrow. "Uhhh," I drawled before looking over my shoulder to see who he was talking to.

When my search came up empty, I glanced back in his direction and found that a behemoth had sidled up beside him. At six-two and two hundred pounds, I was a big guy. But I could only assume that this guy went by the name of Brutus, Butch, or Damien.

"Henry," the giant warned.

The obviously frazzled man strode forward, closing in on me. He was an inch shorter than I was, but while my frame held bulk, his was lean with a toned, muscular build. How a simple pair of jeans, a black V-neck T-shirt, and a pair of boots screamed money, I'd never understand. But he might as well have left dollar bills instead of footprints on the tile as he stormed toward me.

Squaring my shoulders, I stood my ground. "You need something?"

"Please, God, tell me you're not my new pilot."

Ah, yes. The spoiled rock star.

It didn't take but a second for me to recognize him. Hell, most people could have identified Henry Alexander. He was about as famous as they came and had been on the cover of every magazine over the last few years. The moment he released a new single, radio stations across the country joined forces to cram it down the throats of Americans everywhere. His music was good—the first five hundred thousand times. After that….

There was no denying he was a superstar. Women adored him, despite the fact that he was openly gay.

My heart sank at the thought.

Nikki loved this guy. She would have died if she knew he was my passenger today. Something I'd probably never get the chance to tell her.

"No way you're a pilot," he said when I failed to answer.

I'd already been in a shit mood, but thoughts of Nikki only made it worse.

I smiled condescendingly and then smoothed down the white shirt of my uniform. "Nah, but I figured I'd give it a try." I popped a shoulder in a half shrug. "It can't be that hard, can it?"

It was a joke. But, judging by the way his face paled, it wasn't even remotely humorous.

"Carter," he choked out, bending over and propping his hands on his knees.

"Seriously?" Carter, whose name I was disappointed to find didn't fit him at all, said to me as he marched forward. "He's kidding," he informed the drama queen.

"I'm kidding," I echoed when Henry began hyperventilating. "I've been flying for years."

"He…" He stood up, but his chest continued to heave. "He's an infant."

"He's a pilot with an impeccable record," Carter replied.

"No," Henry wheezed.

"It's either this guy or cancel the show. We don't have time.

You're already going to be late. The Red Dot agreed to extend their set until we can get you there, but I don't think your fans are going to like eight hours of an opening act so we can drive."

"Then cancel the fucking show," he ordered, standing up straight but no less panicked. "I'm not going with this guy. Call Jackson and tell him either he finds me someone other than Doogie Howser or I'll take my business elsewhere."

Shit. Jackson was going to hand me my ass if I lost this guy. And I kind of needed a job. I'd become pretty attached to that whole eating thing.

"Okay. Wait. I'm sorry. Let's start over." I extended a hand toward him. "Hi. I'm Evan Roth. I'll be your captain today. I'm thirty-one, but I've been flying for most of my life. My stepfather was a pilot, and we had a small plane he used to let me copilot as a child. When I was eighteen, he helped me get my license. I was qualified to fly commercial liners before I was even old enough to drink. My parents were partial to college though. We compromised on the Air Force Academy." I shrugged and tossed him a half smile. "I did three overseas deployments before getting out of the military almost a year ago."

He didn't look impressed, so I continued.

"I have a degree in engineering, but I knew the only job I ever wanted was in the sky. I've been living that dream for over a decade now. I promise you couldn't be in better hands today."

"A decade," he scoffed. "A decade? Craig has been flying for almost thirty years. And you want me to put my life in the hands of a novice? No fucking way."

It wasn't professional in the least, but I couldn't help but laugh. "Well, he does have me on hours clocked. However, I have him in pretty much every other way possible. I'm younger. My mind is sharper. My reaction time is quicker. If there was any kind of problem, a half a second could make all the difference. I have twenty-twenty vision—no contacts or glasses needed. I'm in perfect health, so you won't have to worry about chest pains or any other kind of illness while we are up there. And above and beyond all that, I own the sky." I pointed to the ceiling. "You may feel safer on solid ground, but up there, that's my home."

It was his turn to laugh. "You own the sky?" He turned to Carter and laughed again. "Who the hell is this guy? No. Just. No."

"Jesus," Carter swore at the ceiling.

Turning on a heel, he called out, "Thanks, but no, thanks, Maverick."

After rolling my eyes at his nickname, I gave my attention back to Carter. "Look, don't call Jackson. I'll call one of the other guys and see if they can get here in time. I'm sorry. I didn't know he was going to freak like that."

Holding my gaze, he banged on the glass of the vending machine, freeing my chips. "We have no time for that shit. Be on the plane in fifteen minutes."

"You sure that's going to be a good idea? I'm not real fond of emergency landings due to a passenger trying to claw their way out of a window."

"He'll be fine. Just fly the damn plane"—he paused, and a patronizing smile grew on his lips—"Maverick."

"Awesome," I breathed with sarcasm.

I watched him walk away in the same direction Henry had left. Before the door clicked, I heard him mock, "I own the sky."

Out-fucking-standing.

chapter three

Henry

"See? That wasn't so bad." I tossed Carter a weak smile when the plane slowed to a roll.

He glared at me. "My leg is numb."

Quickly removing my death grip on his thigh, I replied, "You have health insurance, right? Maybe you should get that checked out."

His glare transformed into a scowl.

After my mini meltdown in front of our pilot, Carter had literally dragged me onto the plane. It wasn't the first time he'd ever had to do it. And it definitely wouldn't be the last. But, in the end, he'd been right. I was fine. Drunk after having chugged three more gin and tonics, but fine nonetheless.

The flight had been remarkably uneventful. Which really just meant it'd been only mildly terrifying. Our pilot had managed to get us on the ground fifteen minutes ahead of schedule. I was still going to be late for the show, but at least my openers wouldn't have to extend their set by more than a few songs. Well, assuming I could sober up in time.

"Let's go," Carter announced as soon as the door was open.

"How far to the venue?" I slurred, scrubbing my hands over my face.

"Less than an hour. You need coffee," he said, snapping his fingers at Susan.

She appeared seconds later with a steaming paper cup filled to the brim.

"Thanks."

She smiled warmly, patting me on the arm. "I put a bottled water and a sandwich in your bag too. Eat it. The food will help."

I returned her smile and draped an arm around her shoulders. "Any chance you're single, Susan? My current wife is failing on his wifely duties." I glanced at Carter and waggled my eyebrows.

She shook her head and slapped my chest. "Have a good concert. I'll see you in the morning."

"Fantastic. Another flight. I can't wait," I deadpanned.

Carter nabbed his carry-on and tossed my backpack to me. His eyes traveled over me before he blew out a loud breath. "You look like shit. Let's hope Macy can work a miracle on the way over."

"You sure know how to make a man feel good about himself," I smarted before taking a sip of the coffee.

He was probably right. God knows I felt like shit.

Shrugging my backpack on, I followed him to the exit.

"How'd it go back there?" I heard Ethan, or whatever the hell our pilot's name was, ask, but Carter's massive body blocked him from my view.

"Great. Thanks, man," Carter replied, patting him on the shoulder and then stepping out of the small door.

Focusing on not spilling my coffee, I shuffled after him.

"I see you survived unscathed," the pilot said to me as I passed, his voice thick with humor.

Keeping my gaze down, I dropped a pair of sunglasses over my eyes even though the sun had set hours earlier. "Yeah. Thanks. And…ya know, sorry about earlier." It was a halfhearted apology, but my mind was on my show and how the hell I was planning to pull it off if I didn't get my shit together—soon.

"It's no problem. I should be the one apologizing. That joke was out of line."

"Make whatever joke you want as long as you get me safely on the ground. See you in the morning," I said dismissively, jogging down the stairs. My stomach sloshed from the movement. "Ugh," I groaned, folding my hands over my midsection and heading straight to the limo door that Carter was holding open for me. "I feel like death."

"You don't look much better," my hair and wardrobe stylist, Macy, said as I slid into the seat beside her.

I moaned, leaning down to rest my head in her lap. "Carter says I need a miracle."

"And a breath mint," she corrected, pulling a small metal tin from her bag and popping one in my open mouth. She tangled her fingers in my hair as I closed my eyes.

It had been a crazy-long day, and add two panic attacks and what felt like a gallon of gin and tonic into the mix and I was spent.

"Well, the good news is your hair is supposed to look like you've slept on it for a week," she said. "Bad news—it takes at least an hour for me to make it look like that."

"I can live with bad hair. Just let me sleep," I pleaded, stretching my legs across the seat.

I heard Carter climb in the other door right before I felt the car pull away.

"If you promise to give me fifteen minutes before we get there, you can relax for now," she said, scratching the top of my head.

"Mmm," I hummed.

"Oh, and hey. I managed to get Robin that new Hermès bag she wanted. It should have been delivered earlier this afternoon."

Whatever sleepiness I'd been feeling left me on a rush. My eyes popped open wide, my gaze landing directly on Carter, who was sitting diagonally across from me. His expression of concern matched mine.

"What bag?"

"The Hermès. She called last week and said you told her to call me since it hadn't been released yet."

I swallowed hard and immediately pushed myself out of her lap. "Who paid for it?" I asked Macy while holding Carter's gaze.

"I put it on your account." Her gaze swung to Carter before turning back on me. "Shit. Was I not supposed to do that? She said it was cool with you."

"How much?" I asked ominously.

She chewed on her bottom lip. "Well, I mean, the collection hasn't been released to the public yet. I got it at a steal."

Clenching my teeth, I lost my temper. "How fucking much, Macy?"

"Ten grand," she squeaked.

Carter and I both cursed in unison.

His phone was at his ear before I'd dug mine from my back pocket.

"I talked to her before we took off…the first time. She seemed fine," I informed him.

"I'm on it. Get some rest and sober up," he replied.

That was going to be impossible though.

The drone of Robin's unanswered phone echoed in my ear as I continuously pressed redial. The shock of adrenaline was more sobering than any cup of coffee, shower, or nap possible.

"Henry," Macy started. "I'm really sorry. I had no idea it would be an issue. I mean, I've done stuff like that for her in the past."

It was a *huge* issue, but it wasn't her fault.

"No. I know. It's okay." I slid my arm around her shoulders and pulled her into my side.

"What's going on?" she whispered as I once again caught Robin's voicemail.

"Nothing you need to worry about."

Mainly because, until I got in touch with Robin, I was going to do enough worrying for everyone.

The show had been a disaster. I'd more than sobered up on the way over to the arena, but I had been left with a splitting headache. There was a reason I didn't drink liquor very often. That "very often" being exclusively limited to when I was forced to fly.

I couldn't imagine how I had sounded as I'd aimlessly wandered around the stage. Sure, I was naturally talented, but most of my success was directly linked to my charisma in front of an audience. Performing was in my blood. Usually, I couldn't be dragged off the stage at the end of a concert. However, that night, I couldn't get out of there fast enough.

Robin weighed heavily on my mind.

She still wasn't answering the phone, and Carter's guys had come up empty-handed at her apartment.

She was gone.

Again.

And I was gutted.

Again.

After a phone call to my assistant, I managed to get our departure time out of San Francisco moved up to first thing the next morning. I needed to get back to check on her. Then I needed to hit the road later that afternoon if I was going to make my next tour stop—the thought of getting back on the bus being the only thing that relaxed me.

I loved life on the road.

Just not in the air.

"Calm down," Carter growled.

I blinked. I was on the verge of passing out. I wasn't sure I could get much calmer than out cold.

"Commercial," I whispered around the lump in my throat.

"We had no other choice."

"I own a private jet," I returned, doing my best to keep from falling apart. It was a lost cause. I'd been a wreck since we'd first arrived at the airport.

"Right now, you own a broken private jet. Call me crazy, but I'm thinking I'd rather travel on a plane that passed inspection this morning."

My hands trembled as I lifted a bloody mary to my lips. I didn't give a single damn that it wasn't even seven in the morning yet. We'd been alerted at five that my plane wasn't going anywhere. Carter had assured me that I had nothing to worry about. I'd assumed he had secured another plane. I'd just never considered he hated me enough to make it a commercial flight.

Not only had the paparazzi and fans stormed me the second I'd exited the limo, but I'd had to fight my way through security and a never-ending terminal in order to voluntarily buckle myself into a flying metal coffin. Then, to top it all off, they didn't have gin and tonic.

If that wasn't a sign of impending doom, I wasn't sure what was.

"I can't do this," I said, yanking my seat belt off and fighting to my feet.

His heavy hand landed on my back, forcing me back into my seat and then shoving me down so my head rested on my knees.

"Deep breath. You're gonna be fine."

"A fiery death is rarely considered fine," I choked out.

"Just breathe."

"I can't'!" I struggled against Carter's pressure on my back, knocking my drink from the cup holder and into his lap.

"Son of a…" he seethed. "Relax."

"Let's rent a car, " I argued as I broke into a full-body sweat.

"Robin has a ten-thousand-dollar purse and hasn't been seen or heard from since yesterday. You have a sold-out venue to be at tomorrow, and unless you've unlocked the magic of adding hours into a day, we don't have time to drive home. Now, you can get your ass off this plane and drive. But you will be doing it alone."

I gritted my teeth.

The legs of a flight attendant appeared at Carter's side. "I brought you some napkins, sir." She paused. "Would…uh…Mr. Alexander like another bloody mary?"

"You happen to have anything a little stronger hidden back there? Maybe a fistful of Valium?" he asked, not a drip of humor in his voice.

"Don't even think about it!" I spat at the floor.

Carter groaned. "Yes. He'd *love* another drink."

"Of course." She stalled for a minute as if she'd never seen a grown man in the middle of panic attack being physically restrained by his bodyguard before.

Fucking amateur.

"How's it going?" a man in a pair of jeans asked as his legs stopped at our row.

"Just another day on the job." Carter's hand squeezed my back as he started chuckling.

"And I thought my job was fun." The deep, masculine voice laughed.

And, quite honestly, it pissed me off. "Move the fuck along," I bit out.

They both ignored me.

"Glad they were able to get you on a flight."

"Yeah. We're back in coach. He gonna be okay?"

"I guess…" Carter started when a loud boom made me jump.

Sitting straight up, I yelled, "What the fuck was that?" My voice echoed off the overhead bins in first class.

"Luggage hatch closing," the guy answered immediately.

I peered nervously out my window. "How can you be sure it wasn't the wing falling off?"

He barked a laugh, but I didn't spare him a glance.

"In my experience, wings don't just randomly fall off. Especially not while sitting at the gate."

"Right," I whispered, smashing my cheek against the window, searching for the wing anyway.

"Well, I'm gonna go sit down. Have a good flight."

Carter harrumphed. "Not likely. But I'll try.

The guy's laugh disappeared as the flight attendant reappeared with my drink. I hastily chugged it down.

She hadn't walked away when another loud bang sounded.

"What the fuck are they doing out there? Strapping explosives on the wings?"

"Jesus Christ!" Carter hissed. "Can you go ahead and bring another?" he asked. "Hold the tomato juice."

"Is he going to be okay?" she whispered as if I hadn't been sitting inches away.

"Why does everyone keep asking that? Do I look like I'm going to be okay? No! I am absolutely not going to be okay. But guess what? I'll be a hell of a lot closer to okay if you'd hurry up with that drink."

I'd barely finished my rant before my drink was gone from my hand and Carter was shoving my face back down to my knees.

"He'll be great. I promise."

"Grrrrrrrreat!" I told my legs with a manic laugh.

"Would you fucking stop?" he snarled in my ear. "I swear to God, if you get us kicked off this flight, I will kill you. We have to get home. Take a deep breath, grab your fucking balls, and act like a man. It's a flight. Not a death march."

Another loud bang made me flinch.

"What the hell was that?"

He sighed. "Man. Up."

"I'd like to meet the pilot before we take off. Get his credentials and all. Maybe he's willing to take a bribe."

"A bribe? Henry, if the plane crashes, he's going to be dead too. I'm pretty sure survival is more than enough incentive for him."

"Maybe, but what if he has a massive gambling debt and needs the life insurance money to take care of his twelve children and handicapped wife?"

He blew out a suffering sigh. "Look, do you think it would make you feel better to know what those sounds are? I mean, if someone could assure that there is nothing to worry about?"

"I don't know…" I snapped before sucking in a resigned breath. "Just…tell Levee I love her, okay?"

"Dear God," he mumbled as his grip on my back disappeared.

I sat up with enough time to see him walk out of first class.

chapter four

Evan

With my baseball cap pulled low over my eyes, I attempted to stretch my legs out in the three inches of space the airline had graciously allowed me. I would have given my left nut for a seat in the emergency exit row. The plane was packed, but I was biding my time, waiting for a chat with the flight attendant to see if I could schmooze my way into an open window seat. For a guy my size, being stuck in a middle seat, sandwiched between two other men, was only slightly above the seventh level of Hell. But I guessed, when the company buys you a ticket hours before takeoff, you get what you get.

I would have way rather been in the cockpit of my own plane, but I didn't have time to wait around for the repairs to be made. I needed to get home and see if I could grab another flight for Jackson. Broken plane or not, a charter pilot didn't get paid unless he actually flew. I needed the money. *Part time* was exactly as *partially lucrative* as it sounded.

"Need a favor, Roth."

Pushing my hat up, I found Carter hunched over in the aisle and staring down at me.

"Sure. What's up?"

After retrieving his wallet from his back pocket, he pushed some bills in my direction. "Two hundred bucks. Switch seats with me and talk him through takeoff."

"I'm sorry. What?" I asked before glancing at the hairy guy to my left, who was clearly unaware that deodorant had been invented.

"He's flipping out up there and, quite honestly, I don't know what the hell to tell him. We need to get home. But, right now, either he's going to get kicked off for acting like a maniac or I'm going to smother him with a six-inch courtesy pillow." He stopped to give me a shrug that said he wasn't kidding. "I'm thinking, if he had someone to explain what was going on, he could keep his shit together. If not, we'll still have the pillow as a backup plan."

My eyes slid to the men on either side of me before I popped my eyebrows in question. "You want to pay me two hundred bucks to move to first class?"

"No, I want to pay you two hundred bucks to talk bullshit about planes."

I smirked then plucked the money from his hands. "What do you know—plane bullshit just happens to be my specialty."

He backed up to allow me out of the row. "You have any experience in crisis negotiation?"

I tipped my head to the side. "Should I?"

He shrugged and clamped his hand on my shoulder. "Couldn't hurt. Good luck up there."

"Uh…thanks," I said skeptically.

He seemed entirely too excited to squeeze his mammoth body into a tiny-ass economy seat.

Whatever. Better him than me.

He shared my feelings.

"Better you than me!" he called out with a laugh as I headed up front.

I got the feeling two hundred bucks, extra leg room, and free drinks weren't going to be an upgrade at all.

And my suspicions were confirmed as I made my way through the magical curtain of opulence that divided first class from the commoners.

Yep. I'd been duped.

"I need a drink. *Now!*" Henry yelled.

Yes. Yelled.

"Sir, you've already had two and we haven't even taken off yet," the busty, redheaded flight attendant said as the other passengers watched on—a few snapping pictures with their cell phones.

"Which only makes my glass that much more empty." He pushed to his feet, and if his glossed-over eyes were any indication, the last thing he needed was another drink.

"Hey. Hey. Hey." I stepped in front of him before he had the chance to exit his row. Placing a hand on his chest, I gently pushed him back. "Let's hold off on the drinks until we get in the air…and maybe back on the ground."

His gaze menacingly drifted down to my hand. "Don't fucking touch me," he whispered as his solid pec flexed against my palm.

I cocked a challenging eyebrow. "Not a problem as long as you sit down and stop acting like an entitled asshole."

He held his ground and studied my face for a moment before yelling, "Carter!"

Yes. Yelled. Again.

Inches from my face.

In the middle of a plane loaded with passengers.

The sound echoed off the overhead bins, assaulting me repeatedly before fading away.

Clenching my teeth, I peeked over my shoulder at the nervous flight attendant and tossed her an encouraging grin. "Go ahead. I'll take care of him. I swear."

"You'll take care of who?" Henry smarted.

I kept my attention on the flight attendant.

Her eyes flashed to mine for only a second before jumping back to Henry. "He can't act like this. It's disruptive for everyone."

I leaned to the side to block her view of him and assured, "I understand. I promise I'll handle it."

Even if I have to use Carter's pillow idea.

She didn't seem convinced, but she nodded and slowly moved away.

Turning my attention back to Henry, I stepped into his space, the bill of my hat nearly bumping his forehead. Being afraid to fly was one thing, but being a dick to a person trying to do their job was something else completely. I didn't care how famous he was.

"I will say this one time and one time only. I don't give a single fuck who you are. You *will* watch your damn mouth. That woman does not get paid enough to deal with that shit from you. She only has to make one call and you'll find yourself banned from flying for the rest of the day." I loomed forward, forcing him to shuffle back. "Now, I don't know about you, but I'd like to get home today. Catering to rich assholes is only a small part of her job. She has safety checks to perform before we can even close the cabin door." I gave his chest a shove. "Now, we wouldn't want her to be distracted while she does those, would we?"

His eyes flared wide in understanding, but he remained silent.

"Sit. Down," I ordered in an angry whisper. Great pleasure washed over me as his cocky attitude melted away.

Breaking our stare, I settled into my new seat on the aisle. Casually crossing my legs, ankle to knee, I blocked him in our row.

He remained standing, glaring down as me as he hunched over

with his elbow propped on the seatback in front of him. He was dressed similarly as he'd been the day before, but today, the V-neck pulled tight over his muscular chest was gray and his jeans appeared to be genuinely tattered from wear rather than the designer denim he'd been sporting. His blond hair wasn't the mass of messy spikes as it had been. Instead, it was naturally sweeping across his forehead. A thin layer of blond scruff covered the curve of his strong jaw, making it obvious he hadn't shaved since I'd seen him last.

He didn't look like a spoiled multimillion-dollar superstar anymore.

But he sure as hell was acting the part.

"That seat's taken," he informed, rudely.

"Yes, Forrest Gump, it is. By me. Now, sit."

He lowered his tall body into his seat. "Um, no. My bodyguard—"

"Paid me two hundred bucks to come sit up here with you."

His mouth fell opened and closed several times before he finally exclaimed, "He did what?"

Ignoring his outburst, I searched for my seat belt. "Better buckle up," I suggested. "Wouldn't want anything to happen to a superstar like you in the air." I winked, knowing good and damn well it was going to set him off.

"Where's Carter?" he seethed. Then he suddenly paused the anger to flash a kind smile at the flight attendant as she walked past.

"Hey, look at you, fast learner," I praised with a wide grin.

As he settled deeper into his seat, his piercing, blue eyes dropped to my mouth, lingering for a beat too long.

My smile wavered under his scrutiny, and for the briefest of seconds, I swear I saw a victorious twitch pull at the corner of his lips.

"Who the hell are you anyway? Air marshal who pulled the short straw on babysitting?" he asked quietly—as if he suddenly gave a damn about the dozen passengers who had been watching his hissy fit.

I narrowed my eyes. "Seriously?"

"Yes, seriously," he bit back. His gaze stayed locked on mine as he tipped his empty glass to his lips, sucking back nothing more than a drop of melted ice before passing it to me. "Take care of that."

I rolled my eyes and then signaled to the flight attendant.

She gave Henry a wary glance before retrieving the glass, switching it for a cup of ice water. "Everything good?"

"Perfection," Henry replied with a saccharine smile. He then held her gaze and tossed back the water as a show of good faith. When she was out of earshot, he grumbled a curse. "Anyway…who are you?"

Tugging my hat off, I ran a hand through my thick, dark hair before rocking it back on. "Evan Roth. *Your pilot.* We met yesterday."

The muscles in his jaw ticked as he gave me a quick head-to-toe appraisal. "Oh. Right. You broke my plane."

"I didn't break your plane. It had—"

Suddenly, ice flew from his glass, landing in his lap when an air wrench sounded outside the plane. His free hand slapped down on my forearm before gripping impossibly tight.

"Shit! What the fuck are they doing out there?"

Lifting my arm with his fingers painfully biting into my skin, I pinched the bridge of my nose.

Deep breath, Roth.

Deep fucking breath.

I pointed out the window. "That's a good sound. You want to hear two of those, actually." I cupped my hand to my ear just as the second one sounded. "See."

His tense posture momentarily relaxed. "Why are you here?"

"I told you. Two hundred bucks. Given the company, I'm not so sure it's worth it anymore. But I've heard there might be some free drinks to sweeten up the deal." I clapped my hands and rubbed them together.

"I'll buy you whatever drink you want if you go get Carter before we take off," he replied with attitude, but it barely masked the shake of vulnerability in his voice.

I actually felt bad for him.

"Look," I said. "He thought it might help if you had a profession-al to answer your questions. Why don't you just sit back and chill. I'll let you know if there's anything to worry about."

His gaze met mine, a mixture of hope and relief filling his face only to transform into terror when the ding of a passenger assistance button sounded.

Leaning toward him, I smiled playfully and whispered, "Relax. Some rich prick just wants a second blanket. She'll tell him no. He'll pout." I sat up and straightened my invisible tie. "In my professional opinion, I don't believe the repercussions of his pouting will be cat-astrophic."

His eyes lit in relief for a fraction of a second before dropping to my smiling mouth again. I witnessed his stare, but I could have been blind and I still would have felt it gliding over my skin.

"So, there you go," I said uncomfortably. "What other question do you have for me? Come on. Fire away. Knowing is half the battle, my friend."

"Awesome. Carter sent me Optimus Prime," he mumbled to himself.

"Optimus Prime?"

He waved off my question. "That 'knowing is half the battle' shit. It's from *Transformers*."

I sucked in a sharp breath, and his nervous gaze flew to mine.

"What? What's wrong?"

"Please, God, tell me you're kidding. *Transformers*?"

"Is that wrong?" He took the safety booklet out and started flip-ping through it when the flight attendant began her preflight announcements.

"That is so far past wrong, wrong isn't even visible anymore," I whispered. "I'm actually embarrassed for you right now. For a man your age, you should be ashamed."

He gasped, slowly swinging a scowl my way. "A man my age? What the hell is that supposed to mean?"

"You're like thirty-seven, thirty-eight, right?"

He was thirty-one. I knew because I'd spent at least an hour the night before reading about him online. After the way we'd met, I was curious about the guy. Plus, I'd been desperately trying to put my phone to a use that didn't involve calling or texting Nikki again.

From what I'd read, he seemed like a decent guy. Charitable. Relatively low profile given his celebrity status. He'd won practically every award offered to a musician, and that included those for song-writing as he'd written over ninety percent of his own music. He owned his own record label—Downside Up Records—with fellow bajillionaire Levee Williams. They had a few big-name artists ranging from country all the way to metal. And, as far as I could tell, the guy had never been arrested or interrupted anyone at an awards show.

Honestly, as much as I wanted to hate him after the way he'd shown his ass when we'd met, I couldn't find anything to seal the deal.

"You," he hissed, followed by a humorless chuckle that had the flight attendant's eyes snapping our way while she demonstrated how to properly use an oxygen mask in the case of an emergency. Lowering his voice, he said, "You can shut your damn mouth. Go see if it's too late to trade back with Carter. At least he doesn't insult me." He paused and swayed his head in consideration. "Not all the time, anyway. For your information, I'm twenty-nine."

I barked a laugh at his lie but decided not to call him on it. "Well, for *your* information, it was *G.I. Joe*. Not *Transformers*. You should

brush up on your eighties cartoons before you start spouting quotes."
I leaned back in my seat and got comfortable as the plane began to
taxi toward the runway.

"*Transformers* was a cartoon before a movie?"

I clutched my chest. "Dear God. You're killing me, man."

A quiet chuckle escaped his mouth, and I couldn't help but smile
over at him.

He held my stare with solemn eyes until my smile faded away.

"I'm not an entitled asshole," he said softly. "I mean, I am, but
only when it comes to flying. It's just…" He trailed off as the plane
accelerated for takeoff.

"Hey, you okay?"

His face had paled, and small beads of sweat had formed at his
hairline.

Reaching up, I turned his air vent on full blast and aimed it at
him.

"Thanks," he replied, staring out the window.

"You want to count with me?" I asked, attempting to distract
him.

He shook his head and doubled his large body over until his
head was resting on his knees.

Normally, I would have laughed at the sight of such a big guy
curled into some sort of fetal position, but I genuinely felt bad for
him. His fear was palpable. While I'd never been afraid of flying, I
knew exactly what it felt like to be ravaged by paralyzing panic.

With every jerk of the plane, the muscles on his back flexed. I
considered rubbing my hand over his back, but touching him in that
state of vulnerability felt entirely too personal.

"Um," I mumbled, looking around the cabin, unsure of what to
do.

Shit. Okay.

Folding over to match his position, I did the only thing I could think of.

"Ten, nine, eight."

His hand snaked out and anchored to my thigh.

"Seven, six, five, four." I sat up and glanced out the window. We were running out of runway, so I rushed through the end. "Three, two, one."

No sooner had I finished than the wheels lifted off the ground.

A strangled cry escaped his throat. "Shit."

"It's all good," I assured as we climbed in altitude. "Just a heads-up: The landing gear is going to lock into place in a second. It's another good sound, okay?"

He nodded against his legs, but the rise and fall of his back revealed that the warning hadn't soothed him in the least.

For some odd reason, I stayed bent over beside him until we reached cruising altitude. I continuously talked him through the bumps and shakes, doing my best not to get too technical but still giving him enough information on what was happening to make him feel informed. If it helped, I couldn't be sure, but I kept talking anyway. He didn't acknowledge me until the flight attendant came over the intercom to announce that the *Fasten Seat Belt* sign had been turned off.

As he suddenly sat upright, I watched a whole new man emerge. Releasing my leg, he calmly lifted a finger in the air and shot a megawatt grin at the flight attendant.

"Another bloody mary?" she asked.

He replied with a flirty wink. "If it wouldn't be too much trouble, beautiful."

She appeared confused by his sudden transformation, but she was worthless to fight the suffocating charm leaking from his pores.

I swear to God, the woman, who not fifteen minutes earlier was contemplating having him removed from the flight, was now batting her eyelashes.

"No problem at all."

I had to give him credit. He'd gone from mental patient to Mr. Suave right before my eyes.

"Thanks, doll."

Doll? Who actually gets away with saying that?

Apparently Henry Alexander.

Retrieving a magazine from the seatback, he pondered, "I saw a stainless-steel wallet in here once. I wonder if they still have it."

"Are you okay?" I asked, completely confused by his abrupt mood swing.

Cool as a fucking cucumber, he tossed me a puzzled expression. "Of course. Why do you ask?"

"Um, because you almost had a nervous breakdown and, now, you're flipping through *SkyShop* in search of a stainless-steel wallet."

With a bright-white, captivating smile, he grazed his shoulder against mine and whispered, "Oh, please. That was nothing."

It was then that I knew exactly why millions of men and women were so hypnotized by Henry Alexander.

I just couldn't figure out why suddenly I was too.

chapter five

Henry

I was well aware that I'd looked like a fool. My heart was still racing as I pretended to absently flip through a magazine. My eyes were glued to the pages, but I didn't see a single word. I couldn't think of anything except for Evan's deep, baritone voice in my ear as he'd counted down to takeoff as if we had been on a space shuttle headed to Mars. That thought was only slightly more terrifying than the shiver that ran down my spine when his warm breath breezed over my skin.

Knowing that every jerk wasn't the worst-case scenario I'd created in my head did more for me than I could explain. Evan hadn't just told me I was "fine" or "okay" like Carter and Susan did. He'd explained why I was okay. And, while I'd still been terrified the entire time, I hadn't felt out of control.

And, recently, that was all I'd felt.

Agents, managers, lawyers, and publicists all made my decisions for me. Even Carter got to decide how I traveled and what restaurants were safe for me to visit. I didn't mind—usually. Or maybe I didn't realize how much it bothered me until then.

I adored my job. I had incredible friends. I fucking loved my life.

What was there left to want for?

Oh, right.

A partner.

And not just a man to lose myself inside. Although I was willing to make an exception for the obviously straight-as-an-arrow Captain Roth.

My cock had gotten me in a lot of trouble over of the years. Its timing was shit. And its taste in men wasn't much better. But it liked what it liked. And, even in the midst of a panic attack, it had decided it liked Evan Roth. It wasn't alone in that. Evan seemed like a good guy. I didn't have much to go on except that he was a pilot, didn't seem overly fond of wealthy people, and could go from gladiator to nursemaid in mere seconds. And, after glancing over at his barrel chest straining against the buttons on his grey button-down, I decided I was completely okay with a little role-play action with him in either one of those scenarios.

In my bedroom.

Or his. I wasn't picky.

"Care for a drink?" I asked with a devilish smirk. My voice was still thick from the panic, but I prayed that it came off as a masculine rasp.

I also prayed that the flight attendant didn't delay in dumping some vodka and tomato juice together.

If history was any indication, I was moments away from the adrenaline shakes. I'd get over those just in time to start the process all over again when we prepared for landing. The flying part of flying wasn't what sent me over the edge. The takeoff and the landing were what damn near crippled me. Those fears were exactly what had driven me to purchase my own private jet, despite the fact that

I only flew three to four times a year—less if I could get away with it. I needed the peace of mind that only came with knowing what pilot was behind the controls. I paid Jackson an exorbitant amount of money to keep Craig available to me at all times. He came with the highest of recommendations from the only pilot I trusted with my life.

Because…well, he'd literally saved my life.

Now was definitely not the time to revisit that day.

Shaking off the memory, I tipped my head at Evan. "Drink? Yes?"

His confusion showed in the tiny creases between his brows. "No. I mean, yes. I could use a drink. But are you sure you're okay?"

"Positive."

His eyes searched my face.

But he wasn't going to find anything. I'd made sure of that.

I held his brilliant, blue stare with every ounce of false confidence I could muster. At any other time, it wouldn't have been false. At a lower altitude, without a death-defying landing in my not-so-distant future, I would have launched full-on defilement mode on him.

Patience. It might have been the only virtue I possessed.

I cleared my throat and jutted my chin toward the flight attendant waiting for his order.

"Right. Yeah. Beer. Domestic," he requested, unfortunately snapping out of my trance.

We sat in silence until she returned with our drinks.

Hiding the shake left in my hands, I shoved the *SkyShop* magazine back into the pocket in front of me. "Thank you, gorgeous." I smiled, dropping my eyes to her chest.

She was completely covered, but her breasts were no less noticeable. If I hadn't been already pushing my limits with this woman, I would have asked if they were fake. Not that I cared. Tits didn't do anything for me. But I found it fascinating, the lengths women went through to enhance those worthless chest ornaments.

I lifted my eyes back up to her face and found that her cheeks had pinked. *Game on.*

"Listen, I'm really sorry about that mess when we first boarded. That's not who I am. Fear is not a pretty color on me." I raked my teeth over my bottom lip and strategically leaned across Evan so my chest brushed his arm.

His thick bicep flexed at the contact.

My smile spread. "I just feel terrible about the way I acted. It was unforgiveable, really. Any chance I could bribe you with front-row tickets to accept my apology?"

Her eyes flashed wide, and I knew I had her.

"Perhaps dinner afterward?"

My sexuality wasn't a secret. Yet, for some reason, women were always easier for me to charm. Men often fell under my spell, but women were intoxicated by it. The thrill of the possibility that they could be the one to change me, no doubt. It was a mindset I understood completely.

"You don't need to do that," she breathed, unconsciously swaying toward me.

We were hovering over Evan's lap at this point. It would have been awkward as hell if his clean, masculine scent hadn't been filling my lungs.

But, then again, maybe my deep inhales as I drank him in were the only awkward part—at least for him.

He pressed back against his seat, but I shifted with him to maintain the connection.

Keeping my eyes on the flight attendant, I purred, "But I really do. What's your name, doll?"

She giggled and then glanced up to see if anyone was watching. "Jessica."

"Mmm, Jessica. So nice to meet you." I started to extend a shaky hand in her direction before I thought better of it. I did the next best thing and dropped it to the shared armrest—right on top of Evan's forearm.

As to be expected, he quickly bent his elbow, moving his arm out of my reach.

"I'm Henry Alexander."

"I know," she whispered, then licked her lips.

"Oh, good. That makes it easier for me." I paused when I got an idea. Fighting back a mischievous grin, I continued. "How about you and one of your girls come out to my show in L.A. next week? My treat. Dinner, drinks, the whole deal. Evan and I would love to take you two beautiful ladies out for an evening."

"Excuse me?" he exclaimed, cocking his head to catch my gaze.

I leaned back into my seat and lifted a hand to massage his shoulder. I was barely able to suppress a moan when the angle of his firm trap muscle met my palm.

Fuck, this guy was built like a brick wall. And I was going to love every second of watching him crumble for me.

"Oh, come on, Evan. It's the least we can do. Double date." I winked at Jessica. "You can fly them out! My plane should be ready by then."

Jessica's eyes jumped to Evan's. "You're a pilot?" Her smile spread irritatingly wide.

Back off, Ginger Spice.

Snapping my fingers in her direction, I corrected, "He's *my* pilot."

Subtlety was *not* a virtue I possessed. Was subtlety a virtue at all?

"Your *temporary* pilot," he amended before shaking his head and then tipping his beer to his lips for a long pull.

"Anyway. Do we have a date?" And, by date, I meant feeding her dinner while I attempted to work my way into Evan's pants.

She pressed one finger to her lips and then nervously flashed her eyes around the cabin.

"Oops. Sorry." I shrugged sheepishly. Lifting my drink to my mouth, I discreetly passed her my cocktail napkin and then not-so-discreetly brushed my forearm against Evan's chest as I pulled away.

He offered her a tight smile just before she disappeared.

I grinned proudly.

"What the fucking hell was that?" he whisper-yelled at me.

"That was me getting a woman's number."

He arched an eyebrow. "A woman. Really?"

"What? Is that not allowed?" I feigned innocence.

He clenched his fist in his lap, and it made me suddenly aware that my own hands had stopped trembling—and in record time, I should note. Evan seemed to be quite useful in the art of distraction.

He leaned closer. "Don't bullshit me. I looked you up. You're…" He stopped, unwilling to say the big, bad "G" word.

"I'm what?" I taunted.

He rolled his eyes and chugged the rest of his beer.

We went back to silence until Jessica came back by with another drink, complete with her phone number written on the napkin.

"I'm not going on a double date," Evan said as I tucked the napkin into my pocket. "You want me to fly them out? Not a problem. Schedule it with Jackson. But that's the extent of my professional responsibilities. And, since I'm off the clock right now, I'd also like to mention that I think whatever play you're planning to run on that woman is fucked up."

My head snapped to his. "I'm sorry. Play?" I asked with more attitude than I had originally planned.

"Yes. Play," he sneered.

I stirred my drink. "Let me get this straight. I'm offering to fly her out in a private jet, feed her dinner at one of the best restaurants in the city, and put her front row at a concert that has been sold out for over a year. That doesn't seem like a play to me. It sounds like I'm trying to do something nice for a woman I was rude to earlier." I casually leaned back in my seat. "My conscience doesn't 'play' when it comes to apologies."

"Right. Well, maybe you should have a chat with your conscience, because she looks like she just won the date of a lifetime. Meanwhile, you don't even like women." He stalled, no doubt looking for just the right word to express his disgust without sounding like a bigot. Judging by his gentleness when we'd taken off, he wasn't the type of guy to go for the fag bomb.

I watched him intently, excited to see how he was going to handle this.

"You're *gay*."

I frowned at his lack of creativity. "Not that it's any of your damn business. But I'll have you know I love women."

It wasn't a lie. I adored women. Especially Levee and Robin.

I just didn't like pussy. *Meh. Semantics.*

He gaped. "You're bi?"

"And I'll repeat: None of your damn business. But yeah. Do you have a problem with that?"

Again, it wasn't necessarily a lie.

Was I bisexual? Fuck no. My cock was in no way an equal opportunity employer.

I was somewhat bilingual though. I knew how to ask for a blow job in English *and* Spanish. I pretended that was what he meant.

Chupame la verga.

He shifted uncomfortably. "I'm sorry. I, uh…didn't know."

"It's cool."

He blew out a loud sigh. "I don't like seeing people getting fucked around with. That's all."

"No fucking around." *Unless it's with you.* I lifted my fingers and swore, "Scout's honor."

He blinked rapidly as his face contorted in disbelief. "For fuck's sake, that's a Vulcan V."

I shrugged and glanced at my hand. "Hm. Okay, well then... Live long and prosper."

He sat stoically for several beats before a huge grin split his handsome face.

My eyes dropped to his plump lips, but it was the sound of his deep, carefree laugh that really transfixed me.

He cleared his throat, dragging my attention up from his mouth. His eyes danced with humor, and for a split second, I could have sworn there was some other indefinable emotion mixed in there as well.

And that was when the alarm bells started blaring in my head.

They weren't in warning.

No. These were the sounds of a casino slot machine screaming after a jackpot.

The landing went much like the takeoff. The moment our pilot announced our descent, I doubled over struggling to breathe. Evan folded over beside me, uttering nearly apologetic explanations for every bump. He finished with a countdown that ended when our wheels safely hit the pavement. He didn't even bat an eye when I once again anchored my hand to his thigh—only removing it when we came to a complete stop.

I would have liked to have left it there longer. I could've made it a sexual joke about wanting him.

But I was too preoccupied lying to myself that I wasn't actually interested in this guy to even get that far.

Carter, along with Macy, met us in first class and escorted us off the plane and then through the airport. Numerous travelers stopped us to ask for an autograph or a picture. And, for the most part, I obliged. Evan was happy to volunteer as cell phone photographer.

I actually loved that part of my job. It never got old. But that wasn't why I smiled for each of those pictures. It had more to do with the fact that, since we were back on solid ground, my senses had fully returned and they were all currently honed in on a broad-chested, blue-eyed pilot with dark-brown hair and a cock-hardening grin.

Once outside, Carter ushered me through a sea of paparazzi and into the back of an awaiting limo. Macy slid in beside me, quickly followed by Carter, and then before I knew it, we were pulling away.

"Wait. Where's Evan?" I moved to the window and searched through the crowd of dispersing photographers. "We can't leave him here!"

Carter quirked an eyebrow. "His boss sent a car to get him."

"Why? We could have given him a ride home?"

Carter let out a knowing groan. "For fuck's sake. The pilot, Henry?"

"What? He's gorgeous," I stated as my answer.

"He really was," Macy cooed, finger combing her hot-pink hair. "Please tell me he prefers women."

I smirked and shot her a challenging expression. "Yes, but only for a little while longer."

She laughed.

Carter cursed under his breath. "So I guess he's not an infant anymore?"

"Nope. But that doesn't mean I'm not going to try to breast-feed him." I waggled my eyebrows.

"Dear. God," he mumbled, cracking a rare grin.

I gasped, clutching my heart. "Did you just smile?"

His face fell. "Don't start with me."

"You did!"

Macy leaned in close and whispered, "It's because you said breast. But I'm not sure if it's because he's hungry or horny."

He glowered at us.

"Hungry," I replied. "Carter's asexual. Best I can figure is he's some sort of robotic super soldier gone wrong."

"You got it," he replied, opening a magazine. "I was a failed prototype. My punishment was being sent here to work for you."

"You want me to give him a lap dance? See if it sparks anything?" Macy offered, digging through her bag before applying a thick coat of lip gloss.

"Nah. I'll go first."

Carter's head shot up, and he leveled me with a death glare.

I threw my hands up in surrender. "Easy there, big man. It was a joke."

"He's scary," Macy whispered as if he couldn't hear from three feet away.

"That's why I keep him. Well, that and because he's so good to me." I smiled. "Hey, Carter. I need the pilot's cell phone number."

He didn't look up when he casually replied, "No."

"Okay, great. Just text it to me whenever."

"No." He absently turned the page.

Macy desperately tried to stifle a giggle.

The corners of my mouth tipped up. "See? He adores me." Shooting her wide eyes, I mouthed the word *robot* at her.

"I heard that," Carter told his magazine.

Macy and I both burst into a loud round of laughter. And, while I couldn't be certain, I swear I saw Carter's lips twitch as well.

"Fine. No phone number, but I want him on my payroll as my new pilot."

Now that got Carter's attention. After abruptly closing the magazine, he tossed it on the seat beside him. "You're seriously going to trust the kid to fly you just to get him in the sack?"

"Who said anything about flying? I don't have to be on a plane again for several months."

He crossed his thick arms over his chest. "Exactly. Why would you hire a pilot now? Do you have any idea how expensive that's going be? Even part time is going to cost you a mint."

Lifting a finger in the air, I corrected him. "Full time. I'll find other duties for him to do in his downtime." I winked.

"I'm pretty sure that's called prostitution."

"Po-tay-toe. Pa-tah-toe. Besides, I only need the time with him. All extracurricular activities will be performed off the clock."

Unless I could help it. In which case, the line between work and pleasure would be seriously blurred.

Macy piped up. "I think this is a fabulous idea. But, if he doesn't bend to your will and stays on the lady train, I want first dibs."

"Deal."

"What is wrong with you?" Carter spat. "Why can't you just sleep with groupies like everyone else?"

I curled my lip in disgust. "Uh, I believe you answered your own question. Nasty ninths aren't exactly my thing. Besides, why do you care?" It wasn't like this was the first time he'd ever seen me trying to seduce a man into my bed. And, honestly, I'd gone through far greater lengths than just hiring someone in order to make it happen.

He rolled his eyes. "I only care because we all know how this is going to end. You have to stop trying to convert the straight guys. It's always a train wreck, and by the looks of Evan, this isn't going to be any different." He scratched the back of his head. "Shit. I really wish you would just find a nice gay guy and settle down."

I gasped, dramatically slapping my hand against the seat beside me, the other clenching my heart. "Did you hear that, Macy?" I whispered, never tearing my eyes off him.

She sucked in a shocked breath. "You're right. He totally adores you."

Batting my lashes, I allowed false tears to pool in my eyes. Then I made a show of quivering my chin. "I...I love you too, Papa."

"Jesus fucking Christ. Forget I said anything," he grumbled.

"What, no hug?" I pouted.

"Fuck off, Henry," he returned.

He wasn't mad. That was just how we worked.

The other way we worked was that I knew with an absolute certainty he'd ensure Evan Roth was added to my payroll no matter the cost.

chapter six

Evan

"'Sup, Man!" **Scott** said, clasping my hand then pulling me in for a one-armed hug.

I closed my front door behind him. "Not a whole lot. Want a beer?"

He looked around my house. "Where's Nikki?"

Good fucking question.

We hadn't spoken since our fight two days earlier. *Was that a fight?* Breakup was more like it. I wasn't ready to admit that yet. I'd called her at least a dozen times, but I'd only allowed myself to leave six messages. Clearly, that was the magical number that toed the line between concerned ex-boyfriend and stalker douchebag ex-boyfriend. She would probably disagree as she deleted them all without even listening though.

Her stuff was still at my apartment. Bobby pins still strewn over my sink and her toothbrush still sat cozied in a cup next to mine. The pajamas I'd stripped off her during our last night together were still in my laundry hamper and the book she'd been reading was still on the nightstand. She hadn't been back while I was gone, and a part of me was almost relieved. I hated it though. I wanted to talk to her, but I had resigned myself to accept that that conversation wasn't going to have some grand outcome. It was still going to end with her being gone and hopefully moving on with her life. Leaving me alone with the impossible task of finally figuring my own out.

"Nikki and I broke up." There. I'd said it. And it'd sucked every bit as much as I'd anticipated.

Scott blew out a low whistle. "Was that mutual or more of a crash and burn?"

I swayed my head from side to side. "Debatable. Honestly, the whole relationship was a crash and burn from the start."

"What? I thought you guys were good together." He settled on a barstool. "She was a cool chick. And one hell of a cook." He moaned and rolled his eyes back in his head. "That bacon cream cheese shit she made last time I was here. Damn. I'm gonna come just thinking about it. Hey. Can I get her number?" he joked.

I made my way to my fridge to retrieve a couple of beers. "Shut the fuck up, dickhead. I made that bacon cream cheese shit." I twisted the top off, passed him a bottle, and then propped my hip against the counter next to him. "You want *my* number? I'll slather that shit all over my balls for you."

"Fucker." He clinked the bottom of his beer on the mouth of mine, causing it to foam out of control.

I quickly moved it to the sink. "Come on, man. Seriously?"

"Don't joke when it comes to food."

I rolled my eyes. "Right."

"So, now that you're single, I think it's only fitting we hit the bars."

Scott's desire to go out had nothing to do with my relationship status. Regardless if I was with a woman or not, his visits always consisted of the two of us going out, getting wasted, and then grabbing a cab home. He'd crash in my guest room until we'd slept the booze off, and then we'd spend the following day miserable while our bodies reminded us that we were in fact thirty-one and not twenty-one anymore.

However, minus the hangover, it'd pretty much been the same thing we'd done when we had been twenty-one.

I'd met Scott Dalton my first day at the Air Force Academy. He hadn't changed much since then. He was bigger than the eighteen-year-old kid he'd been when we'd met. And the tattoos covering his arms were definitely additions, but besides that, he was still that same guy with the buzzed, brown hair and a wicked glimmer in his pale, green eyes. We'd been close at school. But we were closer now. He was one of the few who'd kept in touch with me after I'd left the Academy the summer before my junior year.

Eventually, we'd been stationed together at Travis Air Force Base and picked right back up where we'd left off. He was a pilot too, but unlike me, he was a lifer. The Air Force was going to have to force him into retirement before he'd ever agree to take the uniform off.

During the first few months after I'd gotten out of the service, Scott had made the ninety-minute trek from Travis to visit me nearly every weekend. He'd never admit it, but I think he was secretly worried about my transition into the civilian world. He'd seen how hard it had been for me almost a decade earlier when I'd transferred from the Air Force Academy to the University of California. I appreciated the fact that he cared enough to check up on me. I didn't need it though. My decision to get out of the Air Force wasn't even remotely similar to when I'd left the Academy.

This time, it had been *my* decision.

I'd spent months planning every last step to make it as smooth of a transition as possible. I'd taken my VA loan out, bought a house, and threw myself into making sure all of my licenses were up to date.

It wasn't long before I'd lined up a job with an airline. With as fickle as the economy was, it was a dream come true.

And short-lived.

Three days before I was released from the Air Force, the airline went belly-up.

I scrambled, but it was as though I were drowning in quicksand. The harder I fought, the more impossible finding a job became. There were more than enough desperate pilots searching for work without adding me into the mix. Scott was the only one who saw the hell I was going through. His answer was to ply me with alcohol every weekend to keep me distracted. That's what best friends do. Even assholes like Scott Dalton.

Scott went to a lot of trouble to lead people to believe he was a douchebag. It allowed him to distance himself from serious issues even with his closest friends. It was a trait I'd loved in him when we'd first started hanging out and probably the only reason we'd been able to remain friends after everything had gone down. In reality though, Scott had the biggest heart of any guy I'd ever met—as long as you didn't call him on it.

He was the one who finally convinced me to bite the bullet and ask my stepdad for help in finding a job. He was also the one I'd called two days later when Jackson had formally offered me a job piloting charter flights. It was only part time. And it wasn't ideal. But Scott still celebrated with me as though I'd won the lottery.

While his visits were much less frequent now, something my liver appreciated, we still got together as often as our crazy schedules would allow.

"Sooooo?" he drawled, drumming his hands on the top of my bar. "First round's on me."

"I'm not sure I feel like drinking tonight."

His eyebrows lifted so high they were nearly in his hairline.

After pushing to his feet, he prowled forward. "Oh, I think you do."

I had him by a few inches and at least fifty pounds, but that didn't stop him from getting up in my face.

Typical Scott.

He wasn't serious. I knew this dance well. If I said no again, he'd spend the next hour calling me various combinations of bitch and pussy in an effort to goad me into going. And, if I still refused, when he ran out of creative insults, he'd resort to begging.

"Let's just stay here and drink. I do *not* feel like fighting a crowd tonight."

He groaned, dropping the tough-guy act. "Come on, Roth. I need a night out. Work has been hell. I haven't left the base since Shannon's wedding, and let me just tell you—" He suddenly stopped, but the damage had been done.

And we both knew it.

My body froze as his slipup seared through me. It had been over ten years. I was in no way still haunted by the past. Hurt and anger no longer ruled my days.

But a pain like that never truly left you.

It had changed me.

Actually, it had changed the trajectory of my entire life.

"Dude," he whispered in apology.

Shannon's wedding.

Fuck.

"I'm so fucking sorry, Evan."

Yeah. Me too.

Suddenly, a drink sounded like exactly what I needed.

"You know what? You're right. Let's go out."

Getting up to take a piss at bar number three was the last thing I remembered. But, somehow, I'd managed to wake up in my bed the next morning. I was scared to look at my bank account to see the damage I'd done. If the pounding in my head was any indication, it was going to be extensive. I'd been doing shots—my personal drink of choice when trying to forget that an amazing woman was avoiding me because she loved me and I couldn't return her feelings and also that my ex, the only person I'd ever loved, and eventually hated, had recently gotten married. *Fucking awesome!*

I winced. And it wasn't because of the way my stomach churned as I rolled out of bed. My phone was lying on the ground, the screen cracked right down the center. *Shit.* Add that to my expenditures from the evening and I wasn't sure I could afford to hang out with Scott again until I got a full-time gig.

Sliding my finger across the screen, I found that it was at least still operational. Hopefully it would limp along another few weeks before I had to fork out the dough to fix it. Scrolling through my phone, I noted a missed call from Jackson. There was no possible way I could fly today. *Awesome. Yet another paycheck that won't hit my bank.*

After tugging a shirt on, I made my way to my kitchen for a much-needed cup of coffee. Surprisingly, I found Scott shirtless, sitting at the bar, a steaming mug already in front of him.

"Any more of that?" I asked in a raspy voice. My throat was fucking killing me.

"Whole pot. But your milk is bad. So I hope you like it black."

I lifted my phone to show him the cracked screen. "What the fuck happened last night?"

He chuckled. "Well, let's see. You were half a second from passing out when a song came on the radio in the cab. I swear to God, it was like an exorcism. Your eyes were still closed, but your drunk ass sat straight up and shouted for the cabbie to turn it up. He refused. You called him an asshole."

I groaned.

He laughed, fiddling with the handle on his mug. "Yeah. It was fun. You proceeded to tell us both some never-ending story about how you'd flown the dude singing. I couldn't make out half of the shit you were saying, but at the end, you decided you needed to call Nikki and tell her you'd met Henry Alexander."

My stomach rolled. "Please, God, tell me I didn't drunk-dial her."

"Fuck no! What the hell kind of friend do you think I am? I slapped that shit out of your hand before you even got it to your ear." He lifted his coffee in the air before taking a sip. "Shattered the screen, but that's a small price to keep your cock from drawing up into a pussy. You're welcome, by the way." He finished with a smirk.

"Jesus fuck. We are never going out again. I'm way too old for this shit."

I said that every single time Scott and I went out. Yet, a few months later, he'd show up and put forth a mediocre argument and I'd find myself once again having this conversation. Wash. Rinse. Repeat.

He quirked an eyebrow and pushed his coffee toward me for a refill. "Hate to break it to you, but I'm pretty sure my grandma drunk-dials me after her weekly book club. It's not exactly something you outgrow with age."

I was digging through my cabinet for some ibuprofen when my phone started vibrating on the counter. It was Jackson again. I quickly ended it. I was in no mood for his shit and in even less of a mood to have to say no to a flight when I could really use the money.

After swallowing two pills and washing them down with a bottle of water, I tossed the medicine Scott's way. "Well, thanks for keeping me from calling Nikki, but you're a dick for breaking my phone. And, for the record, I wasn't bullshitting. I really did fly Henry Alexander the other day."

"No shit." He swallowed the pills as I topped his coffee off.

"Yep. Nice enough guy—" I was quickly interrupted.

"Scared to fly. Just on takeoff and landing though. Can be a real dick. But he at least has the decency to apologize for it. Drinks bloody marys like fucking water. Doesn't know shit about eighties cartoons. His only saving grace was that he at least seemed knowledgeable on *Star Trek.*" He stopped, and his eyes danced with humor as he smiled wide.

My face heated in embarrassment.

"Yeah. You may have mentioned something about the guy."

"See? Yet another reason we can't do that bullshit anymore. I'm pretty sure I signed a nondisclosure when I started working for Jackson."

"Roth, don't worry. Your twelve-year-old fangirl secrets are safe with me." He pushed off the stool and stretched, groaning as he cracked his neck. "I need to get the hell out of here. I'm gonna jump in the shower." He lifted his chin toward my phone. "And give you a minute to call back whoever's blowing up your phone."

I sighed. "It's my boss. But I can't fly today. He's gonna be livid."

"Wow. Maybe I was wrong. Your cock must have turned into a pussy a while ago."

I laughed and hurled my empty water bottle at him.

He easily batted it away, but I followed it up with a sponge from my sink. It hit him on the chest with a loud slap.

"Son of a bitch," he grumbled, rubbing the red mark.

I arched an eyebrow. "What were you saying about a pussy?"

"I'm not the bitch too afraid to answer a call from my boss." Scott moved down the hall to the guest room. "Just tell him you started your period. After last night, it's not far from the truth!"

"Dick!" I shouted back only to wince when the loud noise felt like a knife to the skull.

Jesus, I really had to stop drinking. What the hell else had I said to him last night?

My phone began ringing again, and I finally decided to stop being such a bitch. It's not like Jackson could fire me for turning one flight down. I wasn't even on call. I was, after all, part time—however, if Craig was still out, he was probably hoping I'd be available to pick up some of the slack. Hell, I had been hoping that too.

Which made me wonder… Maybe Henry was scheduled for another flight.

"Hello."

"I've been calling you for hours."

"Good morning to you too."

"It's noon, Evan. My morning started at four a.m. It's practically dinnertime for me right now."

And he was in a shit mood. *Awesome.*

"Right. Sorry," I replied curtly.

"Why the hell didn't you tell me you and Nikki broke up?"

Ugh. Fantastic. More Nikki questions. Could this morning get any better?

"Because I didn't realize we were sorority sisters who shared our feelings," I smarted. I immediately bit my lip, hoping he'd laugh and not…say…fire me.

"You know the only reason I hired you is because your stepdad and I go way back. I respect the shit out of him, and he was willing to vouch for you. I gave you every flight I possibly could. But let's be clear here. I have virtually no use for a part-timer."

Shit.

"Jackson, I'm sorry. Yeah, Nikki and I broke up a few days ago. It wasn't exactly a good thing."

"Well, no shit. I figured that out this morning when I had a very awkward conversation with her about you. Her number is still listed on your contact sheet. For fuck's sake, Roth, she was two seconds away from crying. I was on a Goddamn landline and had to fake static just to get off the phone with her."

If it hadn't been for the idea of her crying, I would have laughed. Instead, my stomach wrenched with guilt.

"I'm sorry."

"You should be. But you should be more sorry for ducking my calls because your ass is hungover."

My back shot ramrod straight. "Uh..."

"Anyway, good news is I don't need you to fly today. Bad news is you're fired."

My entire body tensed. "What? No! Jackson, wait—"

"Sorry, son. I lost a client this morning. As much as you know I'd like to, I can't afford to keep you anymore."

I pinched the bridge of my nose as my head pounded almost as loud as my heart. This morning had just gotten a hell of a lot worse. Just what I fucking needed.

"Come on, man. Is Craig back? Why don't you let me fill in for him for a while? I can't afford to be unemployed right now."

I heard him chuckle. "You want to know what client I lost?"

Not really. I mainly wanted to hear the part that ended with me still being able to pay my mortgage without cashing a mutual fund out.

He didn't wait for me to answer. "Henry Alexander."

Oh, fuck. Suddenly, getting fired made a whole lot more sense. I was the last one to fly him. And, despite how he'd acted toward me on the flight back, he wasn't happy at all with Jackson's replacing Craig with me. Not to mention that the fuel pump on his plane hadn't passed maintenance inspection the following morning. Something that had absolutely nothing to do with me, but Henry had implied I'd broken his plane.

I stumbled back a few steps until my ass found one of my barstools. "Did you tell him that a pilot can't fucking break a fuel pump?"

"I sure did. I also told him you were one of the best pilots I'd ever had the pleasure of working with and that it was going to be a great loss to me to let you go."

Story of my fucking life. When the hell did the best become not good enough?

"Right." I mumbled. "Thanks."

"You should be thanking me. I also told him I pay you three times what I really do and that you are worth every penny. You start next week."

"I'm sorry. I start what?"

"Personal pilot for Henry Alexander. Full time. Salaried. One-year contract. He asked for you specifically. The money's some of the best I've seen."

I jumped to my feet. "No fucking way."

"Now, don't get cockier than you already are. I'll still be over-seeing flight plans and maintenance for your aircraft. But he'll be signing your paychecks now."

I wasn't sure how I felt about this new job Jackson had clearly already accepted on my behalf. It worried me that I'd heard Henry only flew a few times a year. I couldn't imagine why he needed a personal pilot. However, Jackson had said three times my current salary. And, if my calculations were correct, that would be doubled again considering I'd be full fucking time.

I was vaguely aware of Scott coming back into the room, but my mind was still counting dollar bills. Making a career as a pilot was a labor of love. The jobs were few and far between, and job security was almost laughable. But I loved flying. I'd take it any way I could. Especially the way where I was well paid, contracted for a year, and captain on my own private aircraft.

Yeah. I'd especially take it like that.

Hope roared through my veins. Maybe this was it. The opportunity I'd been praying for. This could be my *in* in the business. Even if Henry only kept me for a year, I was sure I could get a nice recommendation and move on to some other celebrity with more money than sense. Adding Henry Alexander's personal pilot to my résumé definitely couldn't hurt.

"Please tell me you aren't kidding here," I breathed.

Jackson laughed. "No joke, kid. You deserve this. But hey, considering you informed me earlier that we aren't sorority sisters, I'll let you go giggle with your girlfriends. But you need to get your ass up here. I have new paperwork for you to sign."

And just like that, he hung up, leaving me in state of shock with the phone still secured to my ear, too afraid to pull it away.

Scott nudged my knee.

I lifted my dazed eyes and found him fully dressed and watching me with concern. Water from the shower still dripped from his short hair.

"You okay, man?" he asked.

Adrenaline surged through me.

Was I okay?

I had a job. A real fucking honest-to-God *job*—after almost a year of busting my ass to keep my head above water. Leaving the Air Force hadn't been an easy decision for me. But, as an officer, I'd spent entirely too many hours behind a desk. I wanted to wake up every morning, crawl into the confines of a cockpit, and leave it all behind. I was free from the weight of the world up there. In complete control no matter how out of control my life felt on the ground.

"Evan?" Scott once again tried to catch my attention.

I was lost in thought of what I prayed was my new reality.

Flying.

Fuck yeah.

I stared at him for several seconds longer before a loud bellow of laughter sprang from my throat. "I got fired."

"Shit," Scott breathed.

"And then rehired." I nodded entirely too many times, all the while continuing to laugh. "As Henry Alexander's personal pilot."

"Nice!"

I scrubbed my hand over my face. As it turned out, adrenaline seemed to be the best hangover cure of all. "Yeah, listen, I need to go. Jackson has some shit for me to sign." I pushed to my feet.

"Sure. Go ahead. I'll let myself out." He headed for the front door as I moved in the opposite direction toward my bedroom.

I heard the door creak open just before he called out.

"Hey, Evan?"

"Yeah?" I turned to face him.

He was sporting a huge grin. "I'm happy for you, man. Seriously."

"Thanks." I returned his smile.

"Just be careful, okay?" His tone was serious, but his grin grew to epic proportions.

I twisted my lips in confusion. "Huh?"

"I mean…it can't be easy to work for someone so"—he lifted his fingers and tossed me a pair of air quotes—"'fucking hot.'"

My breath caught in my chest, and my face fell to a practiced blank.

Oh God.

Shit.

Damn.

Fuck.

No more drinking for me. Ever.

He laughed loudly but said not another word before I heard the door click behind him.

chapter seven

Henry

One week later...

"R obin called last night," I told the window at the small private airport I'd been waiting at for the last fifteen minutes.

Levee gripped my hand and intertwined our fingers. "She's probably running out of money."

I nodded. That much I knew.

As much as it had broken my heart, I'd called the bank and had them cut her debit card off. It was a waste of time. Her account was already overdrawn.

"She wouldn't tell me where she was, but she didn't sound right." I sighed. "I told her the apartment would always be there, but I wasn't giving her any more money. I'm done, Lev."

She tugged my arm around her shoulders. Her rounded stomach brushed against my hip as she looped an arm around my waist.

"I think that's smart. I know you love her. I love her too. But, honey, at some point, you have to show her some tough love. You can't save everyone."

Sam came strutting over with three Styrofoam cups of coffee squeezed between his large, callused hands. "Hey, that's my line." He tossed me a sexy smirk that probably could have impregnated me if it hadn't been for the fact that he was married to my best friend.

Sam Rivers was gorgeous, and if he hadn't met Levee first, I can guarantee he would have found himself on my radar. All of that smoldering, tattooed bad boy had practically been begging me to top him. However, if the way he looked at Levee was any indication, I wouldn't have been successful.

I chuckled, taking a cup from the front of his caffeine pyramid. "Thanks."

"Nope. That's Levee's decaf." He flashed her a proud smile.

One she did not return. "I hate you," she hissed at him before retrieving the cup from my hand.

He barked a laugh and raked his eyes over her pregnant stomach. "Your current condition says otherwise."

"No. My current condition says that I liked you at one point in the not-so-distant past. It was probably before you banned soft cheese, sushi, and caffeine."

"What can I say? I'm obviously an asshole." He shrugged with a wide smile.

I went back to staring out the window as Sam moved around me and curled Levee into his side.

"Oh! Is that them?" she asked, pointing out the window to a plane coming down for what I hoped was a landing and not instant death.

"Probably," I replied, quickly spinning away from the window and screwing my eyes shut. I couldn't even watch without having a panic attack.

A few seconds later, Sam's hand landed on my back.

"It's all good now. You want to go out? They're taxiing up."

I swallowed around the lump in my throat. I needed to get my shit together. I had a concert in a few hours. Not to mention a man to seduce.

With just the thought, my pulse slowed and my shoulders rolled back in confidence.

"No," Sam whispered when I turned toward him.

Levee gave me a suspicious side-eye. "I thought you said there were two *women* on that plane? Why do you look like you're on the hunt?"

"Did I forget to mention I hired a new pilot?" I winked. "I guess it slipped my mind."

"This should be fun," Sam mumbled, shaking his head.

Crossing my fingers, I lifted them in his direction as I backed out of the door. "Let's hope."

A member of Levee's security team quickly fell into step behind me.

Carter had flown back to San Francisco after my show the night before. He'd informed me just before the bus had left that he had some emergency business to attend to. I'd had no clue what that could be, but he'd looked amazingly pissed as he'd marched away, so I hadn't bothered asking. He'd been exceptionally cranky recently. I could only hope he'd flown back after discovering there was a robot woman who could give him a piece of ass. Or at least a blowie to take the edge off. She couldn't have been very good though, because he'd called earlier to let me know he would be on Evan's flight to Los Angeles.

Ground crews were busy moving around the plane when Levee sidled up beside me.

"Let me get this straight. I'm fat and pregnant. Stuck at home ninety percent of the time because my husband is so overcautious about me that, if it didn't make me love him more, it would make me hate him. It took me two weeks to get him to agree to my joining you on stage for one damn song tonight."

I smiled and glanced down to see she wasn't kidding in the least. Her eyes were sparkling with tears.

"What the—" I started to ask, but she lifted a hand to silence me.

"My life is so incredibly boring right now. And you—my *best* friend—set your sights on a pilot and didn't even think to call and tell me all about it?"

I sidestepped to get a better read on her face. "You're kidding, right?"

Sam whispered from behind me, "She's totally not."

Waving a finger over her face, I asked, "Is this…a pregnancy thing?"

"No!" she shouted.

Sam quickly nodded until Levee silenced him with a glare.

Tossing an arm around her, I dipped to kiss her forehead. "And yet another reason I'm happy to be gay."

She slapped my chest.

"Okay, since I have so gravely failed at being your entertainment recently, I'll give you a quick rundown. His name is Evan Roth. He's unbelievably hot in that understated nice guy kind of way. He talked me through a flight last week. He has some sort of weird fetish for eighties cartoons but seemed to at least know *Star Trek*. He thinks I'm bisexual. Hence why he's flying two female flight attendants in for me tonight. But, really, he's the only thing on my menu for the evening. I want to have sex with him, but he's straight, so I did what any horny man would do—I hired him to be my pilot."

Levee's mouth fell open as Sam released a string of expletives.

"Now, dry your eyes, Suzie Emotional, and act cool, because they're opening the door." I grinned.

I turned back to the plane just in time to see Flight Attendant

Jessica come teetering down the stairs in a pair of heels. She battled the wind as it whipped her long, red hair into her face. Her low-cut, cream blouse threatened to fly up, but luckily, her short, black skirt appeared to have been painted on, so at least there wasn't any danger of catching my first eyeful of vagina. My virginity was safe for yet another day.

Right behind her was a blonde in a tight, black dress who not even I could deny was stunning. Her long, tan legs devoured the steps as she gracefully exited the plane. Her hair was also caught in the wind, but instead of being a safety hazard as Jessica's had been, this woman's looked as though she were stepping onto a completely different type of runway.

I hated her instantly.

Because I knew Evan would love her instantly.

"Fuck," I whispered as she shot a sexy, white smile in my direction.

"Jesus," Levee whispered. "Please tell me that is not your competition for the evening."

Gnawing on my bottom lip, I made a quick decision that was no doubt going to suck for me. "No. That's my new date," I announced before striding towards the women. "Ladies," I purred over the wind. "Good to see you again, Jessica." I briskly kissed her on the cheek then turned to the blonde. "And hello, gorgeous. I don't believe we've met yet. I'm Henry."

Her eyes turned dark as she gave me an obvious once-over. "Tabitha."

A witch. How fitting.

Lifting her hand to my mouth, I mumbled, "Beautiful name for a beautiful woman." I didn't even gag as I kissed the back of her hand.

Her cheeks blushed as her eyes shifted to Jessica, who appeared none too happy about my interest in her friend. But that's what she got for bringing a fucking supermodel on a double date. Everyone knows you bring the troll friend in this situation. Shit. I was a man and knew that.

"Can you ladies excuse me for a moment? I'm going to have a word with our captain." I jogged up the steps into the plane.

To my excitement, the door to the cockpit was open and Evan's broad shoulders filled the doorway. Another man spoke, but it was Evan's deep, throaty laugh that sent a tingle down my spine.

"Any chance I can get out of here before you start humping him?"

My body tensed and I twisted in the small space. A superiorly disgruntled Carter was glowering at me.

I sighed. "Still cranky. Great. I see you didn't get laid."

His eyes flared wide, but his lips thinned. I made a mental note of the flare but decided not to waste time trying to figure it out. Not with Evan only a few feet away.

Carter grimaced and landed a paw on my chest. "Don't say I never gave you anything." With a hard shove, he sent me stumbling back.

Directly into Evan. Ass to gloriously hard ass.

"What the…" Evan cursed.

Carter called out, "Shit. Sorry, Evan. My bad."

Yep. Cranky and all. It was time to give Carter a raise.

He lifted his hand in a half salute, half wave before disappearing down the stairs.

"You okay?" Evan asked as I turned to face him.

Those dark-brown lashes blinked at me as a timid smile grew on his lips but it faltered before it reached his eyes.

It was still sexy enough to dry my mouth.

"Hi," I said when wit failed me.

"Um. Hi." He swayed uncomfortably as I stared at him.

But the truly unnerving part was that he was staring right back at me.

"Good flight?" I asked nervously. It was a surprisingly unnatural feeling for me.

"Great." He lifted a muscular arm and raked a hand through his short hair. It was barely long enough to style—but more than thick enough for me to grip while he was on his—

"Henry! Let's go. We're going to be late!" Levee called up the stairs.

I lifted a single finger in her direction. "You ready?"

"For?" he drawled in question.

I tipped my head. "Concert, dinner, drinks. Listen, change of plans but Jessica is yours. Have you seen her friend Tabitha?" I sucked in a low whistle.

He furrowed his brow, which caused a sexy crinkle between those gorgeous, blue eyes. "I'm not going to that." He jerked his chin toward his shoulder at his copilot. "Baez and I are gonna grab some dinner and then head back to the hotel."

"What? No. We have a double date. Remember?" Why hadn't I been a dick to two lesbians so that could have been an accurate statement? It would have made my life so much easier.

"No," he said very slowly. "What *I* remember is telling you that I'd fly them here but, after that, you were on your own."

"Right. But then I hired you," I said flippantly.

It had been the wrong thing to say. So, so, so wrong.

"Excuse me?"

But I was me and apparently an obtuse idiot, so I repeated, "I hired you."

His eyes narrowed, and I noted that even that was sexy. I would have wagered that the man was incapable of an ugly expression. But, clearly, that would take more scientific evidence. I'd yet to see his face contorted midorgasm or in the middle of the night with his mouth hanging open and drool dripping from the corner. It was my duty as an American to discover this information. Strictly in the name of science, of course.

I belatedly realized I was smiling when he growled, "Did you only hire me so I'd go on a date with you"—if he had stopped there, I would have had no choice but to answer honestly. *Yes.* Thankfully, he kept going—"and those women?"

Phew. Saved by the details. "What? No!" I adamantly shook my head. "Listen, I guess you're going to make me say this straight out. As you know, I treated Jessica like a dick, and this little trip was my way to say I'm sorry. But she wasn't the only one I was an ass to that day. I want a chance to apologize to you too." I tossed him a charming smile and his eyes instantly flashed to it.

Interesting.

A wave of excitement shot like a drug through my veins. This might be easier than I'd originally anticipated.

"No need to apologize," he said, shoving his hands in the pockets of his navy uniform pants.

My eyes followed the movement down.

A soft smile formed on my mouth as I slowly looked back up. "No. Really. I'm embarrassed. Come to the concert tonight. Dinner, drinks, whatever you want. My treat. I might know a guy who can get you backstage." I winked, raking my teeth over my bottom lip.

His eyes once again jumped down. "I don't know."

"Henry! Stop flirting. We have to go," Carter growled.

Evan's entire body stiffened.

Nope. No fucking raise for Carter.

I shot him a scowl before assuring Evan, "He's kidding." I lifted my hand in the Vulcan V as my promise.

He rewarded me with a chuckle.

"Come on. Let me show you I'm not completely insane." I bent at the waist and leaned toward him. A heady mixture of cologne and pure-male musk intoxicated my senses. My lids fluttered closed as I fought back a groan. "I owe you an apology. I called you Maverick."

"He's Navy. I'm Air Force. But I've been called worse," he replied curtly.

"Really, Evan—"

I was cut off by the sound of a cell phone ringing.

As if he'd been shocked by electricity, he started frantically digging in his pocket. He lifted it to his ear. "Nik? Yeah. Hey, baby."

I felt my lips go tight. *Nick?*

Was he gay?

His eyes jumped to mine. My disappointment must have shown, but he seemed to misinterpret it as annoyance.

Tilting his head to the side in apology, he mouthed, "I'm sorry," and then said into the phone, "Hey, let me call you back in five minutes. I'm just getting off a flight."

As quickly as he'd answered the call, he ended it.

"I'm sorry, Mr. Alexander. That was rude."

Mr. Alexander? We were just engaged in some serious straight-gay eye-fucking, and now, he decides to go for professionalism?

"Boyfriend?" I asked, my voice thick with frustration.

His clear, blue eyes narrowed menacingly as he corrected me. "Nikki. Girlfriend. I mean…ex-girlfriend."

"Right. Of course." I bit my lip and momentarily looked down at my shoes to hide the smile I was struggling to contain. "I didn't mean to insinuate—"

"It's fine," he bit out.

We stared at each other for several beats. His eyes no longer held the levity they had before he'd answered his phone, but there was still something hidden behind that striking gaze. Something I suddenly wanted to figure out.

"How about this? You go to your hotel. I upgraded you to a suite, by the way. Get comfortable. Change out of your uniform. And I'll have a driver come get you after the show. We'll have a late dinner or something."

He eyed me suspiciously and then looked back at his phone in his hand. War visibly waged in his head. I just wasn't sure which side I was on.

"Yeah. I can do that."

A cry of victory escaped my mouth. "Yes! I mean...sounds great."

His lips twitched, and unless hope had clouded my vision, his cheeks even gained a hint of color.

"Okay, then. I guess that's settled," he said dismissively.

"Sure is," I confirmed with a huge smile, but I didn't move.

He slanted his head toward the door. "You should...you know... get going."

"I guess I should." I again didn't move.

And I'll be damned if his lips didn't twitch again.

"I'll see you tonight"—I reached out and glided my index finger over the silver nameplate on his chest—"Captain Roth."

His body tensed as he watched my hand, but much to my excitement, he didn't back away. Not even an inch.

Oh, this was fucking happening.

chapter eight

Evan

I closed the door to the two-bedroom suite in the nicest hotel I had ever seen in my life. Baez had nearly stroked out when we'd pulled up. That is until the cab drove away to take him to the no doubt budget hotel Jackson had put him up in. Working for Henry Alexander definitely had some perks. Although, after our conversation on the plane, I was wondering if he thought my working for him was going to come with some perks too. Or maybe he was only a super friendly guy who really was going out of his way to right a wrong with me. But that didn't explain why I felt the tingle of his presence in my cock.

I hadn't been lying when I'd drunkenly told Scott that Henry was fucking hot. All of his blond hair and lean, sculpted muscles. Even if he hadn't had the voice and the talent he so obviously possessed, he could have easily still graced the covers of magazines. His features were sharp and refined. But, if I had the choice, I'd still favor the strong angle of his jaw covered with a day's worth of scruff that made him more boy-next-door sexy rather than Mr. GQ.

He hadn't looked like that tonight though. Tonight, he'd appeared every bit of the wealthy predator I was starting to fear he was. And, now that I knew he was bisexual, the threat was more real than ever. I was no one's prey, but I was more than willing to hunt the hunter. Gay, I couldn't handle. Bi though… Now, that held some possibilities.

The biggest possibility being that I'd end up losing my job—something I absolutely couldn't afford. I was less than a week in. Even if I didn't get fired, a threesome with my big-time celebrity boss wasn't going to win me any reference letters. No. I needed a cold shower, a drink, and a woman to take the edge off.

Shaking my thoughts off, I made my way over to the huge basket sitting on the side of the bar. Snack foods overflowed from the edges. Wedged into the center was a white card with my name handwritten across the front. I studied it for a few minutes before strategically pulling at a corner, hoping everything didn't tumble out like a game of junk food Jenga.

Evan,

If you change your mind, I left a ticket to my show for you at the front desk. No pressure, but I know hotels can get boring. Even with all the free porn. I wasn't sure what you'd like, but I wanted you to have something to tide you over until our dinner. By the looks of your body, I also considered that you might be a health nut. So there's some fresh fruit and protein bars in your bedroom if you'd prefer. Help yourself to the minibar. It's all on me.
I'll see you tonight.
Hopefully at the show.

-Henry

Wow. It had only been an hour since I'd last seen him. His assistant, no doubt, must have been busy in that time. Although, with references to both porn and my body in only one paragraph, I knew for certain Henry had penned the note. Or at least dictated it over the phone. I laughed at the idea of the poor front desk clerk having to transcribe that onto a card.

Tugging my tie off, I moved to the first bedroom and found a covered dish containing enough fruit to feed a squadron. I inspected the massive bowl before using my fingers to pick a piece of kiwi from the corner and then pop it in my mouth. I moaned before snagging a second piece and heading to the closet while shrugging off my white uniform dress shirt.

After hanging my shirt up, I decided against exploring the rest of the suite and instead opted for a detour to the massive glass shower with four ceiling-mounted heads that would no doubt make me feel as though I were in the middle of a rainforest. Yeah, I could get used to this gig.

I was dripping wet with a plush, white towel wrapped around my waist when I padded across the heated floor of the bathroom. I looked at the clock, and it was nearly eight p.m. Henry's concert would be starting soon. The idea of seeing him in his element on stage was definitely intriguing, but Nikki hadn't answered when I'd returned her call earlier. She met her girls for drinks every Thursday after work, so I figured she'd be calling back any minute.

I wasn't sure what the hell I was going to say to her. Nothing had changed. But I was still desperate to talk to her. The way we'd left things was actually weighing heavily on my mind. Ya know, when I wasn't thinking about Henry. I groaned to myself. What the hell was wrong with me?

Unfortunately, it would have taken far longer than a night to truly figure out that. Settling on the bed, I stared at the ceiling and shook my head, trying to clear my mind with no success.

I'd begun to doze off when my phone started ringing.

I immediately snatched it off the nightstand, but I couldn't make out the caller's name on the broken screen.

"Hello?"

Nikki softly whispered across the line. "Hey."

I sat straight up and rubbed the sleepiness from my eyes. "Hey."

"How's it…um…going?"

I sighed sadly at the nervous shake of her voice. "I'm good, Nik. How 'bout you?"

"Honestly? I've been better."

I collapsed back onto the bed. "God, I'm so fucking sorry."

"There's nothing to be sorry for, Evan," she whispered.

"I know. But I still feel like I need to be apologizing. I hate that you're hurting."

She laughed without humor. "You always were a good guy."

One corner of my mouth hiked. "Not good enough or we wouldn't be here."

"Oh, come on. I'm not sure I'm going to have many more compliments for you in case you're fishing for them."

I chuckled. "No fishing. I swear."

We sat in awkward silence for several seconds.

"Evan…" she trailed off.

"Right here, Nik."

She sucked in a deep breath before whispering, "When did you know?"

I closed my eyes in defeat. I knew exactly what she was asking. It was the same question I'd asked myself every day since we'd broken up. I just didn't want to tell her. I also didn't want to lie to her anymore.

"Your birthday."

"Yeah. I figured."

Fuck. The defeat in her voice was slaying me.

After pushing to my feet, I began to pace the room. "Listen, Nik, it has nothing to do with you. *Nothing*," I swore. And it was the God's honest truth. "It's me. You're amazing. I'm just not built to be in a relationship."

"With a woman, you mean."

I froze midstep. "What…what's that supposed to mean?"

"Evan, just because you call him Shannon doesn't change the fact that he's a man."

Her verbal blow caused me to physically stumble.

I'd made no secret about the fact that I was bisexual with Nikki. It had even been her idea to invite another man into our bed a few months earlier on her birthday. It was a night we had both thoroughly enjoyed. It was also the night I realized I didn't mind sharing her. I would have died a slow, torturous death before ever allowing another human to touch Shannon. I did *not* share what was mine. But, that night, I'd sat on the bed, drinking a beer, and watched a guy she worked with named Neil repeatedly take her.

I'd laid down ground rules before we'd started that I wouldn't be sucking Neil's dick or bottoming for him. Fucking around or not, I wasn't anywhere near ready to expose myself like that to a man—and I feared I never would be again. My rules hadn't seemed to hinder anyone's enjoyment though. They'd both seemed to love it when I'd taken his ass while he'd been fucking her. And my dirty little secret was that, while I'd been inside him, Nikki, a woman I'd thought I saw a future with, had ceased to exist.

I should have walked away from her the very next day. But I'd stayed for three months. Unsure of what it all meant. And, worse, unsure of how I'd felt about it. It dug up emotions and memories of Shannon I had blocked out years ago. And, with every day that passed, I drifted further and further out of Nikki's reach. I had no clue what I wanted anymore. After as badly as I'd been burned, gay men scared the fucking shit out of me. But, honestly, so did women.

So, as I stood frozen in middle of my hotel room, listening to her accusation across the line, I knew she was wrong. Man, woman, T. rex, or mythical god. I was *not* built to be in a relationship—*with anyone.*

"*No.* Not with a man, either."

"Evan, it's nothing to be ashamed of."

I resumed my pacing, but my steps became heavy with anger. "I'm not ashamed of anything, Nikki. How the hell do you even know about Shannon?"

"I went to your place tonight to get my stuff. I was cleaning my clothes out of your closet and your shoebox of pictures fell off the top shelf."

"It fell," I repeated sarcastically. "Bullshit. You were going through my shit."

Her voice rose to match my own. "Maybe I was. But damn it, Evan, you didn't think to tell me that you spent two years in a committed relationship with *a man*?"

"I told you about Shannon!"

"Never with the pronoun him or he!" she shot back. "You knew exactly what you were doing. You knew I'd assume he was a woman."

I had no response. That was exactly what I'd done. I'd done it to every woman I'd ever been with since him. And her next statement explained exactly why.

"You don't think I deserved to know that the man I was falling in love with is gay?"

Labels. Labels. Labels.

The entire fucking world used them.

I fucking loathed them.

For some reason, bisexuality was the black hole of labels. It didn't mean you got two labels—gay and straight. It meant you got *zero.* To gays, you weren't gay enough. But, to straights, you weren't straight, either. You weren't enough for anyone. Most would assume that enjoying both genders would mean your dating pool was so vast you'd have no trouble finding a mate. They would assume *wrong*.

For me, bisexuality was a curse. Despite the widespread theory amongst homophobes everywhere, it didn't go hand in hand with promiscuity. It meant that an individual was attracted to both sexes. Nothing more. And nothing less. Some had a stronger preference. And, for a while, mine was men. But Shannon had more than fixed that. For the last ten years, I'd been living a relatively straight life. (See, even I used the labels!) But that did not mean I was suddenly straight. The one with Nikki wasn't the first threesome I'd ever had. But I emotionally couldn't handle anything more than a casual fuck with a man.

Yet, to hear Nikki tell it, I was still gay.

"No, I didn't think you needed to know! Because I'm not fucking gay!" I roared. "I told you on our second date that I was bisexual. Wait. You are right about one thing. I didn't tell you Shannon was a man. But who fucking cares? You sure as shit didn't while I was balls-deep in Neil's ass."

"And it ruined us!" she shouted back.

"No offense, Nik. But I'd had ass before you. It wasn't exactly my first time."

She scoffed. "Real classy, Evan."

"And you calling me gay is?" I barked a laugh. "This entire conversation is ridiculous. Jesus fuck. How did we get here? I've been waiting for over a week to get the chance to talk to you. To tell you that I *do* care about you. Maybe not the way you want me to, but I do. And this is what I get? Fuck."

"I just want you to accept who you are so you can finally be happy," she whined.

After marching to the minibar, I retrieved a bottle of beer. My patience was gone. I didn't even know the woman on the other end of that phone anymore.

"I think the only thing that I've *accepted* during this conversation is that we're done. And, if you want my opinion, if this is how you view me, we never should have been together in the first place."

"Evan!" she screeched.

"I've got to go. I'll be home tomorrow night. Please have your shit out of my house." I pressed end and tossed my phone on the bed, wishing I could have thrown it against the wall instead.

I drank beer after beer while staring at a tiny, black spot on the ceiling above my bed. I imagined I was flying. Gliding down through the clouds—only a tiny speck of the world below peeking through. It infinitely relaxed me, and slowly, my anger toward Nikki washed away. She didn't understand. She couldn't. Hell, I didn't even understand myself half the time. But there was one thing I knew: I wasn't wrong for being who I was.

I found the remote on the nightstand and set about mindlessly flipping through the channels on the TV. Nothing caught my attention, and before I'd realized it, I had looped back around to where I'd started. Pressing the On Demand button, I hoped there was a movie I hadn't seen.

I must have hoped entirely too hard, because I got *several*.

Front and center on the screen was a previously purchased folder, and though the icons were small, it was impossible to mistake them as anything but porn.

I quickly clicked the folder, and then I gaped before I lost it completely. Howling with laughter, I took in the titles of the videos that had been purchased.

Transformer Trannies, *G.I. Jack Off*, *He-man: Uncut*, and last but not least, *Spock It To Me*.

Yeah. Henry Alexander was a lot of things, but subtle was definitely not one of them. And I was quickly realizing he was shameless too.

But he also made me laugh.

I glanced behind me and saw that the clock only read nine fifteen.

I should have ordered up some room service for dinner.

I didn't. Against my better judgment, I snatched a pair of jeans from my bag and went to the hotel phone.

"Yes. My name is Evan Roth. I believe my boss left a ticket down there for me? Right. Of course. Also, I'll need a cab. Perfect, thanks."

chapter nine

Henry

I was halfway through my set, and Evan still hadn't showed. It had been a long shot, but I was disappointed all the same. For as many times as I'd scanned the front row for him, Jessica and Tabitha may as well have gotten a private performance. My bassist had even noticed my overwhelming interest in that side of the stage and started blocking me in an effort to get me moving around more.

I'd slapped his straight ass. The crowd had roared.

He'd probably quit. *Meh*. It was still worth it.

My biggest concern at the moment was: Why was my biggest concern at the moment where the hell Evan was? Why was this guy affecting me like this?

It wasn't even the chase anymore. I'd just really liked the idea of him watching me perform.

Apparently, I was wrong. *That* was my biggest concern.

Thousands of people were waving cell phones in the air and singing along to lyrics I'd written on a pad of paper while sitting on

Levee's old garage-sale couch when we'd been just two broke kids with dreams. And there I was, giving them a lackluster show because I was lost in thoughts about a man I had little to no chance with. And, even if I had a chance with him, it would be a fleeting experience.

It always was.

With a resigned sigh, I moved to the center of the stage and signaled to the guitar tech. He came rushing out with my guitar and stool.

"How's it going so far, Los Angeles?"

The place went nuts in reply.

"That bad, huh?" I laughed, adjusting my mic stand. "Come on. Let's try that again. I said, 'How's it going, Los Angeles?'"

My lids drooped as I filled my lungs with the mixture of sweat and smoke from the pyrotechnics that had long since been programmed into my olfactory nerves as the smell of home. My body soaked up the loud roars of a crowd, readily transferring them into the fuel that drove me through utter exhaustion.

That feeling of complete and total adoration was why I devoted so much of my life to my work. Friends and colleagues who had been prevalent in the industry when I'd first started had all gradually slowed over the years. Most had taken a step out of the spotlight, opting to work on smaller projects in exchange for time with their family or the anonymity needed to enjoy lazy days on the beach.

Not me. That stage was the only place I belonged.

But, as the high filled me, I found myself squinting past the bright lights to that empty seat in the front row. Disappointment slashed through me all over again.

I shouldn't have cared that much. But I did. Truly. Even if I didn't understand it.

Shaking my head at myself, I waited for the crowd to quiet before I continued. "Now, that was much better." I shrugged my guitar on and settled on the stool. "I have a confession to make," I said, strumming softly across the strings. "You guys probably know this, but I've been on the road a lot recently. Sometimes, it can get lonely."

Catcalls came from women and men alike, making me laugh.

"Not that kind of lonely," I crooned suggestively. "I figured why not bring my family with me tonight?"

There was exactly one person fans knew I referred to as my family. And this was why they lost their damn minds.

Over the deafening cheers, I announced, "Ladies and gentlemen, give it up for the amazingly talented love of my life, Levee Williams!"

In a flowing, red dress that barely masked her very obvious baby bulge, she strutted across the stage with a guitar hanging from her shoulder. Sam was predictably close behind her, dragging her stool. Part of me was shocked that he'd let her carry the guitar. His eyes were aimed at the ground, and a black long-sleeve shirt strategically covered his trademark tattoos. A tech could have gotten her stool, but while Sam might not have wanted to be recognized, he still wanted to be with her. I both smiled and felt my gut twist in jealousy at the sentiment.

That—what they had—wasn't meant for me.

But that didn't stop me from longing for it anyway.

"And who do we have here?" I stood, pulling my mic from the stand. I gave Levee a quick kiss on the forehead before walking over to Sam as he tried to make his getaway. "Whoa. Slow down there"—I paused dramatically before using the nickname Levee had publicly given him years earlier—"Spiderman."

The audience erupted all over again.

Sam glared at me out of the corner of his eye while lifting a hand to the crowd.

"Where ya going, Sam?" I offered him the mic, but he only shook his head. "You don't want to stay and hang out with the wonderful people of Los Angeles?"

He smirked. "I have a feeling it's not me they want to see."

"Oh, but I beg to differ." I tossed an arm around his shoulders and asked the audience, "What do you guys say? Should Sam stay?"

He glowered at me, putting his hand over my mic and mumbling, "I'm texting you seven million naked women tonight."

He'd do it too. I'd long since given up opening pictures from him. He'd scarred my retinas too many times.

Over the audience's resounding yes, Levee called, "Henry! Stop flirting with my husband and get your ass over here and sing with me."

"That baby has made you bossy," I teased, releasing Sam and sauntering back over to her. "Goodnight, sexy!" I called to him, putting my hand to my ear in the universal "call me" signal.

Levee slapped it away, which caused the crowd to laugh.

She shot me a wide grin that made a warmth of contentment fill my chest.

Yeah. This is exactly where I belong.

No matter who was or *wasn't* in the front row.

For the next fifteen minutes, Levee and I sat side by side and played an acoustic mashup of our most popular songs. And, for those fifteen minutes, the world disappeared.

There was no Evan.

No unrequited longing.

No fears.

No Robin.

No hurt.

No pain.

There was nothing but me, a guitar, a woman I'd give my life for, and the music that was my refuge.

When our dueling guitars fell silent, the rush of everything I had been hiding from found me in an instant. My eyes flashed to that seat in the front row. Only, this time, it was filled by the silhouette of a tall, dark, and sexy man I feared my imagination had conjured.

I blinked, waiting for it to disappear.

It didn't.

My heart skipped a beat as my already-wide smile stretched across my face.

I couldn't make his face out amongst the lights, but my gaze remained locked on him. I imagined his strong jaw ticking as he held my stare, powerless to look away. The confusion of why he was there would likely be torturing his mind, but his body would recognize the visceral urge that had forced him to come. He couldn't resist it. He didn't know what it meant. But the weight in his balls and the thickening of his cock would override his mind, making him needy for me.

Any way he could get me.

And every way I could take him.

A victorious growl rumbled in my chest.

But that wasn't the only draw I felt to him.

And, almost as much as it confused me, it made me needy for *him*.

Any way I could get *him*.

And every way he could take *me*.

Levee snapped me out of my trance by wrapping her arms around my neck. "What are you doing? I've said goodnight three times now. Say something so I can get out of here."

"Evan's here," I replied.

Her body shifted in my arms.

"Don't look!" I hissed, but it was too late. She was already offering him a finger wave.

The shadow of his head turned from side to side before he slowly lifted his large hand in an awkward return.

I licked my lips, and a blast of heat flushed my body.

Levee stepped into my line of sight, blocking him. Tugging me into another hug, she warned, "Please be careful. You've got that look in your eye."

Oh. I'd be careful, all right. But I had a feeling that condoms and lube weren't what she was talking about.

I also had a feeling that I wouldn't be heeding her advice.

Nodding, I stepped away. "Give it up for, Levee Williams!" I called to the crowd as she took a final bow, waving with both hands as she walked off stage.

I needed to see him—get a read on his face and figure out exactly why he had changed his mind about coming. My imagination often got the best of me, and the last thing I wanted was false hope if he was clearly only there for one of the girls.

While my band resumed their positions at their instruments, I made my way to the edge of the stage, stopping directly in front of him.

Nerves I had never felt in front of a crowd churned in my stomach.

It didn't matter why he was there. It only mattered that he'd come.

And—no matter what I had to do to make it happen—tonight, we'd both come.

Staggering confidence and overwhelming nerves battled inside me as I stepped around the lights and caught my first real look at him.

Dark jeans hugged his muscular thighs as he lounged casually in his seat. The front row rushed toward me, but Evan didn't budge. His thick arms were crossed over his chest, and those intense, blue eyes swept over me from toe to head before finally meeting my gaze. His expression was impassive, but it gave me hope, because even as Tabitha and Jessica jumped and cheered, his attention never left mine.

Never.

Not once.

In the middle of the sold-out arena, as cameras projected me onto the huge screens on either side of the stage, the world fell away. With his gaze anchored to mine, the six feet that separated us was inconsequential and the air between us became charged, prickling the hair on the back of my neck.

We were two of nearly twenty thousand people.

But we were alone.

His lips twitched in the way I was learning they always did when he thought he was topping me. Maybe not sexually, yet. But that slight tip of his lips appeared in the rare moments when I would drop my guard enough for him to truly see me.

It wasn't supposed to happen like that. But, for reasons lost on me, Evan could strip whatever disguise I attempted to hide behind. Fame, fortune, fear. He saw through them all.

I'd made no secret that I was pursuing him. But, right then, as I was held hostage by nothing more than his gaze, he was no longer in my crosshairs.

I was in his.

The band began playing my intro for the next song, but my mouth had dried and I was already out of breath from simple eye contact. Evan, though, appeared utterly unfazed.

The hand on my mic instinctively lifted to my mouth, but I'd already missed my cue. The band flawlessly looped, repeating the intro.

For the first time ever, I couldn't sing a single note.

Squirming under his gaze while standing in front of a sold-out crowd just became the most arousing experience of my life.

And I knew he felt it too when a lazy smile played at the corner of his lips before his eyes swept back over me.

Dear God. I didn't have to fuck him to get the high.

Evan Roth had just become my favorite drug of all and I hadn't even tasted him yet.

chapter ten

Evan

From what I saw of the show, it was good.

But all I'd really seen was Henry. And *he* was incredible.

I hated to admit the places my mind went as I watched him performing. Part of that was because he was gorgeous up there in the spotlight. His white T-shirt drenched with sweat, clinging to the curve of his pecs, and those black pants that hugged his ass in ways that spoke directly to my cock. His lips against the microphone made my skin heat, but the odd and alluring combination of smooth grit that came from his mouth had me fighting an inferno.

I enjoyed every painful moment, even as I willed time to speed so the show could end and put me out of my misery.

Whatever excuse my head had used for why I'd decided to come tonight was no longer the reason I was still there.

Not after the way I felt when his eyes repeatedly landed on me as if I had been the only one in attendance. Every step he took on that stage was carefully choreographed as part of his performance, but every stolen glance my way was like foreplay. I felt each one in my balls.

He knew what he was doing.

I knew what he was doing.

And, as soon as I got Jessica involved, I knew what *we* would be doing.

I was fucking starving, but it wasn't for dinner.

Henry would absolutely be fed though.

I groaned to myself and closed my eyes, desperately trying to think about anything other than his mouth wrapped around my cock, devouring me from base to tip.

"You okay?" Jessica asked in a gentle voice.

My eyes popped open and I turned my attention her way.

She was cute. Great tits. All of that deep-red hair I could wrap around my fist as I fucked her. Her toned legs would have looked amazing wrapped around my hips as I drove inside her.

My dick didn't even twitch.

At least, not until I added Henry into my little fantasy.

His mouth traveling up my neck, to my ear, sucking before his deep, raspy voice whispered my name. His hands teasing up my abs, plucking my nipples, and then making their way into my hair. He'd give it a hard tug, forcing me to cry out in pain right before he'd seal his mouth over mine, swallowing my pleas for more.

"Evan?" Jessica whispered when I didn't answer.

Blinking rapidly, I dragged myself out of what could have very easily become my first wet *day*dream.

Shifting to hide the bulge in my jeans, I replied, "Yeah?"

"You looked lost." She tucked a piece of hair behind her ear and looked away in a wasted effort to be coy.

I needed her to be brazen. I had enough work in front of me with Henry. If I was going to make this happen, I had to pull his attention away from Tabitha the Twat long enough for him to agree to Jessica.

"I wonder what's taking so long?" Tabitha whined while fixing her hair in the mirror. Again. For the fiftieth time.

Over the last thirty minutes, I'd discovered that, while Tabitha was absolutely beautiful to look at, she was a raging hemorrhoid to be around. She had bitched about everything, including the fact that Carter had escorted us to Henry's dressing room after the show. Despite the fact that Jessica had said that Henry had been preoccupied and distant at dinner, Tabitha had still gotten her thong in a knot that he hadn't worn her on his arm while he did…well, whatever the hell famous musicians did after a concert.

Henry had made it clear to me on the plane that Tabitha was his, but I wasn't sure I could stay hard with her in the same room.

No. Jessica was our girl.

She would be the physical barrier that made my desperate need to be with Henry safe. Her very presence would take our interaction from off-limits to open season.

I smiled to myself, and then I slung my arm around her shoulders and pulled her into my side. "I *was* lost. But I'm back now." I winked and mentally counted the shades of pink her cheeks flashed through on their journey to red.

Four.

None were even remotely as appealing as Henry's natural bronze.

"I bet he fires that guy who put us back here," Tabitha said, pacing the room.

I dramatically rolled my eyes, which made Jessica giggle. She shifted closer into my side, and I smiled down at her. That smile fell seconds later when Henry came flying into the room.

"I'm so sorry! I got out of there as soon as I—" The words died in his mouth when his eyes landed on me.

But they didn't just land *on me*. They landed on *my hand*—which was wrapped around Jessica's waist.

"Hey, baby," Tabitha purred, moving to his side.

Henry remained frozen as she sidled up beside him. The sad surprise in his gaze locked on my hand pained me.

And then it set me ablaze.

I fucking loved the disappointment that contorted his handsome face.

There was no way to misinterpret his feelings.

He wanted *me*.

And he was afraid I wanted *her*.

It might have made me an asshole, but I had to fight a smile back. There wasn't any point in pretending I didn't want him too. As much as I enjoyed a good game of cat and mouse, I enjoyed the bypass-the-bullshit, get-on-your-knees-so-I-can-fuck-your-mouth game more.

"Henry," I called, his mask falling into place as he lifted his eyes to mine. I released Jessica and took two long strides in his direction. "Can I have a word with you in private?"

He nodded robotically, his eyes flashing back to Jessica before he silently followed me out the door.

Tabitha groaned her objection, but Henry's only reply was to snap his fingers to silence her. Her face was priceless.

I nearly took a header into Carter's chest when we exited the room.

"Everything okay?" he asked, glancing over my shoulder at Henry.

"That room empty?" I pointed at the door across the hall. "I need to have a word with Henry. Alone."

His eyebrows popped in surprise, but a slow smirk formed on his lips. "Yep. Sam and Levee just left. It's all yours."

I didn't acknowledge Henry, but I felt him follow me.

Carter's brow furrowed as we passed, and when I glanced back at Henry, I understood why. Deep lines of unease were visible on his forehead.

When we entered the dressing room, I found that it was near-ly identical to the one we'd just left. Minus Beauty and the Beast, though, of course.

It was clean. Well kept. But completely generic. The blank walls were better suited for dirty, drunken rock stars than the kind and classy Levee Williams. Or even the smooth and sexy Henry Alexan-der.

"I'm glad you made it," Henry finally spoke, walking to the fridge nestled in the corner. He retrieved a beer and then offered one in my direction.

We weren't going to be there long enough for me to finish it, so I shook my head.

"You're my boss," I announced, settling on the arm of the brown leather sofa.

He shrugged and tipped the beer to his lips. "So I see you cozied up with Jessica."

I didn't know Henry well at all. I actually barely knew anything about him that I hadn't read on the Internet. But I did know that, re-gardless of how hard he'd tried to play that statement off as innocent, it was still an accusation.

Jealousy wasn't attractive on anyone.

Except for Henry Alexander when it was over me.

Then it was fucking beautiful.

My lips twitched in synchronization with my cock.

His eyes dropped to my mouth and then narrowed.

"I need to know my job is safe," I said, linking my fingers togeth-er and resting them in my lap.

"Safe from what?"

I sighed, and for the first time since I'd found the *Transformer* porn on my hotel TV, I felt a twinge of doubt. "I really can't afford to lose this job. I can't believe I'm even considering doing this with my boss." I closed my eyes and pinched the bridge of my nose.

"Doing what with your boss?" he asked in an ominous whisper.

He must have moved fast, because when I opened my eyes, his beer had been discarded and he was staring down at me, wearing all the confidence in the world. It was a stark comparison to the downcast man from only moments ago.

The air crackled as he waited for me to reply. It wasn't a loaded question, and I had no fear about answering. But, with him so close, holding me captive with the dark desire filling his eyes, I was scared for a completely different reason.

There wasn't a woman in sight, and I'd willingly put myself in this position. I'd gotten too cocky, and in a single moment of weakness, he'd pounced.

I pushed to my feet, attempting to regain the upper hand, but even with my height and weight advantages, Henry was still in complete control. He took another step toward me, forcing me to retreat or collide with his chest.

I regretted my choice to back away, as it only gave him more power.

"You haven't answered me yet, Evan."

My name rolled off his tongue with such a practiced ease that I wondered how many times he'd said it since we'd met.

In the shower?

In his bed?

Late at night, with his hand pumping his dick?

And would it sound as good as it whispered across my skin while I was inside him?

Damn it. I should have brought Jessica with us.

My body jolted when my back hit the wall. I hadn't even realized I'd been moving away.

His strong jaw ticked, and the muscles on his neck tensed. "Do *what* with your boss, Evan?"

Why does he keep saying my name?

Dear God, please keep saying my name.

He put his palm on the wall next to my head and leaned in close. He was careful not to touch me, but the lack of contact only intensified the sparks exploding inside me.

The tip of his tongue snaked out to dampen his lips, and I couldn't help but mirror the action.

"I don't usually do stuff like this," I mumbled, suddenly caring what he thought of me.

"Good," he replied, fighting a grin back.

"I don't want anything to do with Tabitha."

He cocked his head to the side, but his grin grew into a full-blown, breathtaking smile. "Another good."

My heart pounded at his proximity. There were still several inches between our bodies, but our noses could have brushed with the slightest bit of effort. Our lips only slightly more.

God, I wanted the more.

Why, oh fucking why, hadn't I seen this coming and brought Jessica?

And why, oh fucking why, was I standing there like a bitch, unable to formulate a complete thought.

I cleared the suffocating sexual tension from my throat and demanded, "Tell me my job is safe."

His eyes sparkled with amusement. "You have a one-year contract with me. No matter what you *do* with me, that will remain intact."

"Give me your word."

His teeth raked over his bottom lip. "I'll give you anything you want, Evan."

Again with the name.

I shivered in the most non-masculine way possible. "I…I want your word. That no matter what happens. My job is safe. And you don't run your mouth about it. It stays our secret."

His shoulders gave the oddest flinch, which he quickly tried to hide with an insincere chuckle. But the light in his eyes had dimmed so low I was afraid I'd never see them flicker again.

And it should be known that I was desperate to see that mischievous glint again.

Gripping his waist, I spun so fast he didn't have a chance to react. My chest slammed into his as I pinned him against the wall. Hip to torso, our bodies were flush. He could probably feel my cock thickening against his leg, but I was more worried about suppressing the moan at the feel of his growing against mine. Long. Thick. Promising.

Teasing my nose against his, I breathed, "Tell me my job's safe."

He barely managed to squeak, "Your job's safe."

"Good," I breathed just before slamming my mouth over his.

The shock registered in his eyes for only a second before they fluttered shut. Pushing and pulling, our tongues dueled in a rough kiss. He met me stroke for stroke, twisting and gliding.

He lifted his hands and began exploring my shoulders and my back, and my focus faltered, struggling to choose which sensation felt better—his fingers or his mouth. I needed to remove one from the equation, and releasing his mouth wasn't an option. Using a knee, I pushed between his legs, allowing my hips to take over my hold on him. I couldn't risk him trying to regain his control. I had a strong suspicion that, if he did, we'd be finishing this before Jessica could even make it across the hall.

Grasping his wrists, I pressed them to the wall on either side of him. He moaned, and I swear to God I tasted it. His pure, carnal need filled my senses.

Slanting my head at every possible angle, I tried to get closer. It was a futile effort, because with one taste, I knew close enough with Henry didn't exist.

I also knew I was going to try anyway.

With no other way to move, his hips rolled against mine—his hard-on finding brief friction with mine.

Fuck.

Shit. That felt good.

Too good.

And it dragged me out of the moment.

Rules were a real bitch like that.

But the reasons for the rules were even worse.

My chest heaved as I quickly stepped away. I couldn't catch my breath, not while staring at his swollen and bruised lips. The scruff on my chin had left red marks across his mouth, and I'll be damned if the sight didn't make me want to go back for seconds.

With wide eyes, he lifted his hand to his lips. Gone was his confident smirk, but if possible, the sexual fog was even better. It made me want more than just seconds.

And I didn't have to wait long before Henry gave them to me.

He stormed forward, crashing his mouth against mine. His hands flew into my hair, holding me to him as his tongue pillaged my mouth. It was raw but far from harsh.

Sliding his hands down to my ass, he ground himself against me. We both groaned at the contact.

"Please," he breathed into my mouth.

What he wanted wasn't lost on me.

I just couldn't give it to him.

He kept at my mouth while his fingers drifted down my chest. They paused to brush over my nipple before continuing to my abs. The cool air met my stomach as he pressed my shirt up and snuck his hand underneath.

"Fuck. Your body. Insane," he moaned, teasing his way over the ripples of my abs.

A smile crept across my mouth at his praise. Henry could no

doubt have any man he wanted, and there he was—with me.

Hard as a fucking rock.

Speechless over my body.

Me.

And I was about five seconds from letting him have me. At least physically.

If I didn't end this until I could get Jessica in the middle, it was going to ruin everything I had promised myself over the last decade.

I couldn't go back down that road.

Not even for Henry.

Fuck… Especially not for Henry.

His fingers had just slipped into the waistband of my jeans when I backed out of his reach.

"Evan?" he called, but my senses were finally reemerging.

Wiping my mouth on the back of my arm, I said, "That. Can't—" I stopped when a strange emotion passed over his face. It looked a lot like understanding, as if it were a moment he'd been waiting for. I arched an eyebrow but continued. "That can't happen again."

He immediately lifted his hands in surrender but sauntered toward me. "Okay. Just calm down. It's fine."

It wasn't. Because I wanted it—and so much more—to happen again.

He didn't stop advancing until he was in my space.

Not touching me.

Just hovering.

"It's okay. I promise," he whispered.

I wanted to kiss him again.

I wanted *him* to kiss *me* again.

Instead, I fisted my hands at my sides to keep from touching him.

"So let's forget that happened. No one will know." His warm breath breezed across my jaw. "Your job is safe, Evan."

Stop saying my name! I'm the only one in the room!

"Do you still want to go to dinner? We could go back to my suite and order up some food if that would make you more comfortable. I'll get rid of the girls—"

"No." I interrupted. "Get rid of Tabitha. Jessica stays."

His mouth formed a thin line. "Right. Jessica."

I couldn't help the twitch of my lips. A reaction he definitely noticed.

Pointing at the wall where I'd just had him pinned, I said, "That won't happen again. I don't do the gay thing, Henry."

He swayed away, but I caught him at the back of his neck.

"However, if we add Jessica, I think we might be onto something."

His eyes flared wide. "Add Jessica?"

"Threesome. I'm sure you know how to share." I curled my hand into the blond hair at the nape of his neck.

"I, uh…" he stammered.

"That's my offer, Henry. I can't fuck Tabitha. I'm afraid my dick would freeze off."

His eyes nervously searched mine. "Evan, I…"

I stepped away and began smoothing my mussed shirt down. "Don't stress. I'll convince Jessica. Your job is figuring out how to get the house to fall on the wicked witch."

His eyes lit and his smile returned. "Did you just use a *Wizard of Oz* reference?"

I ignored his question. "Deal?"

He swallowed hard and glanced over my shoulder at the door. "Um…"

No *um.*

Um was unacceptable when my balls were aching for this man. He could fuck Tabitha on his own time. If I was going to risk the best job I'd ever had to be with him, *um* shouldn't have been in his vocabulary.

I wasn't above playing dirty.

"Deal?" I repeated, adjusting my hard-on in my jeans.

His eyed jumped down at the movement, and then he swallowed hard. "Yeah. Deal."

A huge smile spread across my face as I headed toward the door. I didn't look back.

But, some hours later, I'd wish that I had.

Because, in my haste to get Jessica and then get the hell to the hotel, I completely missed the paralyzing panic etched across Henry's face.

chapter eleven

Henry

It took every ounce of self-restraint I possessed not to dive across the limo and pull the silky, red hair from her head. I wasn't a violent person. And anyone could see that Jessica was a sweet girl. However, if I had to watch her whisper one more word in Evan's ear, I was going to end up in jail.

She was sitting sideways on the seat with her knees hooked over his thigh, and his hand was lazily caressing her leg.

Caressing.

Her.

Leg.

The same hands that, not twenty minutes earlier, had been cupping my jaw as he'd kissed me to the point of insanity. The same hands that had grabbed my ass in a fevered rush to grind his dick against mine. The same hands I wanted wrapped around my shaft when I came in his mouth.

Those hands were mine.

Yep. *Those hands* were caressing *Jessica's leg.*

If it wouldn't have been such a downer on what I hoped would be a very good evening, I would have shoved her out the door. Or, at the very least, pulled over and dropped her off in a well-lit parking lot, maybe even left Carter with her for safety purposes. I didn't particularly have a preference on which way it happened; I just needed her to get the fuck away from him.

But no, I couldn't do any of that. If I wanted *those hands* back on me, I had to figure out a way to have sex with her. And I assumed that would most likely require me to touch her naked body without gagging.

It appeared my bisexual ploy with Evan was backfiring on me big time.

He had already broached the topic of a threesome with her. I could tell by the blush of her cheeks as he'd whispered into her ear and then the way her eyes had slowly slid over to me.

There was no doubt that her answer was going to be yes. Evan was unbelievably sexy, and I was some kind of prize trophy for no other reason than the world had told her I was.

My fingers had been crossed that she was a prude who'd balk at the idea of premarital sex with just one man, much less two. But my heart sank when she'd enthusiastically nodded in my direction.

"Have another drink, doll," I said, leaning forward to top off her glass of champagne.

She assumed my attention was a flirty gesture and seductively brushed her finger up my thigh.

Evan smiled.

I fought a cringe.

In reality, I was just trying to get her drunk. Not even Evan could argue the merits of seducing a drunk woman.

Blowing out a defeated breath, I settled back on my seat across from them, my gaze returning to his hand at her leg.

What the hell was I doing? I wasn't a coward. I wasn't confused about my sexuality. I wasn't hard up or desperate. It would have only taken one sentence to end this whole charade: *I'm not into women.*

However, Evan's words still rang in my ears. *"I don't do the gay thing."*

And really, I just wanted to do the Evan Roth thing. I wanted his hands on me again. And definitely his mouth. I wanted to peel his shirt off so I could finally get a good look at the muscles that covered his stomach…and his shoulders…and his chest. I wanted to feel his hard body pinning me into a mattress as his fingers threaded through my hair. I wanted to see his blue eyes staring into mine as he slowly pressed inside me.

Really, there was only one thing I didn't want with Evan. And that was for a woman to be involved.

"Where'd you send Tabitha?" Jessica asked, swirling her champagne around in the flute.

"I gave her a private room and then had the hotel send a masseuse up to her. She's probably assuming that I'll be up later." *Because I told her I'd be up there later.* I glanced at Evan. "I won't."

He winked, sending my stomach aflutter like a teenage boy watching *Queer As Folk.*

Jessica started kissing up his neck, and I quickly diverted my gaze. It wasn't necessary to watch. I still felt every brush of her lips against his skin—in my gut.

"Henry," Evan called.

Keeping my eyes aimed out the window, I replied, "Yeah."

"I was just telling Jessica how we met."

A laugh sprang from my throat. I absently lifted my champagne glass in a toast. "It's a good story, Maverick."

"Oh! Since you're Maverick, can I be Goose?" She giggled.

My fingers spasmed around the glass as my patience with the whole situation evaporated.

Snapping my attention to her, I curled my lip as she slid a hand under the hem of his shirt. Those were *my* abs. And she was touching them.

Gritting my teeth, I leaned forward and pointedly whispered, "Goose *dies*, Jessica."

"What the..." Evan said only to trail off.

And then that fucking lip of his twitched, telling me that he was onto me. I would have cared if I hadn't been praying that he'd take note and end this bullshit with her—and then move his ass over to me so we could finish what we'd started earlier.

"She hasn't done anything like this before. I figured knowing a little bit more about us would go a long way in making her comfortable," he said.

And what about my comfort, Evan? What about the fact that I've never done anything like this before and have no fucking idea why I'm even considering it now?

I kept that to myself.

"Great idea," I mumbled dismissively.

After throwing the rest of my drink back, I promptly poured another. We were at least ten minutes from the hotel and my chest was so filled with dread for when we arrived it I felt as though I were a death row inmate.

"Come here, Henry." His tone was gentle, and if I closed my eyes, I could imagine it was just the two of us.

Keeping my gaze aimed at the floor, I moved to his side.

"I never would have taken you as the shy, nervous type," he teased quietly.

I wasn't shy or nervous. I was pissed the fuck off that the one person I wanted needed a woman involved in order to want me too.

His eyes found my mouth as our thighs pressed against each other. Heat radiated like a ball of fire from the point of contact. That was all it took with Evan. A simple brush of his leg and I was rock hard.

"I'll be fine," I replied. And I would be—as soon as she got the hell off him and gave me a turn.

A turn?

God, I seriously hate myself right now.

Refusing to look at her, I couldn't tell exactly what she was doing. All that mattered was that his gaze was still intently aimed at my mouth. Was I allowed to kiss him? Why was I questioning if I was allowed to do anything? Oh, right—because we were playing *his* game now.

Fuck that.

I inched closer, brushing my lips across his in an almost kiss.

"Whoa," she breathed, finally drawing my attention to hers. "How does this work? Do you two…like, make out and stuff too?"

"Would that bother you?" Evan asked.

I didn't wait a single second to hear her reply. I hoped watching two men kiss would bother the fuck out of her. So much so that she would run like hell the moment we got to the hotel.

She gasped when my lips landed on his. His mouth opened with a growl. His hand *finally* left her leg and moved to the back of my head instead. I shifted, shoving her legs off his lap before swinging my own over to straddle his thigh. Most of my weight rested on my knee on the seat by his hip, but I carefully slid my other to the exposed seat at the junction between his legs. His cock immediately thickened at the contact.

Smiling against his mouth, I basked in the knowledge that he hadn't already been hard.

Not for her.

Just me.

For all I knew, Jessica had jumped from the moving vehicle by that point. Because, as his tongue rolled against mine and his hands slipped under my shirt, unabashedly exploring my body, she was nothing more than an afterthought. Or, in my case, a neverthought.

But that's when I felt her.

Her tits brushed against my arm and her lips found my neck. If I'd been forced at gunpoint to tell the absolute truth, I would have had to admit that it wasn't terrible to have Evan's tongue invading my mouth and her lips trailing up to my ear. However, it wasn't good, either.

But, as I opened my eyes and prepared to shut her down, I realized it was totally worth the heebie-jeebies.

His mouth was still moving against mine, but his eyes were slitted, focusing on her lips at my neck. There wasn't even a hint of enjoyment in his gaze. His forehead crinkled and the skin between his eyebrows pinched together. He hated watching her maul me, and the satisfaction that knowledge gave me was immeasurable.

Not so fun with the tables turned, now is it, Evan?

Smiling to myself, I tipped my head to the side, giving her more room just so I could witness his reaction. His lips came to a screeching halt. When her hand landed on my stomach, I recoiled, but it was worth every second because a deep growl rumbled in Evan's chest.

Not a moan. Not a groan.

I'm talking a possessive, animalistic *growl*.

He used the back of her head to peel her off me, and then he deepened our connection. He painfully gripped my hip as his kiss became punishing. It hurt in ways that made me feel as though he were repairing me. Unable to stop, I guided a hand between us and popped the button on his jeans. He broke the kiss long enough to pant his permission, which I hadn't asked for. And then I dipped one finger under his waistband and found the smooth, hard flesh at the head of his cock.

"Fuck, Henry." He lifted his hips and begged for more, but that was as far as I got.

Jessica's hand snaked down to join mine, reminding me once

again that she was there. I roughly caught her wrist, halting her wandering fingers.

I fought the urge to snap at her and instead whispered, "Slow down, doll." I then shot Evan a pointed glare, begging for him to put a stop to this.

He was lying to himself if he thought she was anything more than his safety net. He wanted her involved so he didn't have to admit to himself that he really only wanted me. But, if actions spoke louder than words, he was screaming my name so loud we'd both end up deaf.

Her lips had been at his throat, but the only place his had traveled was against my mouth. He hadn't even kissed her. And, besides his hand on her leg, he hadn't advanced on her at all, either.

He held my pleading gaze for a few beats before releasing an audible sigh and saying, "I can't do this."

Shifting me off his lap, he slid across the seat, leaving me wide open for Jessica to misread the entire situation and swing a leg over to straddle me.

"Wait. Wait. Wait." I pressed myself back into the seat, frantically reaching out for Evan.

This was so fucked up. It was like a comedy of errors without the actual comedy. I was a gay man trying to seduce a straight man who thought I was bisexual while he tried to pretend he wasn't interested in a gay man by requiring that we share a woman. Because that totally made it acceptable to dry-hump another man.

So.

Fucked.

Up.

I absolutely wanted Evan. I'd felt a connection with him earlier. One I would have given anything to explore further, but not by sacrificing a part of myself.

"Sorry, but this isn't going to happen," I told Jessica. I shifted my gaze to Evan. "I'm gay," I told him. "Not bi. Just gay." I laughed humorlessly. "I would do *anything* to be with you, Evan. But not this."

His shoulders fell, and he raked a hand through his hair. I expected anger or frustration from him. I *expected* the spiral down, where he would yell at me to go fuck myself as he reiterated that he wasn't gay. After that, I'd be forced to watch as he took Jessica and cashed in his tickets on the straight train.

"Henry…" he started.

"Don't." I waved him off, refusing to look at him again. I couldn't bear witnessing the regret. Not from him.

"Son of a bitch," he cursed, making me flinch.

I offered Jessica a sad smile. "Sorry, doll. Wrong equipment." I lifted her off my lap, placed her on the seat, and then quickly made my escape to the other side of the limo.

Luckily, it wasn't but a few awkward minutes until we came to a stop. Carter was in the front seat with my driver and didn't even have a chance to fold his giant body out before I bolted.

In my mad dash, I'd forgotten that we were in L.A.—home of the paparazzi. They were lined up on the sidewalk, waiting for me. My stomach was already in knots. I had no bag. No room key. No cell phone. Nothing but my wallet and a face that would ensure I couldn't even walk up to the front desk without being swarmed.

And my heart was breaking for reasons that made no fucking sense.

I needed to be alone.

Using my hands, I shielded my face from the blinding flashes.

"Carter!" I yelled.

The crowd enclosed around me, calling my name in a never ending round. This was the moment when I'd usually smile, sign autographs, pose for few photos, and then shoot the shit with the photogs I recognized. It was nothing new for me.

However, the panic attack creeping up on me absolutely was.

"Carter!" I yelled again, spinning in a circle. "Carter," I choked out one last time before the oxygen ran out. Folding over, I rested my hands on my knees as photographers snapped countless pictures of my breakdown.

Suddenly, a strong arm linked with mine and started dragging me toward the entrance.

"Get the hell out of the way!" Evan yelled, pushing people from our path.

I wanted to snatch my arm away and tell him that I didn't need his help.

I wanted to get my shit under control and take care of myself.

I wanted him to lead me through the chaos and then never leave.

Each was an equally worthless desire.

But with no other choice, I leaned into his side and allowed him to guide me through the clamoring crowd. Once we got into the hotel, he led me directly to the elevator. I briefly made eye contact with Carter just before the doors slid closed. Predictably, he was pissed, but I was too relieved to give a damn.

As the elevator carried us up, I remained folded over, doing my best to slow my breathing.

Evan's heavy hand landed on my back and his breath breezed over my ear as he whispered, "Ten, nine, eight. One in, one out, okay?"

I silently nodded, and he continued.

"Seven, six, five." He squeezed my shoulder reassuringly. "Four, three, two, one." He paused. "Shit…I fucked that up. Let's start at five again. Five, four, three, two…"

The elevator dinged just as the word *one* cleared his lips.

He kept his hand connected to base of my neck as he guided me into the suite and over to the couch.

"Are you going to be okay? I need to go see if Jessica made it up to her room safely."

Jessica.

I nodded.

After tossing a bottle of water next to me, he marched out the door.

It didn't hurt.

Not even a little.

It killed.

chapter twelve

Evan

was the world's biggest dick. Because of my little threesome bullshit, Jessica was now alone somewhere, probably feeling completely rejected, and Henry was in the middle of a panic attack that rivaled any I'd witnessed from him over flying.

He'd lied to me about being bisexual, but I should have known better. The signs were all there. The way he'd stared at me while on stage, basically ignoring the women. The way he'd deflated when he'd walked in and seen me holding Jessica. The way he'd glared at her in the limo. The way we'd both forgotten she was supposed to be involved the moments our bodies had touched. *Fuck.*

I hadn't been with a man since Shannon. Not one-on-one, at least. And especially not with one who unnerved me the way Henry did. Though, the minute we'd climbed into that limo with him, I'd wanted to ask her to leave. I hadn't been able to think of anything except getting another taste of his mouth—and, if I'm being honest, every other part of his body.

I knocked on the door to room 9965, praying that I'd remembered the numbers correctly.

"Who is it?" Jessica called in a soft voice that made me feel even more like an asshole.

"It's me. Evan."

The door immediately opened. She was still in her shirt and her skirt, but she wasn't wearing her shoes. It made her smaller than I'd remembered. Her makeup had worn off a good bit since the concert, and for the first time, I realized just how young she was underneath it all. Shit. She couldn't have been any older than twenty-five. Probably fresh out of college and enjoying her first job in the real world.

And I had been about to fuck her just so I could feel better about fucking Henry.

God. I'm a prick.

"Hey, " she said with a smile.

"Hey." I rocked to my toes and wedged a hand into my pocket.

She pulled the door open wide. "You want to come in?"

"I can't. I just wanted to come down to apologize and make sure you made it to your room safely."

She shyly crossed her arms over her chest. "Yeah. The big guy walked me up when the coast was clear."

"Good," I whispered. "Listen, about that shit in the limo. I'm—"

She cut my apology off with a laugh. "It's okay, Evan. I'd heard he was gay. It was more of a surprise when you said he wanted to mess around."

"Yeah, but I still feel bad. I want you to know that we *both* think you're incredibly beautiful and—"

"Evan, stop. You don't have to do this. I'm not crying myself to sleep tonight because I'm not his type." She shrugged. "Hey, I made it further than my snobby cousin, Tabitha, right? That's a win in my book."

I chuckled. "She really is a snob."

We both laugh for a second before falling into an uncomfortable silence.

"Look, the threesome thing might not have worked out, but a twosome is still on the table." Her eyes flashed to ground as her cheeks blushed.

I swallowed hard. "Jessica…I can't. I'm really sorry."

"It's okay. I get it. Can't blame a girl for trying. But, if you change your mind, I'll be here, drowning my sorrows in the entire room service dessert menu on Henry's dime." She smiled. "Anyway, go on and get out of here. Get back to your guy."

I threw my hands up in defense. "Okay, slow down there. He's not my guy."

She rolled her eyes and propped her shoulder on the doorjamb. "I was there, Evan. Remember? If he isn't your guy, I can promise he wants to be."

Panic built in my chest, but I covered it with a hearty dose of laughter. "Maybe. But that's not going to happen. Trust me."

"Oh, come on. He's Henry Alexander. At least let him take you on a world tour or buy you a Porsche or something."

I laughed. "And, on that note, I'm headed to bed. I'm sorry about everything, but it was nice to meet you tonight." I smiled, backing away from her door.

"It was nice to almost have sex with you, Evan."

I barked a laugh then watched her door close. When I heard the deadbolt, I dashed toward the elevator, shaking my head at the entire interaction.

The shower in the second bedroom was running when I got back to my suite. I was thrilled Henry hadn't left, but I was nervous about talking to him. He deserved an apology too, but I had the feeling it wasn't going to be as simple as it had been with Jessica.

Henry was incredible. Magnetic, really. It was hard not to want him. But the fact remained—I didn't have anything to give. If he hadn't been my boss, I would have taken the coward's way out, cutting my losses and avoiding him completely. That wasn't an option though.

The incendiary spark I felt for Henry needed to be extinguished before it had the chance to explode.

I paced a path in front of the bedroom door, waiting for him to emerge.

And emerge he did, dripping wet and in nothing but a towel wrapped around his hips. Drops of water glistened on his tan skin.

He froze when he saw me. Surprise and excitement passed over his face, but they quickly faded, leaving nothing but bitterness behind.

We spoke at the same time.

"You have a quickie?"

"Are you okay?"

The latter was me.

We responded at the same time too.

"What?"

"I'm fantastic."

I didn't believe him. Sure, he looked edible—but not fantastic. He was hurting, and just from looking at him, I felt the echo of his pain.

"Henry—"

"She kick you out?"

I had to clear the lump from my throat before I could answer. "Who?"

"Jessica," he spat.

My head snapped back at his accusation. "What? No! I just went to make sure she got back to her room, Henry. Nothing happened."

He rolled his eyes, walking to the snack basket he'd bought me. "It's okay, Evan. I get it."

He got it? Thank fucking God, because I sure as hell didn't get it. I had no idea why I felt as though I were constantly fighting a maelstrom of physical desperation every time he walked into a room. I didn't understand how, after all these years of avoiding men, I was suddenly enamored by one I barely even knew. I didn't understand how he had enraptured me with a single stare from across a crowded arena. I didn't know why the heat from his flames consumed me like never before. I didn't know why my mind was screaming at me to run as far away as I could, but my body absolutely refused. I didn't know why I'd felt his pain in the limo as he'd admitted he was gay as if he had been coming out for the very first time. I didn't know why I was still standing in that room with him when I was positive this was going to be a disaster.

But, if he held the answers to even one of those questions, I needed to know too.

I grabbed his bicep and pulled him until his shoulder hit my chest. "You get what, Henry?"

Shock registered in his eyes. "Um…I just meant, if you *did* want Jessica, I'd get it."

"I don't." The words shot from my mouth like an involuntary reflex.

I didn't understand that, either.

"Fuck!" I shouted in frustration.

After reluctantly releasing him, I locked my fingers and rested them on the top of my head.

"Evan?"

Evan. It was like a feather down my spine.

I closed my eyes and painfully whispered, "Please don't say my name."

His hand cupped the back of my neck. "Okay, then, Maverick.

Tell me what's going on."

I sighed at the horrible nickname and opened my eyes. His plump bottom lip was the first thing that came into my view.

"I wish I could, Henry."

His Adam's apple bobbed as he swallowed. "Whatever it is, I can promise you I'll understand. I'm betting I even feel the same way." He dropped his forehead to mine. "All you have to do is just say the words and I'll make it happen. Whatever it is."

But saying it aloud was something I was nowhere near ready for. I couldn't admit why I'd made all of those impossible rules and promises to myself after Shannon had left. No more than I could *forget* why I'd made them in the first place.

The memories sliced through me. Not again. No fucking way.

"Tonight shouldn't have happened," I lied, the words feeling like razorblades coming from my mouth. "It was entirely unprofessional of me."

"Unprofessional?" He leaned away, obviously confused by my sudden switch.

"You're my boss. And I crossed the line."

His hands fell away. "What the hell are you talking about? Evan, *I* drew that line, and *I* invited you to cross it. I've already told you your job is safe. Drop the professional shit."

"Okay. Sorry. Consider it dropped. All of it. I'm just gonna go to bed now. You can let yourself out. Thanks again for a truly unforgettable experience."

I meant the royal treatment at the concert, the lavish hotel, the limo, and the gift baskets. But deep down, I was thanking him for reminding me that fire still existed in the world.

He actually stumbled back a step before recovering. "Ah, yes. The experience." He dropped his voice, but the whisper did nothing to hide his dejection. "You're welcome, Evan." Turning toward the bar, he gave me his back.

That was the end. I'd apologized, and now, I just needed to make my getaway.

And, as soon as we got home, I needed to start job-hunting immediately.

But, regardless of what I told myself, my feet wouldn't move.

My hands wouldn't stop aching for him.

My mouth still craved his.

My eyes couldn't even look away from his back.

Walk away.

I took a step toward him.

Jesus Christ. Go to fucking bed.

Another step.

The pounding of my heart probably could have been heard from across the room. And the closer I got, the more I could feel the heat of his fire searing my skin.

You know how this will end. There won't even be enough of you left to identify the body.

Another step.

It could be strictly physical. That's probably all he wants anyway. Where's the harm in casual sex? Shannon, you dumbass. That is the harm in casual sex.

Another step.

He must have felt me. "Jesus Christ, what now?" he snapped, turning to face me.

I was only inches away.

"Wh-what are you doing?"

"Evan," I prompted. "Say it."

"Oh, for fuck's sake. I'm going to catch pneumonia if you go from hot to cold one more time."

But what Henry couldn't possibly know was that there was nothing cold about me when it came to him. No matter how hard I tried to fake it.

My head was still a jumbled mess, but my body had finally won the tug-of-war.

Closing the last step of distance between us, I loomed over him. "Repeat the question, and use my name this time."

His head tipped back to maintain eye contact, and a new confidence transformed his voice. "What are you doing, *Evan*?"

"I have no fucking idea. Probably making some really bad career decisions."

A smile split his mouth as he swayed toward me, bringing his chest to mine. "Your job"—he brushed his nose against mine—"is safe. Stop talking about it and tell me how long I have until the ice storm hits again."

My lips twitched. "At least until the sun comes up."

"Then we better get busy." He winked.

Nerves surged in my stomach, but I dipped my chin in a nod.

He immediately found the hem of my shirt and peeled it over my head, groaning as he visually fondled my every muscle. "Christ. Your fucking body."

"Evan," I reminded.

He smirked, sweeping his lips across mine before breathing, "Evan."

That was all it took. I crushed my mouth to his. And, this time, I knew I wouldn't be stopping.

Tangling my fingers in the back of his hair, I gave it a tug to tip his head back. "What are you doing to me?" I asked, moving my assault to his neck, nipping and biting as I trailed down to his shoulder.

He took a step forward, backing me toward the couch. "Everything. Repeatedly."

I gave his hair a pointed yank and gripped his jaw so he had no choice but to look me in the eyes. "I'm serious."

He pressed against my chest, backing me toward the couch. "So am I. Now, sit."

Unmoving, I glared my reminder.

"Oh, right. *Evan*."

I collapsed onto the couch, watching intently as his hand slowly made it down to the tent at the front of his towel. He rubbed his hidden length, and I felt it as though it were my own.

"I should warn you, Evan. My balls might be purple after the torture you've put me through tonight."

The corner of my mouth twitched.

He licked his lips in response. "I fucking love when your lips do that, but it's only making things…harder." With one flick of his wrist, his towel was gone. His heavy erection bobbed before he caught the shaft and gave it a quick tug.

My body thrummed and my mouth watered to taste him, but that was one rule I wasn't okay with breaking. At least, not yet.

He jutted his chin toward the raging hard-on battling for a way out of my pants. "Your turn."

My gaze lifted from his hand slowly sliding up his steely rod and caught the victorious glint dancing in his eyes. I was in way over my head. I could feel it in my bones. My need and desire for him made me completely out of control.

"Casual sex. Nothing more," I said, doing my best to ignore his arm pumping in my peripheral vision.

He shrugged nonchalantly. "Works for me."

Shit. Why does that hurt? Yet another thing I didn't understand.

I was going to need more protection—more rules.

"You don't fuck me." I moved my hands down to hover over my button, waiting for his confirmation.

He frowned. "Not even in the mouth?"

"Not at all."

"Fine," he huffed. "Are your rules done? Can you *please* just get naked and be easy for once."

My lips twitched in response to his eagerness. Suddenly, I was in the mood to be easy too.

Pushing to my feet, I crowded his space. And then I uttered the four words I hadn't said to a man in almost a decade.

"Get on your knees."

chapter thirteen

Henry

I **really** *was* a whore, because my knees hit the floor before the final syllable had cleared his lips. Just as quickly, my hands were at his zipper, and then I was pushing his pants down his thighs until his all-but-concrete dick popped free.

He hadn't even stepped out of his jeans before I wrapped my mouth around the head.

"Fuck," he groaned, threading his fingers into the top of my hair.

I circled my fingers around his substantial shaft and slid him from my mouth. I desperately wanted to see what I was working with. I'd been staring at the sizable bulge in his pants for most of the night. He was large. It perfectly fit his massive frame. I might have had him on length, but I paled in comparison to his girth.

I glanced up, fully expecting his eyes to be closed, as I slid him back into my mouth. Straight guys rarely turned a blowie down, but they didn't like to watch. Not Evan though. He was staring down at me with feral intensity brewing in the depths of his blue eyes.

ALY MARTINEZ

He wanted a show, and luckily, I loved to perform.

I released him from my mouth and jerked several fast strokes, twisting and tugging until a bead of precome appeared—fucking perfection glistening on the tip. Then I held his gaze as I laved it with my tongue, moaning when the saltiness registered on my taste buds.

His fingers tensed in my hair, halting any further movement.

I couldn't stop now, no matter what kind of second thoughts he was having.

"Just let me do this, Evan. I swear it—"

"Oh, I'm not trying to stop you. I'm trying to give myself a second so I don't blow my load on stroke number three." He smiled down at me and finished with, "*Henry.*"

I *could* have blown my load without a single touch for no other reason than he used my name.

He might have been confused and fighting it. But he was still with *me*. It wasn't a woman he was imagining at his feet. It was me. And, for that reason, I was going to give him the best blow job of his life—one he would still remember as he took his last breath.

Because, with just one simple word, he'd given that to me too.

Sliding him as deep as I could, I began working him with newfound fervor. I alternated between fast and hard, fisting his cock and sucking the head to the point I was sure it toed the fine line between pain and ecstasy. When I felt his shaft swell with impending release, I let up, switching to slow and soft. My tongue circled his angry crown before tracing up the vein running from base to tip. Squeezing on each upstroke, I forced more of his arousal from his slit.

Each time, I sought his gaze before lazily licking it off.

And, each time, Evan would reward me with something different.

"Henry," he whispered.

"Henry," he groaned.

"Henry," he cursed.

"Henry," he cried.

My name filled his every emotion.

And that filled me in places I hadn't known were empty.

When his legs began to shake, I slowly inched him back toward the couch then lowered my attention to the sensitive flesh just under his heavy sac—flicking it with my tongue. His knees buckled on contact, sending him crashing down. I gave him exactly zero seconds to recover before resuming my assault.

It didn't take long before his hips were bucking into my mouth. His hand remained in my hair, pumping my head into a rhythm I could tell he both loved and hated.

Loved because it guided him to release.

Hated because it guided him toward the end.

"Wait, Henry. Stop. I'm gonna…" He trailed off, but when I didn't let up, he finished the sentence in my mouth. His cock twitched violently as he painted my tongue white.

Squirming under me, he cussed as I milked him with my hand and my mouth, sucking and squeezing until I was positive he had nothing left to give.

And then I swallowed every last drop.

Usually, one of two things happened after a man came in another man's mouth for the first time:

His entire body would go limp as he basked in the glory of an in-fucking-sane orgasm. Feeling as though his very life had been sucked out of him through his dick.

Or…

Without the sexual need calling the shots, he'd fly from the couch in absolute horror at the realization of what he'd done.

And, as I sat between Evan's legs, his breathing still labored from the simple yet overwhelming exertion of coming, I'd never been more afraid of a reaction in my life.

"Henry," he rasped, his voice thick.

I kept my eyes aimed at the floor as I rocked back onto my heels, allowing him space to make his getaway.

My heart thundered in my chest.

"Henry," he repeated a little louder.

I couldn't do it though. I couldn't look up. I couldn't handle the *or*. Not from him.

He pressed two of his fingers under my chin, stripping me of my choice while guiding my gaze to his.

Soft, blue eyes searched my face. They were pensive. Nervous, even. But they weren't angry or filled with disgust. And, most importantly, they held not a single ounce of regret. My heart soared to altitudes that had never before been reached.

"We're gonna need to take care of that," he said.

The high was still so intoxicating that I barely understood him. My mind was spinning. I had no idea what "that" he was referring to, but I didn't actually care either. Not when he was still staring at me from a cool cruising altitude—the spiral down nowhere in sight.

"Henry. " He snapped his fingers.

"Huh?" I said, shaking my stupor off.

He chuckled then repeated, "We're gonna to need to take care of that."

This time, I followed the direction of his finger as he pointed down at my erection, which was still throbbing between my legs.

"Oh," I breathed, but little homemade paper banners dropped in my mind. They all read: *O-motherfucking-h.*

"No fucking me," he reminded.

The celebratory banners in my head rolled back up.

I nodded and waved him off. "No. I understand. Don't worry about…that."

He tilted his head and leveled me with a don't-be-a-dumbass glare.

I quickly corrected. "I mean…uh… Worry about it, then."

That.

Fucking.

Lip.

Twitch.

He bent down, removing his jeans and his boxer briefs from around his ankles, and then unfolded from the couch. "Shower," he grunted as he strode past me.

I blatantly ogled his round ass as he padded away.

Shower? I'm sorry. Say what?

Was that an invitation or an informative statement of his activity?

I blinked at the bedroom door when I heard the faucet squeak and the water begin falling. Was I supposed to follow him? It was going to be awkward as hell if I strolled up on him, offering to wash his unreachables, only for him to kick me out.

On the other hand, I sure as shit didn't want to miss the opportunity of a lifetime for him to take care of "that" in the shower if that was what he meant.

I was torn. Caught between an embarrassing rock and a soapy hand job.

"Hurry up and get your ass in here. I need to get to bed. I have a plane to fly tomorrow," he shouted.

Oh.

My.

God.

I didn't say that though.

What I did do was jump to my feet and sprint my ass to that shower.

The moment I rounded the corner and entered the bathroom, our bodies collided. Evan roughly took my mouth in a scorching kiss while dragging me into the shower. Water rained down on our faces, to the point that it was difficult to breathe, but I was willing to drown before I'd break that kiss.

His hands roamed freely over my chest and my shoulders, exploring every curve before drifting down to my ass. Fire shot down my back when he gripped both cheeks and pulled them slightly apart before massaging them back together. A deep rumble rolled from his throat.

In a flash, his hands were gone, and so was his mouth.

I reached for his hip, desperate to keep the momentum going, but he shook his head, which forced me to still.

Don't stop now. Please not fucking now.

"Evan," I whispered, cautiously lifting a hand to the back of his neck. "Stop overthinking it."

He stared blankly. But he didn't move away, so I pressed my luck.

Dropping my other hand between us, I found his thickening cock. Breath hissed from between his teeth when I gently stroked down his length and back again.

His eyes fluttered closed and his head lolled on his shoulders. "Christ, that feels good, Henry."

Eyes closed.

Still Henry.

My cheeks heated, and a bashful smile played at my lips.

"I'm glad, *Evan*," I murmured, placing a soft kiss at the base of his neck.

His head swayed to the side, and I traced the corded muscles with my tongue. His dick jumped in my hand when I grazed my teeth over his earlobe.

A shuddered, "Fuck," was his only response.

My eyes drifted down in fascination when his hips began to pump into my hand. Every curl deliciously flexed his abs. It was quite possibly the most beautiful thing I'd ever seen.

"You are…" I breathed, glancing up long enough to see that his blue eyes had opened and were locked on me.

"I'm what?"

Everything. Perfection. Mine?

"Gorgeous."

He stared for a minute, his expression unreadable.

Until.

My back hit the cool tile wall before I could process what the hell had happened, and then he was on me. Every inch of his hard body aligned with mine. I jerked my hand away as our cocks became trapped between us. His demanding mouth covered mine, rendering me immobile and pinning me from head to heel against the shower wall.

His hands rested on either side of my head as his tongue skillfully glided into my mouth. In one smooth movement, he rolled his hips, giving me my first taste of glorious friction. Our moans echoed in a harmony. It wasn't going to take but a few more before I erupted between us.

"Fist your cock," he ordered.

It was an outstanding idea, and I eagerly obeyed. I managed to squeeze a hand between our bodies, but I didn't just grab my own shaft. Opening my hand wide, I pulled us both into my grip. His smooth flesh slid against mine and he cursed in my ear when I started working us together.

My hand squeezed on the upstroke, occasionally twisting so my palm grazed over the sensitive tops of our crowns.

We both kept our heads tilted down, watching intently, our heavy pants mingling.

"Two hands are better," I suggested.

But, when he didn't take the bait, I added my other hand into the mix, enabling me to close the circle around both of our cocks.

"Oh, fuck," he cried nearly immediately.

I wasn't far behind him in that sentiment.

"Oh, God, Evan," I breathed when the force of release tore through me.

His soft lips peppered mine as endorphins consumed me. His arm hooked around my waist, keeping me upright as white ropes landed on his stomach.

"Don't stop," he groaned against my lips when my hand slowed.

Though he was still supporting the majority of my weight, I replied, "I've got you," and then resumed my rhythm on his shaft.

Slanting my head, I was attempting to take the kiss deeper when the easy reverence in which his mouth was moving started to tighten the vise on my heart. It was the antithesis of the desperation I'd felt with him earlier.

This was almost gentle. Maybe even meaningful. I couldn't risk reading into it.

It. Him. This connection I felt when his eyes met mine.

It would all be gone soon enough. And, even as his cock in my hand pulsed his release, a weight settled in my stomach. I barely knew the naked man who was absently stroking my back as he rode out the last of his orgasm.

But I knew I wanted to.

I knew that this was more than just the high.

I knew I didn't want him to leave.

But, most of all, I knew he would.

"You're longer than I am," he said, pulling me from my inner pity party.

I smiled and gave him one last gentle tug before letting him go. "You're thicker. And let's not forget to mention that you won the genetic lottery. I'd give anything for that body."

He barked a laugh. "I believe you just had that body."

My heart leapt in my chest. *Was he reminding me of what we just did?* The guys I was used to wouldn't even make eye contact after we finished. Much less compare cocks and reminisce.

"And…it was amazing." I bit my lip to hide the grin.

Using his arm still wrapped around my back, he tugged me forward and planted a chaste kiss on the corner of my mouth. "Good. Now, you need to leave so I can get some sleep."

Just that fast…my heart dropped.

"Right." I stepped back under one of the showerheads and did a quick once over on my stomach.

He was still washing himself when I started to climb out, but I froze when my mind reminded me that I was a fucking idiot.

"Soooo," I drawled. "I don't actually have anywhere else to go."

He cocked a questioning eyebrow and continued with the scrub-a-dub-dub routine.

"I mean, I…" *Jesus, this is embarrassing.* "So, I wasn't sure how this was going to go down tonight. And I really wanted to spend some time alone with you."

He motioned his hand in a circle for me to speed it up. "Henry, spit it out."

"I didn't upgrade your room. This is actually my suite. I just told reception to send you up here. My bags are in the hall closet."

He remained impassive. "Sharing a room. That's pretty presumptuous."

"I prefer to view it as hopeful. I also cashed in, like, a hundred bucks in pennies in the fountain out front and used the wishes from my birthday candles for the next twenty years in order to make tonight happen."

A white, toothy grin formed on his mouth. There was nothing smooth or sexy about it. It melted me all the same.

After turning the water off, he snagged a towel. "So stay here."

Break out the banners again!

"There are two bedrooms."

Just kidding. Pack that shit back up.

I smiled through the disappointment. "You sure you don't mind?"

He lifted the towel to his head and began scrubbing his dark-brown hair dry. "No. I don't mind. However, I'm not dumb enough to think that there aren't any available rooms in this massive hotel. But there's no point in either one of us hauling our shit somewhere else when there are two perfectly good beds here." He shrugged.

I guessed under one roof was a start. We could work up to one bed.

"Great. Well, I guess… Goodnight, Evan."

"Goodnight, Henry." His lips twitched.

I braced myself for the hasty kiss that usually followed.

It never came.

And, moments later, in nothing but a towel wrapped around my waist, I performed the walk of shame for an empty audience.

chapter fourteen

Evan

One week later...

Me: I got my STD results back today.
Negative. Can you send me yours?
Henry: Are you flirting with me?
Me: No.
Henry: Well that's unfortunate. But...hello
to you too, Evan.

It wasn't the same when he typed my name. I missed the sound
of it rolling from his tongue and the sensation of it being breathed
against my skin. I missed his quirky jokes and his infectious laugh.
I missed the way he looked at me—awestruck as though I were the
superstar, not him. I missed the fire he ignited inside me.

And that was exactly why I hadn't replied to a single one of his
texts over the last week. I was in way over my head.

Henry had left on a bus the morning after our little hookup. He'd knocked on my door to tell me he was leaving, but I hadn't even had the balls to open it. It was safe to say I was freaking the fuck out. He'd texted me just after I'd landed with Jessica and Tabitha in tow. It was short and to the point but still very much Henry.

How'd the flight go, Maverick?

I would have laughed if I'd been able to remember how to amongst the chaos in my mind.

What the hell had I done, opening myself up to him like that? It was a casual thing. *Casual sex.* Except nothing was casual about Henry.

Me: Hi. Tests?

Henry: I usually wouldn't share such personal information with an employee. Do you have any plans to utilize this information?

I blinked down at my phone. He could not be serious.

I quickly began swiping my fingers across the keyboard. I still hadn't repaired my broken screen, but Henry had left a business phone complete with his number programmed into the contacts on my seat in the cockpit the morning after he'd left. I assumed he'd gotten the idea right about the time he'd realized he'd never asked for my phone number. But it wasn't like I'd asked for his. I hadn't needed it since I wouldn't be calling him and we went through Jackson for travel arrangements.

Not that there had been any of those in the last week, either. At the rate I was going, I'd have to volunteer to fly Jackson's charters for free just to keep my hours up—and my sanity intact. I loved getting a paycheck, but I was a pilot because I wanted to fly, not sit around watching daytime soaps while waiting for my phone to ring.

I never should have taken the job with Henry.

And I definitely shouldn't have kissed him, gotten him naked, and then let him blow me.

And I *really* shouldn't have wanted more of that so badly I couldn't sleep at night. Honestly, it pissed me off.

So, over the last week, I'd done the smart thing. I'd avoided him. Every text. Every call. That is until I'd caved, jumping at my very first excuse I had to text *him*. And I was already regretting it.

Me: Are you kidding me right now? You should probably share this information with your EMPLOYEE regardless how I plan to UTILIZE it. I came in your mouth last weekend without a condom. I don't think a simple, "Hey I don't have HIV," is too much to ask.

I watched the bubble icon at the bottom of my screen blink on and off for several minutes. He was typing. And typing. And, five minutes later, still typing. I expected one hell of a long message.

Henry: I'm clean. I'll have my doctor send you proof.

"Shit." I raked an angry hand through my hair. That wasn't a long message, which meant he'd spent all that time typing and deleting and then retyping that crap.

Me: What did the first draft of that message say?
Henry: Do you need anything else, Evan?

Yep. It was official. I hated seeing my name typed.
Me: What did the first draft of that message

say?

Henry: Why does it matter?

Because I'm looking for a reason to keep talking to you. Oh, and I feel guilty for avoiding you all week. And for currently being a dick because I have no fucking idea how to handle the way I'm feeling.

I groaned at myself.

Me: I'm sorry, okay? Any chance you'll be needing a pilot soon? Maybe we can grab a coffee and talk.

Henry: Talk?

Me: Talk, Henry. AKA: CASUALLY converse.

Henry: How casual are we talking here? Tic-tac-toe on a paper tablecloth? Or bring my STD results and meet you at a seedy motel?

Me: Wow. Okay. Well, clearly, casual is off the table. Just send over the results when you get a chance.

Henry: Jeez, don't be so sensitive. Fine, here's your original message… I'll be passing through San Fran for a few hours tomorrow night. I'd be happy to hand-deliver the results myself.

Me: Bullshit. That's not long enough.

Henry: Oh, but, Evan, we already established that length is not an issue for me.

I barked a laugh and clapped a hand over my mouth, trying to cover my huge smile even though no one was around. I didn't want to admit how much I was enjoying finally talking to him again—even if it was just through a text.

Me: Don't worry. Haven't forgotten.
Henry: Have you tried to forget?

The corners of my mouth curled upward. That sexy bastard was fishing. Baiting me with a simple question that would give him clear insight into where I stood in regards to him. The only problem was that I didn't have the answer. It was a tug-of-war that had been battling in my head since we'd met. The only thing I knew for sure was that I *wanted* him. My cock grew hard if I so much as thought about him. I couldn't count the number of times I'd jerked off to the memories of our night together.

That's where I stood in regards to him. Plain and simple, I wanted him. I might have been straddling some other lines in the process of wanting him. Mainly, the ones that would explain why I didn't have to be pumping my dick for him to infiltrate my mind.

But I could deal with that later.

Me: Yes. I've tried a lot, actually.

The icon at the bottom blinked to show that he was typing…and probably deleting. I watched for a few more seconds before putting him out of his misery.

Me: I tried in the shower the day I got home. It wasn't as good as our shower.
Me: I tried the next night when I was alone in bed. A bottle of lube and my hand is a sad substitution for your mouth.
Me: I tried again when I got home from the grocery store yesterday. Your lips were on the cover of three magazines. It was torture.

Me: And I'll probably try tonight because I wouldn't want to embarrass myself when you show up at my house tomorrow.

His response was immediate.

Henry: So you ARE flirting with me.

I was. Goddammit. I fucking was. I had absolutely no control over it, either. The only thing I could do was remind myself of what this was. And all it could ever be.

Me: Casually, of course. I'll have the tic-tac-toe board ready.

"Shit. Fuck. Oh my..." My ass was on the couch and Henry was kneeling between my legs. He'd arrived five minutes earlier and this was as far as we'd made it.

No sooner had the door closed than his mouth had landed on mine. And it was just as intoxicating as I remembered. We'd blindly banged against walls and the coffee table before finding the couch. He'd then shoved me down and tossed a piece of paper I vaguely tagged as his STD test results, and then he was on his knees, sucking my length into the back of his throat.

I'd been nervous when I'd heard his car pull up. It hadn't felt casual at all. It felt like a first date. And, given the opportunity, I probably would have gone all teenage boy and asked if he wanted to watch a movie until I worked up the courage to cop a feel.

This was definitely better. My head couldn't get muddled when he kept it right where it belonged—in his mouth.

My pants hadn't even been pushed down. He'd simply popped the button, lowered the zipper, and tugged my cock out. He was still fully dressed, and it was driving me mad. Well, that and the velvet of his tongue as he swirled it around my tip.

"Henry, wait."

He bottomed out, his lips meeting my root.

"Shit. Fuck. Oh my…"

He glided up and popped me from his mouth. "You already said that, Evan."

Evan.

I shit you not, my balls drew up in response.

Making a fist in his hair, I roughly dragged him up until his mouth met mine. "Don't be a smartass while I'm fucking your mouth," I mumbled between kisses.

His tongue rolled greedily and his denim-covered cock ground against my stomach as he rocked against me. "Actually, *I* was fucking *you* with my mouth. Big difference."

I trailed my hand up his throat, then gripped his chin to halt his frenzied lips. "You want me to fuck your mouth?"

His pupils dilated with arousal.

I swiped my thumb over his bottom lip and then dipped it between his teeth. There was no hesitation as he began sucking it with gentle pulls that shot directly to my groin.

"It that a yes?" I asked impatiently.

With a simple nod, his flames consumed me once again.

We rushed to the bedroom and stripped ourselves naked, and then I positioned him face up with his head hanging over the edge of my bed. Henry looped an arm around one of my thighs and lifted it until my knee settled by his head. With a tip of his chin to his chest, I gloriously slipped to the back of this throat on a loud curse.

He was a fucking magician. Because never had anyone—woman or man—been able to suck me so deep.

I started to withdraw, but he gripped my bare ass and pulled me back down. His face was hidden between my legs, and I feared I was going to suffocate him, so I allowed his hands to guide my rhythm.

Resting my palms on his chest, I balanced myself and began drilling into his hot mouth. I stared down at Henry's chiseled, naked body. He had been gorgeous before. But, with his mouth wide as I drove into it, he was unbelievable. Every so often, he gripped my ass, cueing me to switch to shallow glides in order for him to catch his breath. During those moments, he'd tease my head until he was ready again. The sensations were overwhelming, and combined with the visuals of his long, hard cock slapping his stomach with every thrust, I was already teetering on the edge of release.

I very easily could have bent over and sucked him off too, turning our seven into a sixty-nine. But that would have required me to give him a piece of myself. Allowing him the control over me that I refused to ever hand over again. And, given just how much Henry had already thrown me off-kilter, it wasn't a risk I could afford to take. I'd broken nearly every rule I'd made to protect myself from situations like this. I couldn't shred the only two I had left and take him inside me. No matter how much my mouth watered to taste him. To feel him in the back of my throat. To return to him the ecstasy he was freely giving me.

No. I couldn't do that.

Thrust after thrust, his fingers bit into my ass cheeks, forcing me closer and closer to the release.

But what about him? There was no way he was getting off on this. Enjoying it, no doubt. But an orgasm was not about to rip from his body, leaving him limp and sated in its wake.

Unless...

Sucking in a breath, I decided bending wasn't breaking. I wasn't taking him inside me, offering pieces I no longer had to give. I was simply being a decent…. Friend? Fuck buddy? Groupie? *Employee*?

I groaned at my ludicrous—but accurate—thoughts. Labels had no place in this. I was about to explode in his mouth for the second time; the least I could do is take him with me.

Folding over, I balanced on a fist at his hip. "I'm not going to last much longer," I grunted. "I need you to be fast, Henry."

I heard his sharp intake of breath as I wrapped my palm around the base of his shaft. He was so long, more than half still showed from the top of my fist. My mouth fell open as I glided him through my fingers. I could have come from that alone. But, when his abs tensed, magnifying the sexy V that indented at his hips as he lifted from the bed, seeking more attention, I realized I wanted to watch him lose himself under my touch more than I ever wanted to come.

"Stop," I ordered. "Let me do this."

His only response was to take my cock in a relentless rhythm.

"Shit. Fuck. Oh my…" I repeated for the third time since he had shown up at my door. "Slow down."

Henry hummed his refusal and worked me even harder. I pumped him voraciously, unwilling to come without him but unable to hold on much longer.

He stopped sucking more than once, unable to concentrate when the sensations overwhelmed him. Other times, I was the one frozen, trying to fight release back.

Eventually, his mouth won out and I emptied myself down his throat on a deep groan. The tremors were still working through me when he found his, white streams painting his stomach. The last spurt didn't clear his cock, and it trickled down his plump, pink crown.

There was absolutely no way to explain why I did it.

None.

Temporary insanity, maybe?

Orgasm-induced intoxication, perhaps?

Or maybe it was due to the sheer magnetism of the man lying beneath me.

But, regardless of the reason, I leaned forward and, with one swipe, licked him clean. The musky flavor exploded on my taste buds. *Henry.*

Closing my eyes, I allowed the familiar yet completely unique taste to wash over me. We'd only been together twice, but the ground was shaking and my decade-old walls were starting to crumble. I could lose myself trying to rebuild them while the super storm known as Henry Alexander ominously hovered over me. Or I could sit back, relax, and enjoy the thunder. Even the strongest hurricanes had to die out eventually. Maybe Henry was mine.

Or, more likely, he'd be the earthquake that was going to break me down before swallowing me whole.

Either way, I wasn't going to be left standing. I just had to decide how long I wanted to fight.

chapter fifteen

Henry

For as amazing as it had felt when Evan's tongue had sneak-
ily laved my tip, what had come after that was even better. As
soon as we'd both cleaned up, he'd collapsed beside me in the
bed and we'd spent the next two hours bullshitting and laughing. We
weren't exactly cuddling or really even touching, but I could live with
that because there wasn't a spiral down anywhere in sight.

He was incredible.

Once I'd broken through his stoic exterior, he was actually really funny. My cheeks hurt from laughing. We didn't get deep or talk
about the greater meaning of the universe. We mainly just swapped
stories about our friends. I told him about Levee and Sam. And he
told me about his buddy Scott. I told him how my days usually went
when I was on tour, and he told me how he'd been struggling to find
a job after he'd gotten out of the Air Force. I did my best not to stare
at him in awe as he spoke. I had a feeling I was failing miserably
though, because every time his gaze met mine, his lip twitched in my

favorite way.

When it was finally time to leave, he walked me to the door. I'd been playing it safe, giving him his space, but I wasn't sure when or if I was going to see him again. So, just before he pulled the door open, I planted a deep and lingering kiss on his lips. He snaked an arm around my hips, bringing me closer, before reverently filling his lungs.

I was in foreign territory with Evan. I knew how to pursue straight men. The game was simple. I'd gently push them to their limits, coaxing and convincing them that they wanted me. And then, when they finally broke and gave in to the tiniest urge, I'd take over and push it ten steps further to give them what they really wanted. However, if I had to go ten steps past the feelings Evan was pressing against my lips, I wasn't sure I'd ever leave. And, with the way my lungs burned as I held him to my mouth, staying with him was an idea I could get used to.

I was so high on this man I wasn't sure I'd ever come back down. And, in order to protect myself from the fall, I had to play this one safer than ever before. Evan seemed to be an open and willing participant, but his retreat was always lingering around us. When the novelty of being with me wore off, he'd be gone and I'd be faced with the hardest withdrawal of my life.

"Call me, okay?" I whispered against his mouth.

"I will." He tossed me a heart-stopping smile, and it made my bones physically ache.

In that second, that smile belonged to me. But, as soon as the door closed behind me, I would have no claim over it whatsoever. Evan was gorgeous. Surely a woman was waiting in the wings to make her move. A woman I couldn't complete with, especially not from thousands of miles away.

"What's wrong?" he asked, clearly reading my somber mood.

Please don't fall in love with a woman while I'm gone.

"Nothing." I returned his smile, but if the pinch of his eyebrows was any indication, he wasn't buying it any more than I was feeling it.

"Henry?" he said as I quickly stepped out of his embrace.

Forcing a smile, I patted his chest. "I'll talk to you soon."

He opened his mouth, but before I had a chance to cancel my next show or, at the very least, beg him to come with me, I walked away.

Two weeks later...

"I'm in love!" I told Levee over the phone.

She groaned. "Oh, God. Please tell me you're kidding."

"Okay, maybe love is a bit of an overstatement. But I really like him, and if you saw him naked, you'd totally get it. I'm considering purchasing the gym he goes to and installing security cameras so I can watch him work out." I smiled, pulling the curtain on my tour bus back and watching the trees of whatever state we were traveling through rush past.

"Illegal and creepy. Sounds about right for you."

I laughed and reclined back on the leather couch. "There is a fine line between creepy and romantic."

"Word to the wise: Secret security cameras always fall under creepy. But I take it things are going well with your pilot?"

"Fantastic. I mean…I haven't seen him in a few weeks, but he's returned nearly all of my texts and even called me four times." I lifted four fingers in the air as if she had been sitting next to me and not hundreds of miles away. "And twice he's admitted to trying to forget me." I smiled proudly.

"Uhhhh, you've spoken to him four times in two weeks *and* he's trying to forget you? Should I start shopping for my bridesmaid dress now?"

"It couldn't hurt to have one on standby just in case. And no, smartass. Trying to forget me means he was jerking off to me."

"Henry!" she yelled accusingly.

I glanced around as if the empty bus could explain her reaction. Levee and I talked about everything—usually in great detail. A little wanking shouldn't have fazed her.

"What?" I yelled back.

"Please tell me you did not send him naked pictures to jerk off to. You *know* they will be leaked, and you *know* they will end up all over the Internet, and then my daughter will have to grow up in a world where her Uncle Henry's penis is just one accidental click away."

My heart swelled. It didn't matter that she was talking about my dick. It was the way she had called me Uncle Henry that had filled my soul. She'd called me that before, but the reminders that we were a family never got old.

"Please don't call it a penis. You know he prefers his formal title."

"Yes. Sorry. I forgot. Please relay my apologies to Prince Everhard. And then tell me you did *not* send any pictures to Evan."

"You know the prince is camera shy," I said with mock annoyance. However, my smile couldn't have gotten any wider.

"Thank you, Lord."

I switched my phone to the other ear and rolled to my side. "I mean, I guess there is always the possibility that he could have snapped a screenshot during one of our dirty video chats though."

"My poor daughter!" she cried.

Unfortunately, I was only kidding. Evan and I hadn't engaged in any late-night naked video chats. I'd thought about it a lot—dreamed about it, really. But, even though it was killing me, I didn't want to push him too hard too fast. I hadn't been joking when I'd said that I liked him.

As far as I could tell, he wasn't spending his evenings shacked up with a new girlfriend, so I'd decided to stick to the original plan and allow him to take the lead in our little relationship of sorts. I'd texted him just enough to make sure he knew I was interested and dropped everything the minute he called so he knew I wanted to talk to him. But, besides that, I let him make all the moves.

He'd yet to ask when I'd be back in town. As much as I would have loved to know he wanted to see me again, I didn't need the temptation. I wasn't going to be back in San Francisco for at least another few weeks. It sucked, but I was just happy that he wasn't avoiding me anymore.

The first time he called, he tried to play it off as a business question. By the second call, we'd exchanged enough texts that he'd loosened up a bit. We chatted for over an hour about absolutely nothing. I did the majority of the talking, but he still listened and interjected with the occasional question. He was engaging, and that was more than I ever could have hoped for weeks ago.

Evan was funny, tossing out dry one-liners that had me rolling. He also laughed at my jokes, and that throaty chuckle of his gave me chills down my spine every time I heard it. I thought about him more often than not. And I secretly allowed myself to wonder what it would be like for him to call me every day. For him to go to award shows with me. For me to hide in his house for weeks on end where no one could find us. Those were the thoughts that disturbed me most. My entire life was in front of the crowds. Not hidden behind locked doors. But with Evan…

"What if she searches 'celebrity peen' and you pop up?" Levee exclaimed.

"Then you have bigger problems than her seeing my junk. Levee, your daughter will be fine. Styles will have shown his dick at least a hundred times by the time she's of age. He should dominate the search engine results."

"Oh, good," she retorted sarcastically. "Wait...are there nudes of him now?"

"I don't know. I'll search as soon as we hang up and forward any I find to Sam."

She giggled. "Stop sending my husband naked men."

"Then tell him to stop sending me women. I swear he's taken this game too far. I opened a text the other day and there was a half-naked woman wrapped in nothing but a sheet and she appeared to have a massive tumor growing in her abdomen."

"Those were the proofs of my maternity pictures, you ass."

I choked on a laugh. "Truly beautiful, by the way."

"Hilarious," she deadpanned. "But let's get back to your pilot."

I jokingly breathed his name on a dreamy sigh. "*Evan.*"

"Yes, him... Spill it."

"I don't have a whole lot to say. I wish I did though. I'm trying to play this one cool and give him plenty of time to fall for my coy charm."

She barked a laugh. "Coy. Right. Okay, so you like the guy. I take it you aren't just trying to fuck him."

My teeth sawed over my bottom lip. I absolutely wanted to fuck Evan. I also wanted him to stay when it was all said and done though.

"I want what you and Sam have," I admitted.

"I want that for you too. But, honey, I'm not sure you're ever going to find that if you keep chasing straight guys. Even if they hang around for a while, you can't expect a man to go against everything he knows just to be with you. It's just not realistic."

But I needed that.

I needed it desperately.

When I was three hours old, my father signed his rights away and my mother lost hers later that day when I tested positive for cocaine in the nursery. No grandparents, aunts, uncles, or cousins stepped forward to take care of the innocent baby who hadn't asked to be born. They didn't even give me a name. From what I'd heard over the years, the little old lady who volunteered to rock the crying babies named me after her son who was killed in Vietnam.

Really, my life was a rags-to-riches story that could rival most Lifetime movies.

I was seven when my mother, who I'd never met, finally lost her rights permanently. And let's be honest: The market to adopt a troubled boy with more attitude than sense wasn't exactly booming. Over my eighteen years in the system, I spent time in six different foster homes. Some were better than others. We were always poor, but they were all relatively decent people. Not great. But I survived.

Let's face it: Growing up "the gay kid" was difficult no matter what the circumstances. Even if I'd had two biological parents who adored me, the struggle with society would have still been overwhelming. But toss in religious bigots as foster parents, relentless kids who believed different equaled wrong, and a confused boy who had never felt even an ounce of love…

It was the recipe for disaster.

But it had produced me.

I had several sexual experiences with gay guys when I was in high school. But it wasn't until I was with my first straight guy that I really came alive in my sexuality. The worthiness I felt in knowing they were going against their own DNA just to be with me was unrivaled. Those brief encounters were the ones that made me feel something I'd never experienced before—special. No one could or ever would have them like I did. And, after I'd felt a high like that, I'd never gone back to gay men. I couldn't, not with knowing what else was out there.

I understood why Levee worried about me. She loved me and hated the idea of me being hurt. But I didn't have any other choice. I'd been irrelevant, inconsequential, and extraneous my entire life. But, when it came to men, I refused to accept that role. I needed to be the only exception—the one person capable of bending the laws of nature.

It was the only way my heart absorbed love.

"Henry? You still there?" Levee asked over the phone.

I rolled off the couch and made my way to my bedroom at the back of the bus. "I'm good, Levee. You know me. I'm just out for a good time."

She breathed a sad sigh. "I hate it when you lie to me."

I hated it too. But I didn't want another lecture on something she couldn't possibly understand.

She started to reply, but she was cut off by the beep of an incoming call.

I pulled the phone away from my ear and saw Evan's name flashing on the screen. My heart squeezed and my breath hitched at just the sight. My whole body began to thrum with excitement. Shit, I was in so much trouble.

"Hey, Evan's calling. I gotta go."

"Okay, go, but this conversation isn't over."

"Sure, sure. Whatever. I love you, babe." I didn't wait for her reply before I switched calls. "Well, hello, sexy," I purred.

He chuckled. "I guess that's a step up from Maverick. What's going on, Henry?"

"Oh, not much. The usual. Lighting the world on fire one mile at a time from the inside of a tour bus in Bumfuck, Egypt."

"I don't know how you do it. I'd lose my mind being on the road that much."

"It's not that bad. But I do get bored being alone so much."

"Are you telling me megastar Henry Alexander doesn't have an entourage?" His voice smiled, and I longed to see it.

Closing my lids, I tried to picture him. Those lips hiking at the corners as he stared down at me, warmth brewing in his eyes as he curled into my side, unable to go another minute without the contact. It would probably never happen, but the fantasy alone soothed my soul.

"Hardly. The band is on a different bus. Carter rides with me sometimes, but as you can imagine, he isn't the best company. He just scowls at me a lot."

I sucked in a sharp breath as he laughed freely, reminding me of how sexy he was when he momentarily let down his guard long enough to enjoy himself. It was something of beauty, and I missed it more than words could translate.

"Yeah, he did some scowling at me when I picked him up yesterday."

I sat bolt upright. "I'm sorry—what? You picked him up yesterday?"

"You didn't know?" He sounded thoroughly perplexed.

I was just thoroughly pissed.

It wasn't a big deal that Carter had taken my plane back to do whatever urgent task he'd needed to take care of back in San Francisco. He'd told me that he'd meet back up with me at my next stop. And I was happy someone was using Evan's services. However, I was nearly livid that that someone wasn't me.

"Why didn't you tell me you were going to be in town? I could have at least come to the airport to see you before you took off," I snapped entirely too roughly.

"Uhhh… I figured you were busy. You are, after all, *Henry Alexander*." He flourished to make me sound like a pretentious dick.

"And?" I drawled.

"And I'm not going to be one of your groupies waiting with bated breath for you to work me into your schedule. If you wanted to see me, you could've called."

"First, I don't have groupies."

He actually laughed at my statement.

"I'm serious."

"Henry, I'm not stupid. You don't have to bullshit me. Half the world wants your attention. And you want me to believe that you're just sitting around, waiting for me to let you know I'll be in town for less than an hour?"

Clearly, he had no idea what I was capable of in less than an hour, but that wasn't why I was upset.

"Yes! That's exactly what I want you to believe because that's what I've been doing since the day I met you. I would have dropped everything for less than an hour with you. Christ, Evan, I would have dropped it all only to wave at you from the runway as you took off. I just had no idea you were going to be in town. You should've called."

"Orrrr...you could have called me. Seems like I'm always the one calling you. Phones work both ways, Henry."

"I text you all the time," I defended.

He laughed without humor. "Right. Once-a-day texts are the same thing."

His sudden attitude made me cop my own. "I'm giving you your space!"

He immediately shot back, "Well, don't!"

I blinked. *Well, don't?* What was that supposed to mean? Don't give him space?

"I need to go," he said just seconds before he literally *went*.

The silence filled my ear as I sat befuddled by the entire exchange. I pulled my phone away to look at the screen. *Are we fighting? Does he want me to call him more? Does he want me to be interested?*

I stared at my phone for several seconds before I typed a message out.

Me: Fine, Maverick. No space. But I'm not positive you can handle the truth. (Gratuitous Tom Cruise reference.)
Evan: Try me.

And there it was—the defining moment. Bracing myself, I typed out what would be either the truth that opened the door for me with him or the truth that would cause him to slam it in my face for good.

Me: I'm pissed that I missed a chance to see you yesterday. I've thought of absolutely nothing but you for the last two weeks. And I don't know how to show you that without going too hard too fast and risk scaring you off.
Evan: Christ, Henry. What the hell are we doing here?
Me: I can't answer that. It's your turn to be honest, Evan.
Evan: I fucking hate when you type my name.

I swear I needed a decoder ring to read between the lines with this guy.

Me: I don't even know what that means.
Evan: The scary thing is I don't either.

I squinted at my phone, trying to see if some sort of sense could be made from our current conversation. I typed out several messages in reply, but the words didn't feel right, so I deleted them all.

"You're Henry Alexander." His words rang in my ears.

In my world, I wasn't Henry Alexander. I was just Henry, smartass extraordinaire. But I'd forgotten that Evan wasn't of my world—no matter how much I'd wished he were.

"Shit!" I dropped my phone.

So, now, on top of convincing his conscience that it was okay for him to be with a man, I had to overcome the stigma of my fame.

There I was, worried about him meeting a woman, when he was worried about me meeting...well, everyone else.

I hated that I'd made him feel this way, but this revelation immeasurably filled my damaged soul. The potent high sent me spinning, and the warmth brewing in my chest made me brave.

I couldn't lose him over a misunderstanding. For the first time in years, I'd found someone I could actually imagine a future with. I'd been handling him with caution because I wanted more than just a cat-and-mouse game. But, if Evan wanted to be chased, I'd cat the fuck out of him.

My hands began to tremble as I reached for my phone, knowing what I had to do.

chapter sixteen

Evan

"**D**o I need** to slap that shit out of your hand again?" Scott joked, pulling my attention away from my phone.

I'd been staring at it for the last five hours. That damn text bubble would occasionally pop up, taunting me that Henry was typing, but no messages had been sent.

It was official. I was a bitch. But, for over two weeks, Henry had been driving me insane. Baiting me with texts but never calling. He hadn't even mentioned wanting to see me again. Every so often, I'd give in and call him, and he'd always act like he was happy to hear from me. But I had no interest in another one-sided relationship.

Relationship?

My head was a jumbled mess when it came to him. Just the thought of being with a man again sent me into a tailspin, or that's what I told myself. When, in reality, Henry's indifference toward me was what really had me on the edge of sanity. I wavered from minute to minute between what I wanted—him—and what I needed—

self-preservation.

I reminded myself every day that this thing with him was as casual as I'd told him it was. Unfortunately, the more I got to know him, the less I wanted it that way. I couldn't deny that I was attracted to him, but wasn't everyone?

He was charismatic, charming, and unbelievably sexy.

But, on the other hand, he was so charismatic that bullshitting me would be easy for him.

And he was charming with everyone—not just me.

And, sure, he was unbelievably sexy, yet I was supposed to believe he'd set his sights on only me? For fuck's sake, I knew firsthand that life didn't work like that. Much less when you add in fame and fortune.

But, despite what I'd told him on the phone, I didn't care that he was superstar Henry Alexander.

I did, however, care that, for some reason, I was starting to develop feelings of the non-naked variety for him.

And, tonight, I'd broken, making myself more vulnerable, because now, he knew I cared. Pretending was safe. I could even convince myself sometimes. Now though? I'd exposed my hand, and he had absolutely no response. Watching that text bubble flicker was like salt in a wound.

"Dude," Scott laughed. "You're missing the fight. What the hell is wrong with you?"

I shook my head. "I don't know. Tired, I guess." Pushing to my feet, I headed to the kitchen to grab a beer. "You need another?"

"I'm good," he replied before yelling at one of the fighters on the TV.

We'd been planning to go out to the sports bar, but when he'd gotten to my house, I'd been in a shit mood. So shitty that he hadn't argued when I'd told him that I'd rather stay in and order the pay-per-view.

I was once again preoccupied with my phone when I heard a knock at the door.

"You expecting someone?" he asked.

"Not that I know of." I popped the cap on my beer off and followed him to the door.

The second he pulled it open, we both froze.

We were shocked, but for two totally different reasons.

For him: Celebrity Henry Alexander was standing on my front porch.

For me: The man who scared the living shit out of me was standing on my front porch and not hundreds of miles away like he'd been earlier.

His eyes met mine and an apologetic smile spread across his mouth. Tipping his head to the side, he shrugged.

Simple. Silent. Stunning.

Henry.

My mouth dried and I momentarily lost the ability to speak. He appeared tired and slightly disheveled but still sexy as sin, and it caused my hands to itch to touch him.

"Hi," he said, shifting the two large brown paper bags he was holding to one arm in order to extend a handshake Scott's way. "Henry Alexander. I'm Evan's boss."

Scott clasped his outstretched hand, but his surprised gaze jumped to mine. I felt it, but I couldn't drag my eyes off Henry long enough to acknowledge his silent question.

"Scott Dalton," he replied.

"What are you doing here?" I asked Henry. It was an accusation, but it came out as a whisper.

He flashed his gaze to Scott then back to me. "I, um, have some *business* to talk to you about."

I pointedly looked at the bags in his hands in question.

"And I thought you might be hungry." He smiled, but his Adam's apple bobbed as he swallowed hard.

I couldn't help it. My lips twitched as I fought a grin. "It's almost eleven."

He blew out a breath in mock frustration. "Okay. Fine. *I* was hungry." His smile spread.

Scott interrupted our stare off. "Great timing. I was just about to get out of here."

He hadn't been. The main event hadn't even started yet. His offer to go was just one more reason why he was my best friend. But I was his, and as much as I wanted to be alone with Henry, I couldn't let him leave.

"You aren't going anywhere. You've been drinking, and you're on the bike. I don't have any desire to scrape your sorry ass off the pavement tonight."

Henry pounced. "I have a car." He swung an arm toward my driveway. "I mean…if you need to go. My driver can take you wherever you'd like."

I opened my mouth to object, but Scott slapped me on the shoulder.

"Perfect. See you later, man. Nice to meet you, Henry." He grabbed his boots from beside the door and didn't even waste the time to put them on before he jogged out.

The best part about Scott was, unless I brought it up later, he would never speak of the eye-fuck I'd just been throwing my male boss.

We both watched him jog away, and Henry threw a thumbs-up to the driver as he quickly got out of the black SUV to open the door for Scott.

"What are you doing here?" I asked Henry again when he'd finally turned back to face me.

He didn't wait for an invitation before he came inside. "Is it going to be a problem for you that he saw me here?"

"You *are* my boss," I deadpanned.

He studied me for several seconds and then blew out a relieved breath. "Good. That could have been bad. Anyway, we need to talk." He strode past me, toward the kitchen.

As I raked my eyes over his ass, talking became very low on my list of things I wanted to do.

"Are you hungry? I really did bring food."

I shook my head and asked, "How'd you get here? I thought you were on the road?" I folded my arms over my chest and watched him settle his two bags on the counter.

His blue eyes smiled as they lifted to mine. "I was. But you weren't. And I wanted to see you. So I flew back."

My eyebrows nearly hit my hairline. "You flew?"

"I also might be slightly drunk now." He smiled, but I didn't return it.

He'd flown? Why did that make my stomach wrench? I pretended that it was because I hadn't been the one in the cockpit, but I knew that it had more to do with the fact that he'd done something so terrifying just to come see me.

"You flew?" I repeated in a whisper.

"My last name is Gilchrist," he randomly announced, pulling a takeout container of wings from his bag. He nabbed a piece of celery and crunched a bite.

"Answer me. You flew? To see me?"

He ignored my question. "Henry Alexander Gilchrist. For obvious reasons, I dropped the last name when I started the music thing. I grew up in foster care, and my most prized possession was an out-of-tune guitar I'd bought at a garage sale. I taught myself to play, and I'm not going to lie, at first, it was like nails on a chalkboard even to my ears."

I tilted my head to the side in confusion. "Why are you telling me this?"

He tore off a paper towel from the holder next to the sink and wiped his mouth. "Because, earlier, you told me I was Henry Alexander. I'm not. I'm Henry Gilchrist. I'm a simple man who makes music the same way you're a man who flies planes."

I took a step toward him. "And you decided to face your biggest fear of flying to tell me this? You could have texted."

He grinned proudly. "Texting did cross my mind, but where's the romance in that?"

The walls around my heart began to shake, and I instinctively took two steps back before firing off the first thing that came to mind. "Romance doesn't sound casual."

His eyes darkened at my retreat, but he didn't let it dampen his mood. "No, it doesn't, but you didn't sound all that casual earlier, either."

"I was in a bad mood."

With a confident smirk, he closed the distance between us. "Yes. You were. And so was I. I'm sorry for being short, *Evan*." He winked when my breath caught. Leaning toward my face, he rubbed his jaw against mine and whispered in my ear, "Suddenly, I'm feeling better. How about you?"

I was.

Actually, I was fucking elated.

And suspicious.

And worried.

I backed away. "Why did you come here?"

He moved back to his bags on the counter and started digging through them. "I like you. I believe I mentioned that on the phone. However, my favorite part of that call was when you, in a roundabout way, admitted you liked me too."

Fan-fucking-tastic. I'd fucked up when I'd caught an attitude. I just hadn't realized I'd opened a door too. And I sure as hell hadn't had any idea just how quickly Henry was planning to storm through it.

I squared my shoulders. "Maybe, but I don't think that required you to fly across the country to see me."

He propped his hip on the counter and crossed his arms across his chest. "You want me to leave?"

Fuck no. But what I did want was for him to stop talking so I could stop thinking. "No."

He shot me wickedly seductive smile. "Good, because I brought dessert too."

Now, dessert I could do, because I had a sneaking suspicion that it involved being naked. But this—whatever he had to say—I wanted over as quickly as possible.

"So talk," I said.

"Well…okay. I figured we could eat first, but—"

"Talk," I ordered sternly.

"Stop barking at me. My nerves are shot after the flight."

And, with that, I felt guilty. Pinching the bridge of my nose, I sighed. "I'm sorry. If you want to eat—"

Only I didn't get to finish before he rushed out, "For the first time in my life, I have no idea what to do." He laughed. "I mean, seriously. I feel like I've been holding my breath since that night in L.A. I'm starting to become a little delirious. So I've been letting you run the show. All I want is for you to be comfortable." He paused to smirk. "Well, I mean, that's not *all* I want, but your being comfortable is an integral part in getting what I do want. Which, just in case you've misunderstood any part of me being here, that something is *you.*"

My body tensed as my mind flooded with a million things I *wanted* to say and even some I told myself I *needed* to say. But my brain wasn't firing in the proper directions at all. His words should have terrified me, but they only made me want to kiss him that much more.

I cleared my throat. "That *really* doesn't sound like casual."

He smiled, reached into one of his brown bags, and pulled out a bouquet of deep-blue flowers. "I guess I'm not a casual kind of guy after all."

I blinked. "Did you seriously bring me flowers?"

"Guys can like flowers!" he defended.

I shot him an incredulous glare. "None I know."

"Well, none I know, either, but I was hoping you would. I was on a serious time constraint while shopping." He looked from me to the flowers and back again and then twisted his lips. "Okay, so no flowers." With a dramatic toss, he threw them over his shoulder.

They bounced off my pantry door before falling to the floor.

I did my best not to laugh only to fail miserably. "What else you got in there, Casanova?"

He bit his lip and then began digging through his bags again. Next out was a bunch of chocolate-covered fruit in a clear, plastic container.

"I tried, but they didn't have kiwi. Sorry. I noticed that was all you ate out of the snacks at the hotel."

I couldn't even remember if I'd eaten kiwi in front of him, but he'd not only *noticed* but also *remembered*.

Why did that feel so good?

Why did it make my stomach twist?

Why did it fill my chest with a warmth that I swear seeped into my bones?

I had no clue how to react to any of those things.

When I didn't respond, he discarded the fruit on the counter.

"Right. Stupid. But look what I have that goes with them?"

"Henry..."

"Whipped cream!" he exclaimed, pulling out a tub of Cool Whip.

"A tub?"

His shoulders fell. "Come on. Cut me some slack. It was all I could find." The disappointment on his face made me burst into laughter.

I walked the final two steps to him and squeezed his hips. "Anything else in your magic bags?"

"Um…" He reached inside with both hands and pulled out a giant bottle of lube and a box of condoms. He fought his own laugh as he unceremoniously dropped them back into the bag. "Nope. Nothing else."

He was gorgeous as he stared at me with that mischievous glint in his eyes, but that had nothing to do with why my heart was swelling.

Nipping at his bottom lip, I said, "You flew to see me?"

He nuzzled his nose with mine. "I did. And it was terrible, but this makes it worth it."

I rushed on a breath, "Jesus, I wanted to see you too." I held each side of his strong jaw as I pressed a reverent kiss to his lips.

His arms folded around my waist. "I'm treading in uncharted waters with you, Evan. I don't want to fuck this up." He slid his hands into the waistband of my pants and gripped my ass.

When our hips met, our hard-ons gloriously rubbed together, shooting sparks to my balls. I groaned and dropped my hands to his ass.

His lips caught mine just seconds before his tongue swept my mouth, igniting me. Threading my fingers into the back of his hair, I tipped his head back and sealed my mouth over his. After that, we were all hands and mouths as I backed him against the pantry door. When he hit, I went for the button on his jeans.

"Wait," he panted. "I came here with something to say."

I ground my hips into his and shifted my attention to his neck. "Then fucking say it so I can get you naked."

"I want to fuck you," he blurted.

My entire body stiffened, and my heart began to race.

"Not now," he quickly clarified. "I'll wait. However long you need. But I want to be very honest with you so there are no doubts in your head about where I stand. Look at me, *Evan*."

The purr of my name left me helpless but to obey. Slowly, I lifted my head and met his heated gaze.

Trailing his hand over my abs, he ducked behind me and flattened his chest to my back. Chills spread over me as his teeth raked the flesh at the base of my neck.

"Actually, I want a lot of things from you, Evan."

"Son of a…" I groaned when he rolled his hips and pressed his hard length against my ass.

"This being just one of them," he whispered.

Snaking a hand around my hips, he found my shaft through the denim and gave it a quick once-over. That paired with his hard-on at my ass had my knees damn near buckling. I threw an arm out and supported myself against the door.

"Shiiiit," I groaned.

"But I want more than that too. I want you in my bed on my tour bus, waiting for me after a show. I want to watch movies and order takeout with you on lazy Sundays. I want you shirtless, lounging on a beach with me when we need a vacation to clear our heads. I want your voice in my ear, counting down from ten when the panic sets in. I want you sitting beside me for family dinner at Levee's. I want you parked beside me at every boring-ass award show I'm forced to attend. And, *Evan*, I want every woman who so much as walks past you to know that you're *mine*."

My mouth was dry and I wasn't sure I was even breathing when his agile fingers popped the button on my jeans open and dipped inside. A hiss escaped through my teeth when his cool hand wrapped around my length.

"But, more than all of that, I want you to want it too." Using his other hand, he forced my jeans and my boxers down my thighs and then began a merciless rhythm on my cock. "I'm a patient man. I'll wait. And, when I'm positive you want all of that too"—he ground his denim-covered erection between my bare ass cheeks—"I'll fuck you, Evan."

And his promise was all it took to make me explode. I dropped to an elbow against the door, barely remaining upright in the midst of the sensorial overload. He caught my release in one hand as he continued to work me through my orgasm with the other.

Slowly, my head and my body returned to me as I came down, but there was a piece of myself that would never reemerge.

Because, no matter how hard I'd tried to fight, that piece now belonged to Henry.

chapter seventeen

Evan

Henry left the next morning. It sucked, but when his lips brushed mine, it felt like we were finally starting something real. And surprisingly, I wanted that real more than ever before. We kept in touch with multiple daily calls, and as the weeks passed by, I found myself falling for the man on the other end of the phone.

To say Henry was a busy man was an understatement, but he always made time for me. It wasn't enough though. He still hated to fly, but it was kind of my specialty, so the first day off he had, I grabbed a red-eye and flew out to see him. We didn't leave the hotel room for a full twenty-four hours. We didn't exactly put clothes on, either. While my walls were crumbling, I wasn't ready to give myself to him completely. And he never pushed me. His mouth touched every inch of my body, including the few times he snuck his tongue down the seam of my balls. I nearly came unglued the first time his tongue swirled around the sensitive flesh. But, then again, this was

Henry. He had that effect on me regardless of where his tongue was touching.

After that, it was two long weeks before we saw each other again. But it was for the best. We got to know each other, and that kind of comfort only turned my already-desperate desire to be with him up a notch—or twelve.

There wasn't a ton of conversation when Henry showed up at my house that night. Those seconds were better spent with our mouths crushing together as we blindly made it to my bedroom, clothing left to litter the hallway. I didn't even make it to the bed before I came down his throat. I couldn't get enough of him. And, as quickly as he'd lost himself with my hand working between his legs, it was clear he couldn't get enough of me, either.

He was lounging like a sated god on my pillows with his hands folded behind his head when I returned from the bathroom and tossed the damp washcloth on his stomach.

"Shit. Cold," he gasped, his abs rippling as he scrambled to pull it away.

I fought to suppress my smirk. "Sorry."

"Yeah, you look real sorry."

I swayed my head in consideration. "Actually, I'm not sorry."

A glowing, white smile formed on his lips. "Not at all?"

Judging by the hope etched on his face, we weren't talking about the washcloth anymore, but my answer remained the same. "Not at all."

If possible, his smile grew wider as he looked down and cleaned his stomach.

That smile did something to me. I couldn't put my finger on what, but I gave up trying to figure it out and decided to put my fingers on *him* instead. Crawling into bed, I flipped to my stomach and draped an arm over his hips.

Part of my mind screamed for me to get up, get dressed, and use any possible barrier to distance myself from him. However, I didn't care what my head had to say anymore. With his breath on my neck and his heart slamming in my ear, I knew what I wanted.

Him.

He tangled our legs together and brushed the hair off my forehead. "What are you thinking about?" he asked.

"Nothing." But it seemed distant even to my own ears.

"Look at me," he urged gently. "What's going on in that sexy head?"

I smiled, tilting my head back to catch his eyes. "Just thinking about us. That's all."

The skin on his forehead wrinkled. "What about us?"

"How good this feels. Just being here with you. I never expected—" *To crave you so deeply. And not only in the bedroom. But in everyday life.*

"Evan. This. Me and you. It's not a bad thing."

"I know."

"Don't fight it, okay? Just trust me that I'm in this with you. One hundred percent. Every step of the way," he implored before leaning down and placing a reassuring kiss on my lips.

Filling my lungs with all that was Henry, I allowed his promises to infuse me. The calm left behind was confounding, but I'd never wanted to embrace something more.

"Do you trust me?" I asked.

"Yes," he replied immediately.

"Good. Let me fly you to your next show."

His arms spasmed. "Evan…"

I pushed up on my elbows. "That's my job."

"This isn't about jobs."

"No. You're right. It's about me. And I fucking hate the idea of anyone else flying you. Or even driving you, for that matter. I should be there."

His blue eyes warmed. "You hate it?"

"Despise might be the better word."

He bit his lip and bashfully cut his eyes away. It was so unlike Henry it made me chuckle.

"I despise it too," he whispered.

"Then let me fly you. You want me to trust you? Consider it done. But you have to trust me too. I swear on my life I won't let anything happen to you up there."

His eyes dimmed. "It's just... I had a really bad experience in the air a few years ago."

I rolled to my back, and he followed me over until his front was plastered to my side.

"You know this is where I give you the whole 'flying is safer than driving' inspirational speech. They teach it the first day of flight school. Plus, I'm a damn good pilot. You'll be safe with me."

He dragged his finger over the curve of my pecs. "Maybe, but even the best can't prevent an act of God?"

I narrowed my eyes on his blank stare as he watched his finger swirling circles on my chest. "Okay, I guess you could worry about that. But I assure you—"

"You can't assure me of anything." He lifted his gaze to mine. "Two years ago. There was a bad storm. My flight was struck by lightning while we were descending toward the airport. We lost power. Blew an engine and suffered a good bit of damage to the body." His hand stilled as his eyes filled with overwhelming fear at the memory. "There was this loud banging rhythm from a piece of metal flapping in the wind, and all I could think about was that it was going to be the bassline of my death."

I blinked in shock. "No fucking way. AirUSA Flight 219?"

He chuckled humorlessly. "That would be the one."

Awestruck, I announced, "I would have given anything to be on that flight."

He curled his lip in utter disbelief before rolling away.

I caught his elbow. "Henry, that flight is legendary in the world of aeronautics. No one, and I mean *no one,* should have survived that flight."

"Yeah. I got that much when I was wearing an oxygen mask and praying to a God, who obviously hates me," he scoffed.

"No." I tugged on his arm until he turned back to face me. "See, you and I, we look at this differently. Sure, lightning is considered an act of God. Fine. But the real act of God I see is that you had Captain John Wyatt in the cockpit that night. That man is the most talented pilot I've ever met. He was quite possibly the only person in the world who could have gotten that plane back on the ground with zero casualties. And, out of the thousands of pilots who could have been behind the controls, you got *him.* That was your act of God." I laughed quietly. "I can't believe you were on that flight. The jealousy actually hurts a little."

His mouth slacked open. "Jealousy?"

"I've heard all the stories at least a dozen times, but I'd have given anything to experience that landing firsthand."

His lips formed a hard line. "Is there something wrong with you? It was the most terrifying experience of my life, not a rollercoaster at an amusement park."

"That's not what I meant. It's just—"

"You should have heard the cries from the other passengers, Evan. There was this mom with her baby…just shrieking." He paused when the emotions lodged in his throat. "The whole ordeal lasted only a few minutes. But, for those minutes…we were all dead."

I tugged on his arm until he begrudgingly stopped trying to escape my bed. "Okay, okay. I get it. I swear I do. We just have a different outlook on things. I'm sorry." I pointedly held his gaze until he relaxed. And when he did, I pressed a gentle kiss to his lips until his body sagged. "I'm sorry," I repeated softly. "I'm sure it was scary."

"Terrifying," he corrected.

"Terrifying," I confirmed. "But did you ever get a chance to meet Wyatt afterwards?"

"Yeah. I thanked him. Donated a bunch of money in his name. Shit like that. I actually harassed him for months to be my new pilot. I'd fly with him again. I threw a ton of money at him, actually." His entire face lit as his lips lifted up at the corners. "He told me to fuck off in three different languages."

I sucked in a sharp breath. *That. Smile.* Millions of people were captivated by just the image of it on television and magazines, but up close, with only mere inches separating us, it was damn near spellbinding.

Henry was afraid to fly.

I was afraid of that smile. And, the longer I spent with him, I was starting to fear the man behind it—in the best possible way.

Shaking my stupor off, I replied, "I'm surprised it wasn't more. He's fluent in at least six."

His brows knitted together. "You know him?"

"Yep. He taught me everything I know about flying."

"Really?" he drawled in shocked interest.

I chuckled. "He's my dad, Henry. Well, stepfather, really. But same thing. He's the only dad I've ever known."

He gaped in disbelief. "Shut up."

I laughed again. "Is he the one who told you to use Jackson for your pilots?"

He nodded quickly.

"Yeah. That makes sense. I always thought it was strange that a big shot like you used him. He's good, but he mainly charters to animal transports and medical emergencies. He and my dad have been best friends since high school. John got me the gig with Jackson when my first job fell through."

"No fucking way," he breathed.

ALY MARTINEZ

"Scout's honor." I lifted my hand in a Vulcan V.

His smile was epic.

If the question had been how long I wanted to fight, that smile would have been the minute I threw in the towel.

"You do realize your dad basically set us up. It was fate, Evan." He teasingly waggled his eyebrows.

"Hardly." Dipping my head, I caught his mouth and mumbled against his lips, "I think we should stop talking about my dad though."

He moaned when our tongues glided together.

After sliding a hand into his hair, I tugged his head back and kissed down the hard, masculine curves of his neck.

I knew he was kidding. Henry's coming into my life wasn't fate. At best, it could be considered a fluke. But, as I made my way down his sculpted chest, ten years' worth of resolve disappearing, it was clear: For once, luck had been on my side.

"This is going to end badly, isn't it?" I mumbled—more to myself than him.

"Not if I can help it." He arched his back off the bed as I teased my tongue down the hard planes of his torso.

"Evan," I ordered, grazing my teeth over the sensitive flesh on his stomach.

He squirmed under me. "*Evan*. Shit."

"What if you can't help it? You know, random acts of God and all."

"A few inches lower and I'll talk to God myself."

I started to laugh when I peeked up and found him watching me. The blistering heat in his gaze crashed down, enveloping me.

My heart was thundering, but I wanted this—to take him in my mouth so I could give him one of the tiny pieces of myself I'd been protecting since Shannon had left me broken.

I wanted the freedom I'd been denying myself for too long.

And I wanted it with *him*.

Unfortunately, I would have to wait.

The *Sesame Street* theme started blaring from his phone on the nightstand.

chapter eighteen

Henry

"Nooooo!" **I yelled** as Evan continued to kiss toward my rock-hard cock. Fucking inches away—and my phone was blaring the only ringtone I couldn't ignore. "Hold that thought. Okay?" I said, blindly slapping my hand on the nightstand to find my phone.

He eyed me skeptically.

I scooped my phone up and pressed it to my ear. "Hey, kid. Now's not a good—"

"I need help," Robin cried on the other end.

My heart lurched, and I sat straight up, forcing Evan to roll to the side.

"What's wrong?" I rushed.

A man's voice cursed in the background just as she shrieked, "I'm trying. Back off."

"Robin!" I called, jumping from the bed. "What the fuck is going on?"

"There's this guy…and I owe him some money."

"Fuck."

She continued to cry, but she lowered her voice to a desperate whisper. "I know, I know…but please. Just one more time. I swear. I'll get clean. Please."

Blood boiled in my veins, but guilt overwhelmed me. I pinched the bridge of my nose and squeezed the phone painfully tight as I ground out, "How much?"

She blew out a relieved breath. "Twenty-two hundred."

I clenched my teeth together, but my hands began to shake. Marching from Evan's room, I tagged my jeans and my shirt from his hall floor. Frantically pulling them on, I barked. "Where are you?"

"You can just transfer it to my bank account."

And that was when I lost it. "Where the fuck are you?" I roared.

She sobbed. "Please don't send Carter! Please. I'll do anything…"

Oh, I wasn't sending Carter. It was time I handled this shit with her myself.

"I'm in town."

She gasped, "No."

"Where are you, Robin?" I repeated, barely keeping it together.

"Henry, no! You can't come down here."

I was searching for my other shoe when I caught sight of Evan walking from his room fully dressed. He was eyeing me closely, but he didn't touch me as he walked to his hall closet and dragged a hoodie out.

"Last chance," I growled. "Either you tell me where you are or I'm hanging up."

"Send someone else—"

I closed my eyes so tight it's a wonder I didn't disappear. I wished I had. Because, one second later, I felt the jagged pain of my heart shattering.

I hit the end button and dropped my phone to the floor. My

knees quickly followed.

"Oh, God," I breathed when the reality of what I'd done consumed me.

Evan was there immediately.

Kneeling, he pulled me into his arms. "Jesus, what the hell is going on?" he asked as I broke down.

It had been a long time coming. I'd barely been fighting off that breakdown for the last five years.

"I've…I've never hung up on her," I stuttered, trying to catch my breath, but it was one race I wasn't going to win.

"Okay, let's calm down." Tucking my face into his neck, he counted into my ear. "Ten, nine, eight."

If anything happened to her, I'd never forgive myself. But that was the problem. Something had already happened to her…because of me. She was probably in some dirty crack house, track marks running up and down her arms, scared to fucking death, and I'd hung up on her.

My throat nearly closed, and I struggled away from him, but he moved with me.

"Shhhh. Seven, six, five." One of his hands was anchored on the back of my head, and the other smoothed up and down my spine. "Take a deep breath. Four, three—"

The *Sesame Street* theme interrupted him.

We both looked down at my phone vibrating on the floor as if it were some kind of ticking time bomb. But what he couldn't possibly have known was that, for me, it was.

"Who is she?" he asked.

I wasn't sure I could do that question justice. I could write a love song that would make grown men cry, but I'd never be able to find the words to explain who Robin Clark was to me.

When I'd told people that I was going to be famous one day, they'd all laughed. And then, a few years later, they'd nearly blown my phone up. Some called with genuine congratulations, but most greeted me with their hands held open. Whether they were asking for money to buy shit they refused to work for, a shout-out on my record to give them five minutes of fame, or me to put in good word with my recording company so a talentless, lazy asshole could get a deal, they all wanted something.

It didn't matter that they hadn't supported my relentless climb to the top or that they discouraged me at every turn. Seven degrees of separation was all that was required for them to feel entitled. People I barely knew scurried out from the woodwork.

With Levee at my back, I donned a steel spine and told almost all of them to fuck off. And lost not a wink of sleep over it.

But it was the "almost" percentage of that equation that kept me up at night for the majority of the following five years.

I adored my life, but if I could turn back time, I'd be willing to accept a dead-end job teaching guitar lessons at the local music store if it changed her path.

Staring down at the picture of her wide smile flashing on the screen of my phone, I replied into his neck, "She's my sister."

"Shit," he breathed just as the ringing fell silent. Using my shoulders, he gently shifted me away so he could catch my gaze. "What's going on?"

There was no point in trying to explain. He probably would have just laughed at me if he'd known how many times I'd gotten that exact call over the years. I could only imagine his face if I told him about the hundreds of thousands of dollars I'd spent supporting her, sending her to rehab, or, in cases like this, paying some dealer who no longer accepted her word as credit. The money didn't matter. However, the hollowness in my chest that expanded each and every time she used me was embarrassing. After all of this time, it shouldn't have hurt anymore, but a pain like that never went away. And, one day, when I inevitably lost her, it would devour me.

I decided to give him the abridged version. "She's an addict and needs money. I refused to put it in her bank account, and she refused to tell me where she was." I pointed to my phone and tried to crack a joke. "Tough love. Doctor Phil would be proud." My voice was the only thing that actually cracked though.

"Come here." He tugged until I was once again against his chest. "It'll be okay."

I barked a humorless laugh. "I don't know anymore. This might just kill me."

"It won't kill you."

My breath caught as I choked out, "But it might kill *her*."

His hands froze on my back as he bit out a curse. But, besides that, the talking portion of my breakdown was over. For several minutes, Evan remained kneeling on the ground and silently holding me. He was the only thing keeping me together.

I was trying to collect myself when the phone started ringing again, and before I had the chance to stop him, Evan yanked it up.

"Where are you?" he greeted, standing up.

"Evan, no!" I jumped to my feet after him.

He extended an arm to stop me from advancing. "Don't worry about who I am," he told her. "Tell me how much money you need and where you are." He walked to his bar and found a scrap of paper and a pen. His blue eyes lifted to mine before he turned away. "No. I understand. Don't worry. He's not coming."

The hell I'm not.

I kept my objections to myself because he started writing something down. I could argue with him later as long as he got her fucking address.

"Right. Yeah." He glanced at his watch. "I'm about twenty minutes out." He hung up. Turning to face me, he shook his head—and read my mind. "You're not going with me." He stomped past me to the door, where he grabbed his keys off a metal hook.

"The hell you say! She's my sister!"

"And she sounds high as a motherfucking kite, but she's right. You show your face in the middle of that neighborhood, the only thing people are going to see is dollar signs."

"For fuck's sake, it's San Francisco, not South America. I'm pretty sure we aren't dealing with the Cartel here."

"Which only makes them more dangerous. They're desperate and stupid. And, if you want to talk about 'for fuck's sake,' your fingernail clippings are sold for a cool grand on eBay. You're a liability, Henry. Let me go pay this bastard and bring her back here. We need a good night of sleep so we can figure out how to deal with the rest of this in the morning." He paused and pulled his wallet out. "How much cash you got on you?"

I blinked. Then I swallowed hard and blinked some more.

We.

"So we can figure out how to deal with the rest in the morning."

We.

It was the single most romantic thing anyone had ever said to me.

He was counting twenties when I managed to squeeze the syllable past the lump in my throat.

"We?"

His head popped up, and his face softened when he met my gaze. Three steps and his long legs swallowed the distance between us. When he stopped in front of me, vulnerability flashed in his eyes.

"Depends. Do you want that to be a we?"

I nodded enthusiastically and fought the emotion back as I joked, "I totally meant to include rescuing Robin from drug lords when I told you all the things I wanted with you. It must have slipped my mind."

He chuckled and looped an arm around my waist. With a tug, he pulled me against his chest and dropped his forehead to mine. "Then yeah, Henry. It's a *we*."

"Okay," I breathed, unable to utter anything else.

He squatted an inch to bring our eyes level. "Now, you gonna give me any more shit about staying here while I go get her?"

I shook my head and smiled weakly. "Nope."

His hand drifted down to my ass, where he dug my wallet out of my back pocket while gratuitously groping me.

Smirking, he lifted my wallet into view. "How much cash you got? I need to get out of here"—he paused to brush his lips across mine—"so I can hurry up and get back."

I was terrified to fly.

But, right then, wrapped in his arms, Evan made me soar.

Minutes later, he left.

But, for the first time in my life, I didn't feel alone.

"Cookie!" Robin cried as she rushed through Evan's front door. Her long, black hair blew behind her as she sprinted into my arms. She was all of five foot one and maybe a hundred pounds, but her tiny body still managed to rock me back a step when she slammed into me.

Loud sobs ravaged her as she buried her face into me.

"I'm so sorry."

My bones ached to tell her that everything was okay, but that was exactly why we were in this situation to begin with. Clearing my throat, I bent to kiss the top of her head.

"You fucked up, kid."

"I know. God. I'm so sorry. It won't happen again."

Gripping her shoulders, I pushed her away from me. "Yes. It will. And, every time I bail you out, it basically ensures that it *will* happen again."

She adamantly shook her head as tears streamed from her dark-brown eyes. "No! I'm serious this time. I'm done." Fighting my grip off, she buried her face back into my chest and continued to cry.

Profuse apologies rolled from her mouth. Those I believed. The promises that she'd quit were a different story though. I'd heard those lies a million times. And, if history was any kind of indicator, I'd hear them all a million more.

I glanced up and found Evan standing in the doorway with his shoulder leaning against the jamb and a hand shoved in his pocket.

"Thank you," I mouthed.

He nodded and offered me a smile.

"He's"—she sniffled—"hot." She didn't even attempt to be quiet.

I chuckled and held Evan's eyes as I replied, "He is."

"He like men?" she asked.

"Uhh…" I bit my lip and popped my eyebrows at him in question.

He laughed and rolled his eyes as he became unstuck from the door. After sauntering over to me, he stepped to my side, brushed a kiss across my jaw, and then replied, "I like one."

My heart seized. Those three magic words spoke to my soul.

Who needed love when you were the only exception?

I was still making dreamy eyes at Evan when his front door flew open. We all jumped. I squeezed Robin tight, and Evan quickly stepped in front of us.

"Where is she!" a deep, gravelly voice I barely recognized rumbled.

Robin went solid in my arms, but my body slacked.

"Jesus Christ, Carter. Can we maybe chill with the Incredible Hulk act?"

"She's fine," Evan announced, stepping aside to reveal her tucked against my chest.

Carter's nostrils flared as scary muscles ticked on his neck and his jaw.

He strode across the room. "Let go of him," he growled.

She shook her head and squeezed me tighter.

"Robin, I'm not asking again."

She squeaked but didn't reply.

I shot Carter a puzzled look he failed to notice through his palpable anger.

"Did you call him?" she accused into my chest.

"Well…yeah." I bulged my eyes at Evan, who was watching the whole interaction equally as perplexed.

"Why?" she whined.

I had opened my mouth to answer, but Carter got there first.

"Okay, I'm done." He bent down and scooped her off her feet. "Let's go."

"Carter! Put me down," she protested.

"Hey! Where are you taking her?" Evan shot in front of him, clearly concerned that Carter was caveman-carrying a woman from his house.

Even in the chaos, I took a minute to note what a good guy he was.

"Home," Carter grunted and then turned to look at me. "I'll take her back to your house and keep an eye on her for the rest of the night."

I shrugged. "Okay."

Evan's mouth gaped open and he shot me a scowl. "Okay?"

"Uh…I mean. Is that cool with you, kid?"

She never once looked up as she grumbled, "It's gonna have to be, apparently."

"There. Decision made." Carter nodded at me and then at Evan before storming out the front door with Robin in his arms.

Evan closed the door behind them and then raked a hand through his hair. "What the fucking hell was that about?"

"No clue."

"And, just to be clear, you're not concerned at all that maybe letting her go with him was a bad idea? He was pissed and she didn't seem all that excited about going."

I waved him off. "Nah. She'll be fine. Carter and Robin are tight and fight like siblings. He's good to her. He's just pissed she's using again. Trust me. She's safer with him than any other person in the world."

He twisted his lips skeptically and glanced back at the door. "If you say so."

I smiled at his concern. "She's fine."

He strolled over and cupped my jaw. "And what about you?"

"I'm better now." I brushed my lips over his.

"Good. You want to tell me who she really is now?"

Leaning away, I cocked an eyebrow. "She's my sister."

"Really? Because she told me you were her dad."

chapter nineteen

Evan

A loud groan rumbled in his throat. "She has got to quit telling people that shit."

On our little trip back, I'd learned that Robin was twenty-one—only ten years younger than Henry. There was no possible way he was her father. But, after having witnessed Henry's breakdown over her, I was incredibly interested to hear more about the dynamic between the two of them.

"So, then why don't you tell me who she really is?"

"I already told you. She's my sister," he said defensively.

Gripping the back of his neck, I tipped my forehead to his. "We're a 'we' now, remember?"

His eyes flared and his lips parted. "We."

I nodded. "I'm just trying to understand what happened tonight. I hated seeing you like that, and I'm going to need all the facts if I'm going to prevent it from happening again."

With a sigh, he wrapped his arms around my hips and pushed

his hands into my back pockets. "She was my foster sister."

I pressed my lips to his and then pulled him over to the couch with me. He settled into the corner, and I sat beside him with my leg curled up on the couch so I could face him. He was notably uncomfortable with the conversation, and I needed him to understand that he had my undivided attention—and support.

Taking his hands, I encouraged him. "Keep going."

He glanced down at our linked hands and trailed his thumb over my knuckle, smiling like I'd just offered him the world. "She was five when she was placed in my foster home. I was fifteen and had a job washing dishes at a dive restaurant. The owner's daughter had a bakery across town, so he sold her stuff as dessert. I can't even tell you how addicted I was to those damn peanut butter cookies. You'd never catch me leaving work without one."

He puffed his cheeks, insinuating he'd been fat. My only response was a teasing side-eye. He shook his head and continued.

"I got home one night and found her crying in the bathroom because she'd wet her bed. Poor kid was scared to death. I helped her clean herself up and fix up her bed. She was so damn cute it didn't take but one sentence for her to wrap me around her finger. But it was what she asked that changed my life." He paused and sucked in a shaky breath. "She asked me if I'd stay with her until she fell asleep. It was the first time anyone had ever *needed* me." He swallowed hard. "I wasn't a burden to her. I wasn't a gay kid who needed to be fixed. I wasn't a poor, pitiful foster kid no one gave a damn about. When those big, brown eyes looked up at me, I wasn't Henry Gilchrist. I felt like Superman. That little girl saved my life, because she made me feel worthy."

"Jesus," I breathed, leaning forward to kiss his temple. I officially hated this story, but I adored that he was telling it to me. That made *me* feel worthy.

"Every night for the next three years, we shared a peanut butter cookie before she went to bed."

"That's why she calls you cookie," I filled in as it dawned on me.

"Yeah. I was her Cookie Monster." He laughed at the memory. "I had a whole lot of nothing back then, but she was always there, waiting for me with a huge, goofy grin. She used to beg me to play my guitar for her—even when I sucked at it. It took me a week, but I learned the theme to *Sesame Street* for her. God, I loved that little girl." Pain was etched into his face, but he swayed toward me as though I could take it all away.

I couldn't. But I sure as hell was going to try.

"When I graduated high school, I was forced to leave her behind. She had a really hard time with the transition, but in some ways, I think I struggled more. As much as I wanted to be out on my own, forging my own path, I wasn't ready for the loneliness I felt. Robin and my guitar were the only two things I wanted to take into my new life with me.

"I went out on a limb and asked permission from my social worker to keep in contact with her. Thankfully, it all worked out and we got to talk on the phone a few times each week. While it wasn't the same as seeing her every day, it definitely helped us both. I visited her for birthdays and such, but it became harder and harder over the years when she started being moved around foster homes. In the name of full disclosure, I feel the need to tell you Robin was always a good kid. But the girl hit puberty and I swear she became a different person."

I chuckled. "Teenage girl. I can imagine."

"It was bad, and I knew she wasn't getting the emotional support she needed to feel worthy too. The day she turned sixteen, she called me crying. She'd gotten into it with her new foster father and he put his hands on her. I lost my fucking mind. I'd already made it big in music and had been trying to figure out how to get her out of there, but that one call sped up the process. The very next day, three attorneys were at Social Services, filing adoption paperwork on my behalf."

My head snapped back in surprise. "You adopted her?"

"Well, I tried. I canceled a month of tours and threw every re- source I had into getting her placed into my custody. But the state of California wasn't keen on giving a sixteen-year-old girl to a sin- gle twenty-six year-old guy. Besides, it would have taken forever to jump through all the hoops required to adopt, and I wanted her out of foster care immediately. That's when my attorney's came up with another idea. A few days later, I transferred a large sum of money into a trust fund in her name and we petitioned the courts for her emancipation. With the money to support herself long term, it was an easy win."

He paused and the light in his eyes dimmed. "It was the greatest day of my life when I moved her into my house. Now, five years later, I wish she'd stayed in foster care. I had no idea what the hell I was getting into with her. That money I gave her may as well have killed her. She was young and suddenly loaded. I made her get her high school diploma, but she didn't have to work. I travel all the time, and though I hired people to be there with her, she was still alone a lot. With a virtually bottomless bank account, she turned to drugs to keep herself entertained. And, for the rest of my life, I have to live with the fact that I'm responsible for that."

I ran a soothing hand over his thigh, unsure what to say. He didn't want my opinion, I was sure, but to me, it didn't sound like Robin was the only young, dumb kid with too much money in that equation. But his heart was in the right place. I didn't have any sib- lings, but it was easy to understand how Henry thought he was help- ing her.

Now, I just had to figure out how to help *him*.

"You aren't responsible for her decisions, Henry."

His pained gaze lifted to mine. "I gave her almost a million dollars."

My eyes bulged as my mouth fell open.

"Yeah." He laughed without humor. "On top of that, I bought her an apartment when she wanted to move out of my place and gave her credit cards for whatever she wanted to buy. And yet, three years later, that million was gone. I have no fucking clue where it went, but the resources that were meant to set her up for years, if not life, are completely tapped out. And I have no fucking idea what to do about it." His sad, blue eyes searched mine, but I held no answers. All I had to offer was comfort.

"Come here." I gripped the back of his head and pulled his face into my neck. "We'll figure it out."

His shoulders shook as the emotions fought their way out. "I can't give her any more money, Evan. It's killing her. Every fucking dollar, she pumps into her arms. She's been through rehab four times. I can't keep doing this with her. I'm killing her. Just being in her life, I'm killing her. But I can't tell her no. I'm all she has…" His voice caught. "She's all *I* have."

"That's not true," I quickly said. "Not anymore." Tipping his head back, I guided his gaze to mine. "You are *not* alone anymore, Henry. I swear to you I'm right here. I'm not going anywhere."

"You will," he whispered as though it were a promise.

"No, I'm not," I said adamantly.

Even I was surprised by the ease with which it had left my tongue. There was no longer a fight—my mind and my body were both finally on board. The walls had crumbled and I was clambering over the wreckage with only him in my sights.

I was in it with Henry.

Plain and simple.

"I'm here," I reiterated, needing him to understand how serious I was.

"For now. You can't see it now, but if time has taught me anything, it's that everything is temporary."

"Not me. Not us. Jesus, Henry. I've been caught in your web since I first laid eyes on you. Yeah, I've been scared. But this thing with you was hard for me to accept. Maybe you were right. I needed some time to get used to it all. But it's done now. It's time for you to get used to the fact that I'm here to stay as long as you want me." I pressed a hard kiss to his lips.

He closed his eyes and breathed in as if he were trying to inhale me.

I wanted that too, and seconds later, his exhale filled my lungs.

"You aren't alone anymore. *We'll* figure out Robin." I kissed him again, this time opening my mouth and touching my tongue to his lips. "*We'll* figure it all out."

His mouth briefly opened with mine before I leaned away. "*Evan*," he breathed, following me forward.

My cock thickened the way it always did when he said my name, but it was my mind that made me want to take it further. And it was the swell of my heart that made me want to take it all the way.

I slipped off the couch, settling on my knees and holding his gaze. "*We'll* figure out how to get me in your bed on a tour bus after your shows."

His mouth slacked open and his eyes heated. "Wha…what…"

I winked, shifting between his legs. "*We'll* go to family dinner at Levee's house anytime you want." Gliding my hands up his thighs, I found him quickly thickening behind the denim. I paused at his button. "I'm not big on takeout, but I'll cook dinner for you, and then *we* can watch whatever the hell movie you want on lazy Sundays." I watched him intently as he remained frozen, but his breathing had begun to speed. "*We'll* sit on whatever beach you want when you need to get away from it all."

"What are you saying?" he finally asked on a whisper.

I smiled up at him as I pulled his zipper down. "I guess I'm saying I want it all too."

Understanding morphed his face into something so beautiful, I knew I was done for. There would be no coming back from this. Not from Henry. And, for the first time, I was completely okay with that. No reservations.

I hadn't even gotten his pants down when I felt his hand in my hair, urging me away. My eyes jumped to his as he suddenly stood off the couch.

"Be specific here. You want what?" he asked.

"*Evan*," I corrected, and a sinister smile tipped one side of his mouth.

His grip in my hair tightened as he repeated, "You want what, *Evan*?"

"You. Every way I can have you."

The weight of a decade floated from my shoulders, freeing me.

I was still on my knees when he bent down and brushed his lips across my mouth, hovering out of my reach so I couldn't take it any deeper.

"There's no going back from this, Evan."

"I know." I teased the waistband of his jeans.

He caught my hands to stop me. "You can't wake up in the morning and ask the universe for a redo. I won't be able to let go."

"I don't want a redo, so don't let go." I pressed up on my knees until I caught his lips.

It started out gentle, but it quickly progressed. Our lids never drifted closed as he dominated my mouth. However, it wasn't confidence he was blinking back. Nor was it desire that made his hands shake as he fought to maintain his grip in my hair.

I wasn't sure what was going on in his head at all, but I knew one way to make it stop.

"I want it too. All of it," I whispered into his mouth.

"I need to hear you say it," he urged.

"Fuck me, Henry."

A loud growl rumbled in his chest, and suddenly, I was going over. My back landed hard on the carpeted floor, and Henry crashed on top of me.

Our teeth clanked as he wildly kissed me. His hands traveled over me, frantically tugging at my shirt until he was able to get it over my head, and seconds later, he was dragging my pants down my legs. The air was cool as I lay naked in front of him, but it was Henry— there might as well have been a fire crackling beside us for the way his heat engulfed me.

"Get naked," I ordered, pushing up on an elbow to watch.

But, for once, Henry didn't seem in the mood to put on a show. He was naked and straddling my hips before I had the chance to enjoy the view. Folded over, he kissed his way up my chest to my neck. Our erections ground together, sending sparks shooting down to my balls.

I lifted my hips, desperately seeking more friction.

"Easy," he soothed into my ear. "This is not going to be a fast fuck, *Evan.*"

I groaned in both frustration and excitement.

He chuckled, raking his teeth over my earlobe. "It's going to take me a little while to get you ready, but I swear you will fucking enjoy every second of it." Arching his back, he made room for his hand to squeeze between us and grip my cock.

"I'm ready," I mumbled as though it were a curse when his thumb spread a bead of precome around my head.

"You're wrong, but if you think you are, then the next half hour should be torture."

He wasn't wrong.

I lost track of how many minutes passed as he alternated between kissing me and working my cock with his hands and his mouth. Every so often, his damp fingers would drift down to my ass,

ALY MARTINEZ

teasing my rim before disappearing. I almost came at least a dozen times. It was a sheer force of will that kept me from emptying down his throat when the tip of his finger slipped inside me. It was agonizing, but there was no way I was complaining.

Well…at least, not until he got up and walked away.

He returned seconds later sporting a sexy smirk that made me want to be the one fucking *him*, but my ass clenched as I caught sight of him pouring lube into his hand with the square packet of a condom clamped between his teeth.

"I thought there wasn't anything else in your magic bags," I joked as he kneeled beside me.

"There wasn't. I pay a little gay fairy to follow me around with condoms and lube. It's a perk of being rich."

I laughed, but it ended on a curse when his slick hand slid over me from base to tip. The condom landed on my stomach just seconds before his mouth covered mine.

"You're killing me," I groaned as he fisted my cock.

"It'll be better this way. I swear."

I reached out and gripped his hard-on. "I don't need better. I just need you. Inside me. Now. Stop fucking around."

His eyes were wary, but biting his lip, he nodded in understanding.

My whole body seized as his hand glided down my crease and circled the sensitive flesh. It had been too long for me. I'd loved to bottom with Shannon, but I'd never let anyone else touch me like this, not even the women I'd been with over the years.

And this was Henry. That alone had me perilously close to losing it.

"Relax," he urged, using his other hand to generously drizzle lube over my balls until it dripped down to my ass.

"Oh God…" I trailed off, throwing an arm over my face.

The anticipation was killing me and once he was inside me, I wasn't going to last more than a second. But I wanted that one fuck-ing second with him stretching and filling me more than I'd wanted any orgasm in my life.

Misreading my reaction, he stilled his finger and used his other hand to remove my arm from over my face. I hated the look in his eyes. It was all wrong for what he was doing to me. The heat and fe-ral desperation that usually filled his gaze had disappeared, leaving something hollow behind.

It pained me.

"Henry, wait," I said, sitting up, but I didn't have a chance to ask him what was wrong before one of his fingers filled me. "Fuck," I breathed, falling back down.

My lips fell closed as he worked my ass with one finger and his other hand followed the same rhythm over my dick. It was over-whelming and intoxicating—but not nearly enough. I wanted the sting as he penetrated me. I wanted his breath on my shoulder as he pumped into me, giving me back everything I'd lost all those years ago.

And I wanted it from him.

Only him.

"Look at me," he ordered.

My eyes popped open just as he added another finger, delicious-ly stretching me in preparation. I barely managed to hold his gaze as he curled his fingers and nearly sent me flying over the edge of release.

A knowing smile tipped his lips and his blue eyes branded me as he promised, "This doesn't make you gay, *Evan*. It just makes you mine."

I fucking hated labels. Always had.

But maybe that was because no one had ever given me the right one.

At least, not until that moment.

Gay. Straight. Bi. None of them fit me the way *mine* did rolling off Henry's tongue.

Suddenly, it was the only label I'd ever wanted.

chapter twenty

Henry

His hips lifted off the ground as I gently fucked him with my fingers. He'd been rock hard for nearly half an hour. He was close—just the way I wanted him. When I was done with Evan, I didn't want him to remember the pain of his first time. I wanted him teetering so close to orgasm that, the moment I got inside him, he'd come damn near instantaneously.

I needed him desperate for seconds. Thirds. Fourths.

Forever.

I couldn't lose him. That would be one crash I wouldn't survive. We'd only been a *we* for hours, and I knew I never wanted to be a *me* again. Deep in my soul, I knew that Evan was it for me. While I had never been a praying man, right then, as he got his first real taste of pure ecstasy under my touch, I prayed to whatever god was willing to listen that I was it for him too.

I found hope in the fact that he had so freely given me his body. And, as soon as I got inside him, I'd claim him completely once and for all. No woman in the world could take him like I was going to.

He was beautiful writhing under me. The strong muscles of his stomach and his thighs tensed every time I pressed in deep. And the breath that rushed from his mouth when I'd start to withdraw might as well have been whispering erotic pleas to my cock. I'd never been so turned on in my life.

But I wanted his heart.

"Henry. Please. I can't hold back much... Fuck."

I curled my fingers inside him and his hard-on jumped in response. A few strokes more and he was going to lose it.

But I wanted to feel that from the inside and not with my fingers.

"Roll over," I ordered, snatching the condom off the floor.

"Thank fuck," he huffed, climbing to his knees, but he didn't roll over at all.

Gripping the back of my hair, he crushed his mouth over mine. Greedily, our tongues tangled and his hand slipped between my legs, massaging my balls before gliding up my shaft.

"Shit," I cursed as he punishingly pumped me.

Biting my bottom lip, he mumbled, "Not so fucking fun on the receiving end of torture, is it?"

I moaned, barely able to force my smartass reply out. "Oh, I don't know. Torture has its merits."

His lips twitched against mine as he snagged the condom from my hand. "So does you fucking me."

He continued his steady strokes as he ripped the foil wrapper open with his teeth. With a practiced ease, he rolled the condom on me and then picked up the bottle of lube. "There. Now, we're both ready."

"Are we?" I whispered when unexpected nerves churned in my stomach.

A sexy smirk hiked one side of his mouth. "*We are.*"

We.

The nerves faded, leaving nothing but an all-consuming need coursing through me.

"Turn around," I demanded, pouring lube over my wrapped erection.

He obeyed.

My heart raced as if I were the virgin in our little scenario. And, for the way I knew both of our lives would be altered after this, I might as well have been.

It was his first time.

For me, it was the culmination of what I hoped was the final hunt.

Pressing my chest to his back, I allowed my cock to glide between his cheeks. His head lolled to the side and a loud growl rumbled in his throat as he swayed back against me. On our knees, we were nearly the same height, and our bodies lined up perfectly.

After looping my arms around his hips, I found his thick cock jutting out in front of him—waiting for me. Evan moaned and arched his back when I took him in my hand. His cheeks parted slightly from the movement, taking me deeper without actually taking me anywhere.

Lube was everywhere, but I needed more if this was going to be good for him. And I *needed* it to be good for him. I was reaching for the bottle on the floor beside us when he caught my wrist.

"No more. I'm good." He bent over, resting his hands on the ground and forcing his ass up.

There was nothing left to do—except risk losing the only person I'd ever truly wanted to keep.

Nerves roared inside me.

Leaning over, I grazed my teeth over his shoulder. His breathing faltered as I guided myself to his entrance.

"Breathe," I whispered. But, as I gently pressed past his tight ring, he wasn't the only one holding his breath. "Relax," I urged when

ALY MARTINEZ

I felt him tense around me, halting any further progress. I stroked his hard-on from behind until his body gave in to my demands.

"Oh, fuck," he groaned, his whole body sagging and allowing me just enough leeway to ease all the way in.

It was too much.

His back muscles rippling.

His strangled moans.

My body joined with his.

Mine.

"Move," he ground out.

I couldn't if I'd wanted to. "No. Just relax for a second." I squeezed his hip with one hand and gave him another stroke with my other.

Suddenly, he reared up and caught the back of my head. Turning his neck, he pulled my head over his shoulder until I met his mouth. "Okay. Then I'll fuck you," he murmured, sinking backwards onto my cock.

He held me tight for balance as he forced my ass to rest on my heels. As soon as I was settled, he rose out of my lap before gliding back down.

I was speechless as he brazenly began to ride me. The visual combined with his tight heat wrapped around me and his mouth finding mine on every down stroke, made it clear I wouldn't last long.

"Jesus, Evan," I breathed before biting his shoulder.

"Faster," he pleaded, folding his hand over mine, which was still wrapped around his cock.

I attempted to match his rhythm but found it nearly impossible to concentrate. I was going to ruin this for him, but I couldn't do anything but feel as he moved over me—bottoming out, circling his hips in my lap, and then rising again.

I gave up waiting for his mouth and dropped my forehead to his back as he thoroughly worked me over.

"Yessss," he hissed as he sank down onto my lap one last time.

Cupping the head of his cock, he caught his release. I was worthless to help him, because as he pulsed with his own orgasm, it sent me over the edge as well.

And I fell.

And fell.

And fell.

And fell.

Until I crashed so hard there was nothing left of me but broken pieces littering his floor.

The sex was off-the-charts, indescribable, ruin-me-for-life amazing.

And that was exactly why my heart shattered into a million shards before I'd even pulled out.

And it wasn't because I was afraid he would leave or freak out.

It was because I knew I could never stay.

There was no fucking way possible that had been Evan's first time.

Evan

The world tilted on its axis for those brief moments Henry was inside me. I'd forgotten how good it could be. But, like a flash of blinding color, I realized exactly how black and white my life had been for the last ten years.

It was time to stop punishing myself for Shannon's mistakes.

And, as if the stars had aligned, Henry was my reward.

"What the fuck was that?" he panted as I shifted off his lap.

Smiling, I turned to kiss him. Only the absolute horror that painted his face stopped me in my tracks.

"Uh…" I stammered when coherent thought failed me. "What's

wrong?"

He scrambled to his feet, blinking at me as though I'd just maimed him. He hadn't even removed the condom before he started snatching up his clothes.

"Henry?" I called, standing up with him. I took a step toward him, but he backed away. "What's going on?" I asked cautiously, thoroughly confused.

He shook his head and started tugging on his shirt.

I lifted my cupped hand in his direction. "Let me clean this up. I'll be right back."

He nodded, but it was empty. The shell of the man was standing in front of me, but his mind was a million miles away. And I was clueless as to where he'd gone or, better yet, *why* he'd left. The sex had been incredible, but clearly, something grievous had happened in Henry's head.

By the time I returned from the bathroom, he was dressed and pulling on his shoes.

"Where are you going?" I asked in shock.

He didn't lift his head when he replied, "Home. I need to check on Robin."

I tagged my jeans off the floor and tugged them on. "Fine. I'll go with you."

His head popped up, and the blue eyes that usually ignited me landed on me like a bucket of water extinguishing the coals. "No. I'm good. Besides, I have to leave in the morning."

"Yeah. I know. I'm flying you."

He scoffed. "No. You aren't."

I narrowed my eyes. "Yes. I am. There is no fucking way I'm letting you get on a plane with someone else. We discussed this."

"*We* didn't discuss anything!" he roared, every muscle in his neck straining under the exertion.

My mind was spinning from his sudden eruption, but as he

darted toward my front door, I knew I wasn't letting him leave. Not like that.

Catching his arm, I spun him to face me. "What the hell is going on with you right now?"

With a pointed glance at my hand, he growled, "Let me go."

I laughed humorlessly. "Have you lost your mind? I'm not letting you go. Not now. Hell, maybe not ever."

His face softened for the briefest of seconds, but he quickly covered it. "There's nothing to hold on to. You were never mine to begin with."

The pain was staggering. His words felt like a thousand tiny daggers, each one slicing through me in rapid succession. Unable to formulate a response, I stumbled back from the verbal assault.

"Yeah," he breathed, taking a menacing step in my direction. "I don't date gay guys, *Evan*."

My name was his kill shot, and for the way it seared through me, it hit right on target.

I wasn't even sure why I was under fire, but I sure as hell wasn't going to stand there and take it without a fight.

"I'm not fucking gay."

He patronizingly tipped his head. "No? Then what do you call what we just did? And, better yet, what do you call all the times you've done it with men before me? Because I know good and damn well no straight man fucks like that."

Story of my Goddamn life.

Not gay.

Not straight.

Not enough.

"I never said I was straight, either," I seethed through clenched teeth.

He snatched his arm from my hold. "You never said *anything*!"

"Bullshit. I said I wanted *you*."

In an eerie whisper, he shot back, "And what guy did you want first?"

I crossed my arms over my chest and held his angry gaze. "Could you speak fucking English for me here? I don't have a clue what you are pissed about."

"You've been with a man before!"

I arched an eyebrow. "Never claimed to be a virgin."

"Oh, God," he choked, running a shaky hand through his hair.

Even with as upset as I was, every fiber of my being ached to soothe him. But, as I took a step toward him, he threw up a hand to stop me. The gears in his head were turning, and within seconds, his anger dissipated.

His teeth worried over his bottom lip. "It was just sex though, right? How many men have you been with?"

My lips twitched, and like a moth to a flame, his eyes fell to my mouth.

"I suppose you'd be okay with me asking you the same question?"

"You could," he said matter-of-factly as he began pacing the room. "And I would give you the only answer that mattered: more than *one*."

My lips twisted in a grimace. "How is that the only answer that matters?"

"It just is!"

I threw my hands out to the sides in frustration. "Fine. I've been with less than five. Does that help?"

Hope flooded his eyes. "So, like, two, including me?"

I swayed my head from side to side in consideration. "So, maybe it's less than six now."

"Oh, God." He pinched his nose and dropped his head back to stare at the ceiling.

"Jesus Christ, Henry. You're openly gay. It seems a little hypocritical for you to be judging me for sleeping with a few guys. Why does it matter?"

Lowering his head, he leveled me with the most tormented expression I had ever witnessed. And not just from Henry, but in my entire life.

"You were supposed to be straight!" He stabbed his thumb into his chest. "I was supposed to be the exception—not number fucking five."

It started in his fingers. Then the tiniest of twitches traveled through him until it became an all out tremor. And, seconds later, his chest heaved and a red flush swept its way up his neck.

I was pissed, but I couldn't just stand there and allow a panic attack to overtake him. With two long strides, I closed the distance between us. His body jumped in surprise as I folded an arm around his hips and pulled him against me. Cupping the back of his head, I tucked his face into my neck.

"Take a deep breath. This is nothing to get worked up about. I'm right here."

His arms fell to his sides, but he didn't melt into me. We were inches apart, but he felt more like a stranger than he had the day I'd met him. It was all wrong. But it was a feeling I knew all too well.

It was the end.

And, once again, I was helplessly holding on to a man who had already let me go.

Wrenching my eyes shut, I started counting. I pretended that it was for him, but suddenly, he wasn't the only one panicking.

"Ten, nine, eight." I kissed his temple and murmured, "We're okay."

His heart slamming in his chest said otherwise.

"Seven, six, five." I squeezed him until he was plastered to my front. "Catch your breath and we'll talk. Everything is fine."

He shook his head, but I ignored it. Or, at least, I tried—my pulse skyrocketed.

"Four, three, two—"

"Don't say one," he pleaded. "Just don't say it. Not yet."

I nodded, pressing my lips to his temple again, this time letting them linger.

And then, for several minutes, I held him impossibly tight. Slowly, his breathing returned to normal and his trembles stilled. However, there was nothing I could do to calm myself. Every minute we stood there, a ball of fire grew in my chest.

That embrace burned like a goodbye.

And I was helpless to extinguish it.

We hadn't even talked yet, but Henry was checking out.

He wouldn't magically disappear when I let go.

But I knew he wouldn't be there, either.

"You're bisexual?" he finally asked my neck.

I sighed. "Something like that."

"Why didn't you tell me?"

I leaned my head away to get a read on his face, but he followed me forward, unwilling to look me in the eye. "I figured it was fairly obvious after I kissed you at the concert."

"It probably should have been. But you were so skittish at first…"

I cleared the emotion from my throat. "I had…a…really bad relationship with a man. I vowed not to repeat the process."

"Oh, God. It wasn't just sex, then? You actually dated men?"

"Just one," I whispered.

His body immediately stiffened.

I hadn't meant to say the word that would end the countdown.

And I definitely hadn't meant to end the shortest yet most poignant relationship of my life.

And, more than all of that, I'd had no idea how deeply that single solitary word would wound him.

"One," he whispered as though it were a confirmation.

"Please don't do this." I fought to hold on to him, but he struggled out of my arms. "Just talk to me. What are you so scared of?"

His hand was already on the doorknob when he froze. The crack of his voice was agonizing. "You."

"Henry!" I called, but he was out the door and jogging down my driveway before I could stop him.

His car wasn't out front anymore, but he didn't slow as he rounded the corner onto the main street.

"Shit," I cursed, rushing back inside to grab my shirt and my keys before taking off after him barefoot.

Henry

There was no reason why I should have been gutted. Deep down I had always known there was something different about Evan. Denial was a cruel bitch like that. The signs had been there. I mean, I was good, but it usually took more than one night to get a man into my bed—or, in our case, my shower. And, as soon as I had thrown down the gauntlet and let him know I wanted something serious, he hadn't hesitated in picking it up.

But I liked him, so I was blinded by hope. I was willing to pretend that I was irresistible to him, because God knows he was to me.

Aimlessly, I was wandering down a street in his neighborhood when my phone started ringing the theme song to *Transformers*. I didn't even retrieve it from my pocket. I had no words left for him.

I was famous beyond my wildest fantasy, but somehow, after years of working my ass off, I was still alone. And I was walking away from the best thing I'd ever had because I feared he could never love me the way I knew I would—and probably already did—love him. Even I could see the ridiculousness of the situation. I should have been stoked beyond all reason that the man I so desperately wanted to be with wanted to be with me too. And we didn't have the impossible hurdle of his sexuality to overcome.

We could just be together.

But that knowledge didn't slow the anguish growing in the pit of my stomach.

It was four in the morning and Evan's cozy neighborhood was still fast asleep. So, when I felt the high beams on my back, there was only one person it could be.

Quickly ducking around the side of a corner house, I watched his SUV fly past. What was I doing? Well, besides being minutes away from being arrested for trespassing.

The hammering in my chest told me to go back to his house.

To talk to him.

To get over myself and follow my heart for once.

Nothing had changed. He was still the same man who made me want to settle down and be more than just Henry Alexander—recording artist, celebrity, *star*. With Evan, I saw more than stages, screaming fans, and casual encounters. It was the first time I had ever seen picket fences, family, and a future.

But the nagging in my head told me that it was all too far out of reach.

In the end, it was that voice that won out.

I didn't go back to Evan's house.

But I didn't go home, either.

chapter twenty-one

Henry

The dog barked as I used my key to let myself in. Soon enough, he was wagging his tail and welcoming me back. It had been a while since I'd been there, but when faced with the need to forget the madness brewing in my head, there was only one place I could go.

After turning the security alarm off, I silently made my way to the bedroom. Not even the moon peeked through the window, but I was able to make out his solid body sleeping soundly under the covers.

Unable to resist myself, I toed my shoes off, climbed into the middle of the king-size bed, and draped my arm around his stomach as I spooned up behind him.

"Mmm," he purred, shifting back against me. His hand slipped back over my ass, squeezing before he drifted to sleep again.

I chuckled, nuzzling into the back of his hair. "See? I knew I could turn you."

His body went solid just before I caught a hard elbow to the stomach. "What the…" he yelled, scrambling off the bed.

I hadn't even had the chance to defend myself before his hand was at my throat.

"Stop. It's just me!" I croaked through the pressure, the light thankfully clicking on to illuminate the room, revealing his fist reared back and aimed directly at my face.

"Henry?" Levee said sleepily from the other side of the bed.

With my hands up in surrender, I repeated to both of them, "It's just me."

I held Sam's gaze as recognition hit his face.

"Jesus, fuck, man!" he shouted, but his hand fell away from my throat.

"What are you doing here?" Levee asked, groaning as she heaved her round stomach over so she could cuddle into my side.

Sam marched to the dresser and pulled a T-shirt on, mumbling curse words under his breath.

"Sorry. I didn't know where else to go." I kissed her forehead.

"I can tell you a few places to go," Sam sniped.

"Do any of them involve you grabbing my ass again? Because, if so, I'm there."

Levee giggled. "You grabbed his ass?"

I nodded and waggled my eyebrows suggestively while Sam stood at the foot of the bed, fuming.

"I thought it was you!" he defended, raking a hand through his hair. "Jesus, you scared the shit out of me."

"You should probably keep an eye on that one," I told Levee. "He obviously has some latent tendencies hidden beneath all those tattoos."

"Oh, fuck you," he retorted, but he did it while motioning for me to scoot over so he could get back in bed.

I climbed over Levee and got comfortable on one of her down

pillows. Before Sam had come along, lounging in bed together was a nightly occurrence for us. I missed it a lot. But, as she rested her head on my chest, I would have given anything for it to have been Evan instead.

She yawned. "Is it seriously four thirty?"

"Yeah. Sorry about that."

"I didn't know you were going to be in town."

"Yeah. We drove all night so I could spend less than eighteen hours with Evan."

She pushed up on an elbow. "Eighteen hours?"

"I wanted to see him."

"So, then what are you doing crawling into my bed in the middle of the night? Why aren't you tangled up with your lover boy?"

I groaned and threw an arm over my face. "We had a fight. So I took off. Hitchhiked my way here."

"You hitchhiked!" she shrieked, sitting straight up.

I laughed, dragging her back down. "Technically, I paid a cab driver. But, for the way he watched me in the rearview mirror like he was Buffalo Bill and wanted to wear my flesh as a new set of pajamas, it feels like I hitchhiked."

She blew out a relieved breath as Sam chuckled behind her.

"Why didn't you call Carter?" she asked.

"He's babysitting Robin."

Sam laughed. "I bet he is."

Levee and I both turned to look at him, but he waved us off.

"Nothing. Bad joke. Sorry. Can you get to the part where you tell us what happened so she can fix it, and *I* can go back to bed?"

Rolling my eyes, I propped myself up on an elbow so I could see them both. "Evan's bisexual. Apparently, he's dated a guy before."

"Oh my God," Levee breathed.

"I know. It's terri—"

She interrupted me. "Fantastic!"

"And sleep is out." Sam mumbled, rolling out of the bed. "I'll make the coffee."

I wolf-whistled as he walked from the room in only his boxers and a T-shirt. His response was to flip me off over his shoulder.

Pushing off my chest, Levee bent her knees to sit cross-legged beside me. "Please, God, tell me you aren't freaking out about this?"

"I'm in your bed at four thirty in the morning," I stated.

"But why? This is the best possible scenario."

"Are you kidding me? This is horrible. Levee, he's been with men before."

"Aaaand?"

"And he's been with men before. I might as well just draw a number and wait for my turn at the deli counter."

She slapped my chest. "Don't be a dick. I happen to know you've been with your fair share of men."

"Right, but I've never been with a woman."

She squinted at me in disbelief. "I'm sorry. What? I've seen Evan. No way he's a transsexual."

I curled my lip. "No. He's hung like a horse. He's just bi."

"So, not a woman?"

"No."

"So, what does you being with a woman have to do with this?"

"I've never been with one."

She tipped her head in confusion. "Did he ask you to be with one?"

"No!" I snapped, having lost my patience with her inability to follow the conversation.

"Then I officially have no idea what the hell you are talking about."

I groaned in frustration. "There's a reason I seek out straight men. I need to be special, Levee. I don't want to be another notch on someone's belt," I said, imploring her to understand.

She didn't. "And he's made you feel like just another conquest?"

"Well, no."

"Then what?" she shouted, having lost her patience as well.

I rolled off the bed and began pacing a pattern around her bed. "You don't understand."

"Not at all," she replied, propping herself up on the pillows and folding her hands over her swollen stomach.

"I need him to be straight."

"No. You *need* him to be gay. You're gay, Henry. This isn't exactly a newsflash."

I nibbled on my thumbnail. "Right. But, if he likes all men, how will I know that he truly loves *me*? I mean, he could leave me tomorrow and just move along to the next guy. Or, fuck, even woman."

"That would be more likely to happen if he were straight though."

I shook my head. "No, you don't understand. Shit, I'm not explaining this right."

"You want to find King Kong," Sam declared, appearing in the doorway with two steaming mugs of coffee.

I tapped my finger on the tip of my nose. "Yes! That!"

He rolled his eyes and passed me a mug.

"You don't have enough body hair for King Kong. Too much manscaping," Levee said, taking the other cup from him as he settled next to her on the bed. "Ew…decaf." She passed it back.

He threw his arm around her shoulders. "King Kong was a gorilla, but he fell in love with a woman and ultimately fought to the death for her. She was his one and only mate despite their vast differences in basically every other way—including species. If you forgo the battle with the T. rex and stegosaurus, I can see what you're going for here."

"Thank you, Sam." I smiled proudly.

"You're also a delusional idiot who believes wooing a straight man into bed will ever turn into anything more than sex."

My jaw fell open as he casually sipped Levee's coffee.

"Well, aren't you chipper this morning," I deadpanned, resuming my pacing.

"I'm not trying to be chipper. I'm trying to be real. While you're here pissed off that your boyfriend actually *wants* to be with you for once, there is a line of men out there waiting for you to fuck this up. I don't know Evan well. Only met him once. But, if he's willing to put up with your brand of neurotic, he's got my stamp of approval."

Levee pinched his nipple through his shirt. "He's not neurotic."

He tenderly smiled down at her. "Yes, he is. And you are too. But I fucking love your brand. And, if Evan loves his, then that, in and of itself, is more rare than any King Kong he's ever going to find." He took another sip of the coffee and then lifted his eyes to mine. "Maybe you need to figure out why you chase straight guys to begin with. You didn't drive all the way back today just because he was straight. You did it because you wanted to see *him*."

"But I never would have given him a chance if I'd thought he was bisexual. So, really, it all goes hand in hand," I countered.

"Aaaand there's your problem."

Levee gasped, "Oh my God."

Sam looked down at her and grinned painfully. "I told you."

My eyes flashed between them as Levee's face paled and she used a hand to cover her mouth.

"You told her what?" I asked anxiously. "Have you two been talking about me behind my back?"

"Of course we have!" Sam replied at the same time Levee breathed, "No."

"Somehow, I'm not believing that," I smarted.

"You don't want them to get to know you," Levee damn near cried.

I barked a laugh. "What are you talking about?"

"You only go after men who won't want you."

I shot her a confident scowl. "Oh, please. They *all* want me eventually."

"No, they don't! They want whoever you become when you're trying to get them into bed. That's not you. At least, not the Henry you show me. That's the cocky asshole you are on stage!"

I swirled a finger next to my temple. "I'm pretty sure it's still me, crazy."

Sam sighed. "It's not. Trust me. I can tell immediately when you're on the hunt. You find men who are just as confused as you are and then you use the whole sex thing to keep your distance. Nobody stays with you because they don't know what the hell they want any more than you do. It has nothing to do with gay or straight. And everything to do with you being too damn afraid to expose yourself to someone for fear that they will see the real you and still walk away."

I scoffed. He was so fucking wrong I was almost embarrassed for him. "Okay, slow down there, Doctor Rivers. I'm not afraid of that at all. I just like straight men, the same way you like women." I waved a finger between him and Levee.

"Straight men are not a gender, Henry." Levee piped up. "You just like *men*."

"Who like women," I corrected, leveling her with a challenging glare. "It's a type. Everyone has a type."

She rolled her eyes. "Bullshit. You like the ones who do their best not to get to know you. The ones who will play your little game of chase and not ask a single question about you in return. Let me guess: Evan wants the real you. It freaked you the fuck out. And you hauled ass here so you could avoid doing the one thing you really need to do."

I blew out a loud breath, becoming more annoyed by the second. "And what's that?"

"Let him get to know you!" she yelled, rising to her knees and moving down the bed until she was right in front of me. "For God's sake, Henry. Does he like you?"

"He apparently likes a lot of men," I snapped.

She poked me with a finger. "I asked if he likes *you*."

I opened my mouth to reply only to close it. Did Evan like me? I mean really like *me*? A million moments of him flashed through my mind. From his face in the limo when I had announced I was gay to him counting down with me in the middle of a panic attack, all the way up to tonight when he'd forced me to tell him every detail about Robin just because he was genuinely interested in why I was so upset.

If it had been a movie, that would have been the moment of realization where I took Levee's face between my palms, planted a kiss on her lips, and then ran from the room while an upbeat ballad played in the background. A camera would have followed me all the way back to Evan's house, where I'd throw cash at the cabbie and tell him that he didn't need to wait. I'd run through his front door to find him waiting for me with surprise covering his handsome face. And, when he asked what I was doing, I'd have some grand line about being just a boy asking him to love me or something equally as unrealistic. Then we'd kiss while the cameraman panned a circle around us until we faded to black in an implied happily-ever-after.

But life wasn't a movie. At least, not that kind.

In order to accept that someone as incredible as Evan Roth wanted to be with Henry Gilchrist and not the façade I paraded around as, I'd need far more than a pep talk from my best friend. I didn't even want to be with that guy, but for a brief moment in time, I'd convinced myself that Evan did.

I didn't care that he wasn't straight. But I couldn't risk him seeing the dirty and broken parts of me, because if he didn't return my feelings after I'd opened myself up, I'd never recover.

Evan had given himself to me that night. What we had experienced together wasn't even in the same category as sex. It was the joining of two souls, and we'd both felt it.

Only I'd felt it too much.

Too deep.

Too hard.

Too permanent—at least, I wanted it to be.

So, clearly, the obvious answer was for me to leave him before he could leave me.

"Henry." Levee snapped her fingers and repeated, "Does he like *you*?"

"I don't think so. I'm pretty sure it was only physical for him," I lied. Only I couldn't muster a fake smile to go along with it.

I liked him. That was all that mattered. And it hurt like hell to be standing in her bedroom instead of falling asleep in his arms.

"Jesus. Get him in bed," Sam whispered when Levee wrapped her arms around my trembling shoulders.

She pulled me down beside her. "You're so fucking stubborn."

"I'll give you two some time alone." He kissed Levee's hair and squeezed my shoulder. "Not accepting it doesn't change reality, Henry. Life is a struggle, but it's who you chose to take on the journey with you that matters the most. And, if you ask me, it sounds like you already chose. Don't let the bullshit details get in your way."

I squeezed my eyes shut, nowhere near ready to internalize his words. "I'm doubling my efforts at sending you naked men from now on. Warning: They might even include a few selfies."

His laugh traveled out of the room before disappearing with the click of the door closing behind him.

Levee tugged a giant body pillow between her legs and faced me. "You want to talk or sleep?"

"Sleep. But I feel the need to admit that I lied to you about how I felt about Evan a few weeks ago."

Her eyes softened as she trailed her thumb over my eyebrows. "I know."

I sucked in an agonizing breath. "Well, it was only a half lie. I don't know if I really love him yet. But I want to. So fucking bad."

She smiled warmly. "I know that too."

chapter twenty-two

Evan

I sat at the airport all day, hoping Henry would show and at least let me fly him to his next concert.

And maybe talk to me.

And kiss me.

And tell me that he was sorry.

And, most importantly, tell me that *we* were okay.

He never showed.

My heart broke a little more each time my call went to his voicemail. I couldn't wrap my mind around the fact that he was avoiding me.

But, by the second day without so much as a text, I got pissed.

At him for having run out on me for reasons I still couldn't comprehend.

At myself for having trusted him with the jagged pieces of my heart.

At Shannon for having made them jagged to begin with.

At myself for having allowed Shannon to still have any part of my life at all.

Then, at Henry again, for having proven me right about men.

It was emotional upheaval at its finest.

On day three, I sent him a text telling him that I quit. It probably would have been more effective if I'd actually ever flown him anywhere since he hired me.

He didn't reply.

So, on day four, I gathered my company cell phone and the few bits of clothing he'd left at my house and dropped them off at Jackson's office. It was unlikely that Henry would get them any time soon, but just having them out of my house did wonders for me.

Or that's what I told myself as I drunkenly destroyed my bedroom.

By day five, the anger had ebbed, but the pain was more prevalent than ever. The walls around my heart had long since been demolished, having left me raw and exposed. I couldn't figure out how to start over after someone like Henry Alexander.

On day six, I found myself trying to manipulate a situation where I got to see him again. I spent hours mapping out his tour routes like some kind of sociopath. I needed to talk to him and naïvely thought, if I could get him into a room with me, I could fix things. I wasn't sure what was truly broken, but I would have torn the gates of Hell down in order to fix it.

I was drowning.

At the one-week mark, I decided to fuck him out of my system with as many women as I could find. Scott came over, we went out, and, instead of taking home the busty brunette eye-fucking me from across the bar, I proceeded to sit at a table and stalk Henry's twitter account, which I knew he didn't even run.

There wasn't enough booze in the state of California to make me forget him.

I went home alone that night. It was a good fucking thing too. Because, the next morning, someone finally threw me a lifeline.

I was still basking in an alcohol-induced, pain-free slumber when I awoke to a loud knock on the door. Prying one eye open, I felt the world came crashing back down around me. I had no idea who was at my door at what felt like the crack of dawn, but I knew who it wasn't, and for that alone, I dragged the pillow over my head and tried to block it all out.

However, when my unwelcome guest had the audacity to begin knocking in a cheery, musical beat, I was left with no other choice but to drag a pair of pants on and put a stop to the pounding before my head split in half.

"What?" I snapped, jerking the door open.

"Evan!" The woman tipped her sunglasses down her nose and raked her eyes over my shirtless torso while mumbling to herself, "Nice job, Henry."

"Can I help you?" I impatiently bit out.

"Hi! I'm Levee—"

"Williams," I filled in when I finally recognized her.

Chestnut-brown curls covered her shoulders, and her pregnant stomach might as well have been inside my house even though her feet were firmly on the other side of the threshold.

"Well, technically, Rivers, but yes. We met briefly in L.A. at one of Henry's shows."

The mere mention of his name wrenched my heart.

I nodded, crossing my arms over my chest as though it could mask the pain. "I remember."

"Right. Well, anyway. I'm here to do the obligatory cleanup mission." She shot me a megawatt smile.

"Cleanup mission?"

"Yeah. You know… Henry fucks shit up, I come in to save the day, and we all live happily ever after." She shrugged. "I would have been here sooner, but you'll find, with Henry, it will be quicker in the end if he has time to really stew on things."

"Funny. I'm no longer interested in any kind of 'happily ever after.'" I tossed a pair of exaggerated air quotes her way. "I've been *stewing* too."

It was a lie of epic proportions, but my pride wouldn't allow me to fall to my knees and beg her for help the way I so desperately wanted. He'd left *me*. Not the other way around.

Her eyebrows popped in surprise. "Oh. So, you aren't interested in knowing how miserable he's been for the last week?"

I ground my teeth. Part of me hoped he had been worse than miserable. Lord knows I was.

"Not really."

She adorably twisted her lips. "Hmm… Well, that makes this a little more challenging, then. You mind if I give you my speech anyway? It would be such a waste. I've been practicing for a week."

"Maybe you should give it to Henry, then."

She pouted her bottom lip and stomped her foot. "Come on! It's a good one."

My head was killing me and my heart was aching, but my only lifeline to the man I had been pining over was standing in front of me. Fuck my pride.

My shoulders fell as I let out a resigned sigh. "You want to come in?"

She had the good grace to look surprised. "Why, that would be fantastic."

I stepped aside and motioned her in. Just before closing the door, I caught sight of a giant leaning against her black SUV.

"You want to invite Hercules in too?"

She laughed. "Nah. Linc is fine out there. He's not Henry's biggest fan anyway. He probably wouldn't help my cause."

I slanted my head in silent question.

"Oh, it's nothing. He just doesn't sympathize with Henry's equilibrium issues."

"His what?" I asked.

Giggling, she waved me off and settled on one of my barstools. "You'll have to ask Henry."

"I would if he would answer my calls." I rolled my eyes as I made my way to the fridge. "Or, ya know… texts, e-mails, Morse code, smoke signals."

"Have you tried the Pony Express? I have it on good authority he likes horses." She winked as though I should have gotten her joke.

"Right. I'll hop right on that. Coffee?" I asked as I caught sight of Scott meandering shirtless into the room behind her.

"Dude, you're up early. I figured you'd still be cry— Shit." He froze when Levee spun to face him.

"Oh, shit," she breathed, swinging her head between Scott and me—her eyes growing angrier every time they landed on me. "No fucking way."

My lips twitched as she got the completely wrong idea.

"Are you…" Scott started in awe.

"Levee," I said in both an answer and introduction. "This is my best friend, Scott. Scott, this is Henry's best friend, Levee Williams." I scratched the back of my head. "Er…Rivers."

Levee's murderous glare leveled me. "Best friend?"

The woman was more than a tad pissed off on Henry's behalf. If it hadn't been for the gaping hole in my heart, I would have burst into laughter.

Even still, I released a quiet chuckle and elaborated. "Straight best friend."

"Totally straight!" Scott proclaimed after me. "Super straight. So straight, straight men wish they could be me. Straight as an arrow. Ruler straight. No! Make that yardstick straight."

"You done yet?" I glared at him, unimpressed.

He bulged his eyes and tipped his chin to her while mouthing, "Holy shit!"

I shook my head and looked back at Levee. "You'll have to excuse Mr. Straight. He has problems."

Her cheeks pinked in embarrassment. "Sorry...I thought..."

"Coffee?"

"Yes! But no. Sam would sense the caffeine hitting my taste buds and show up like the Kool-Aid Man busting through your wall to stop me." She propped her chin on a hand and frowned. "Any chance you'd be willing to indulge my voyeuristic needs and let me stare at you while you drink it? I'll do my best to suppress the creepy moans."

The first genuine smile in over a week teased at my lips, but it fell just as fast. There was a reason Henry and Levee were so close, and that similarity was almost more than I could take.

"I'll be happy to indulge you. No suppressing necessary," Scott flirted, sauntering into the kitchen, his abs flexed so tight it was a wonder he was able to speak. "Nice to meet you, Levee." He extended a hand over the bar.

Levee took his hand and turned to the side to expose her stomach, politely—and pointedly—saying, "Nice ink. My husband would love it."

Scott barked a laugh, catching the hint loud and clear. "Can't blame a guy for trying."

"I would expect nothing less from the consummate straight man," she replied.

I pressed brew on the coffee pot and then leaned my hip against the counter, crossing my legs at the ankle. "So, let's get back to Henry."

Her eyes flashed to Scott in question.

"Oh, don't hold back on my account," he said. "I know all about Henry's premature departure. Evan hasn't stopped crying all week." He nabbed an apple off the counter and polished it on his flexed pec.

I swung a fist out to the side and landed it hard on his shoulder. "Asshole."

"What? It's true. Besides you know beautiful women are my kryptonite. I'd spill all of your deep, dark secrets for one this gorgeous." He winked at Levee while crunching into the apple.

Her eyes lit as she leaned over the bar and asked, "Is he in love with Henry?"

"Don't answer that!" I shouted.

He mocked insult. "Man, I would never answer something so personal." Then he turned to Levee, nodding as he shot her a shit-eating grin.

"Oh, for fuck's sake. Can you go home now?" I growled at him.

"Sure can." He turned back to Levee and shook his head while mouthing, "No."

"Go," I ordered.

He threw his hands up in surrender. "Okay, okay. I'm going. Nice to meet you, Levee."

"You too, Scott the straight man," she laughed.

I rolled my eyes and not-so-patiently waited for him to get dressed and actually leave. After one last round of goodbyes, Levee and I were alone again.

"So...Henry?" I prompted.

"Ah, yes. Henry." She intertwined her fingers and rested her linked hands on the bar between us but said nothing else.

After several seconds of staring at each other, I was the one who finally broke the silence. "You're killing me here."

Placing a hand over her heart, she feigned innocence. "Oh, I'm sorry. I thought you weren't interested."

I shot her a don't-be-ridiculous expression that had her smile spreading so wide I feared for her lips.

"Okay, okay... You freak him out."

I hitched a thumb at my chest. "*I* freak him out? *Me*? The one he ran out on approximately ten seconds after we had sex for the first time? The one he has avoided at all costs since I fucking pulled up my pants? Yeah. Sorry. Didn't mean to freak *him* out so badly."

"Well, I didn't say it was a rational fear. I'm just stating the facts."

Groaning, I pinched the bridge of my nose. "You know what? On second thought—I can't do this. Maybe it's for the best he took off the way he did. Save us the trouble down the road."

"He's scared. This is not the time to quit on him."

I laughed, and it held God's-honest humor. "Actually, I'm pretty sure that is the exact moment to quit. I don't have it in me to play games. You want to talk scared? I'm fucking terrified of your best friend. And you want to know why?"

"Evan..."

"Because I was scared he would do exactly what he did. Work his way into my life, consume me, and then leave my ashes blowing in the wind as he traveled to the next guy."

"Evan, he didn't leave. He's crazy about you. He just doesn't know how to come back."

I pointed at the front door. "There's a door right fucking there. All he has to do is walk through it."

"It's not that easy for him," she said defensively.

And that's when I lost it. "Yes, it is that easy! I would take him back zero questions asked. Jesus, Levee. I miss him. His laugh. His randomness. The way he can captivate me from across a room. The rush I felt when we were together. It was the closest thing to flying I've ever experienced with my feet on the ground. I would do anything to have him back. How fucking sad is that? He damn near breaks me, and I can't even slam the fucking door in his face."

She smiled. "That's not sad at all. That's why I'm sitting here. Let me give you some info on Henry and then you can decide what you want to do with it. Okay? Just hear me out."

I leaned forward, propping myself on my fists on the counter.

"And who's going to hear me out? Sure as fuck not Henry. He ran out of here like his ass was on fire because he found out I was bisexual." I laughed, but it held no humor. "I wasn't straight enough for the man I was falling in love with. Do you have any idea how much that hurt?"

Her smile fell flat. "I do now."

I instantly felt guilty. She didn't deserve my wrath. She was only trying to help, but the longer we talked, the more jaded I became. I wanted him back more than anything, but I couldn't magically be who he wanted me to be. That's not how relationships worked. People seek out a mate who can offer comfort and unconditional acceptance. But the way Henry had made me feel that night as he'd lost his shit because of my sexuality had been anything but. There was nothing wrong with who I was. So fucking what I wasn't straight. So fucking what I wasn't gay. If he didn't accept that, I was better off alone.

"I'm sorry. You should go."

"His name is Henry Gilchrist," she announced.

"I know," I called over my shoulder, walking to the front door.

"He— Wait. What? He told you that?" she gasped.

I yanked the door open and motioned for her to go. "Yep. Weeks ago."

A sinister smile pulled at the corners of her mouth, but she didn't budge from the stool. "Now, we're getting somewhere."

"Any way you can get there faster? I have shit to do today," I smarted.

"Sure." She grinned confidently. "He loves you."

My back shot ramrod straight, and as much as I wanted to deny it, hope swirled in my chest. "Don't say that."

"Why? It's the truth. He loves you, Evan." She tipped her head to the side. "I mean, he's a dumbass, but he loves you. For the last week, I've been listening to him bitch and moan about how much he misses you. He hasn't been out gallivanting around town or moving on to the next guy. There is no other guy for him."

I raked a hand through my hair and tried to pretend that that little bit of information hadn't ignited a spark inside me all over again. "I think you're wrong."

She pushed to her feet and lowered her voice to a scary whisper. "Did he tell you about Robin?"

"Yes," I replied curtly.

Her brown eyes lit and the proverbial light bulb flashed over her head. "Did he tell you how he grew up?"

"Yes."

"Oh, wow," she breathed.

I chewed the inside of my cheek, equally interested in and dreading whatever she was going to say next. I was barely hanging on to what little resolve I had about asking her to leave. I hadn't needed her "oh, wow" to make me curious, but it really fucking had.

"Evan, that's huge for him." She walked over and gently pulled the door from my hand before swinging it shut. "You can Google all of that about him. It's not a secret. But never, not once—including with me—has he voluntarily told someone about his past. He doesn't trust people with it. He wants people to see the confident and successful man he is now, not the broken, insecure boy he still secretly harbors inside."

I blinked. Henry had openly given me that. I'd had no idea what it'd meant to him at the time or I would have offered him the broken parts of my past too. However, now, I was happy I hadn't.

"Can you just listen to me for ten minutes? I'm not wrong about this. He loves you, and after this conversation, I'm pretty sure you're in love with him too."

I clamped my mouth shut.

There was a massive difference between *being* in love and *falling* in love.

Being in love was like a never-ending flight through the clouds. Storms were likely. Turbulence a given. But they didn't last forever. The clouds always returned.

Falling was more like a terrifying test of trust where you're expected to leap from death-defying altitudes with nothing more than one flawed person with his arms held open, acting as your safety net.

Sometimes, you crashed, shattering into a million pieces, when the person you trusted wasn't there to catch you. I'd learned that firsthand.

But, as I stared at Levee's pleading eyes as she asked for ten minutes of my time to hopefully enlighten me about the man who had me plummeting in an all-out free fall, I couldn't help but wonder if Henry was falling too.

And if he was…was I the one who was supposed to be catching *him*?

chapter twenty-three

Henry

As a successful songwriter, I prided myself in not only the
music, but the ability to transfer simple words into tangible
emotions. Over the week without Evan, I realized something truly remarkable.

I didn't miss him.

Not at all.

Because, according to the dictionary, the word *miss* meant to
notice or discover the absence of something.

I *missed* how content I felt in his arms.

I *missed* the way his breath felt whispering across my chest as he
slept at my side.

I *missed* his stoic smiles and their ability to fill my soul for no
other reason than they were aimed at me.

I *missed* the idea of forever and the promise of a future.

No, I didn't miss Evan at all.

Because you don't *notice* or *discover* the absence of a man like that. That pain was engrained so deeply it was inescapable. It devoured me on a second-by-second basis and consumed my every thought—conscious or not. Sleep wasn't even a reprieve.

I craved him on every level.

But especially the level where I got to walk into his house and have him wrap me in his strong arms while I hid from the world, or the one where I collapsed naked and sated next to him in bed, knowing that the mind-blowing orgasm wasn't even going to be the best part of my evening.

I told myself that it was irrational to feel so strongly about a man I had only been seeing for a couple of months.

But, in reality, I knew that the only irrational part was when I'd walked away.

"Henry, where's Carter?" Levee called from the doorway of my dressing room as I stared at my phone, willing it to ring.

Evan had stopped calling a few days earlier. It was for the best. It meant I didn't have to have a nervous breakdown every time it rang.

"No idea," I replied, pushing to my feet and walking her way. "Hey, beautiful," I purred, pulling her in for a tight squeeze. "How's my baby?"

"She's good, but I can't find Linc and I need someone to escort Sam past the press so he can get to his seat." She huffed anxiously.

We were in L.A. for a special all-acoustic charity concert Levee was heading. It was a cross between a formal affair and a drunken night of entertainment. The floor level of the arena had been transformed into a lavish dinner party, with tickets having been sold for tens of thousands of dollars. Meanwhile, the upper levels had been sold for donations of any size on a first-come, first-serve basis. It had been Levee's idea to make tickets affordable to everyone, despite their tax bracket. And it had been a smashing success, bringing out the best in everyone. Those tickets had sold out in a matter of minutes, ranging from one dollar to ten thousand. With the average of each seat going for over seven hundred dollars, it was far more profitable than we'd ever hoped. But, then again, it was the concert of the year. There were over fifteen of the biggest names in the industry, spanning all genres, slated to perform that night.

First up? Me.

"Are you okay?" I rubbed her stomach. "I'm sure he'll be back in a minute."

"I'm just stressed about the show—Oh my God, did you feel that?" Grabbing my hand, she moved it just below her belly button. "Shhh…" she said as two hard thumps landed on my palm.

"What the…" I yelled, snatching my hand away as if her spawn had been about to claw its way out, *Alien*-style.

"Give me back your hand," she demanded. "Bree wants to say hi. She's really active right now."

I backed away as quickly as possible without breaking into a dead sprint—which was not-so-secretly what I wanted to do. "Can she maybe say hi when she isn't floating in a sack of bodily fluid at Spa de Levee?"

"Stop being an ass and give me your hand. This is important to me. *You're* important to me."

My chest warmed, and as much as it grossed me out, I begrudgingly lifted my hand in her direction. "That's not fair. You know I can't say no when you con me like that."

She smirked mischievously. "No con. But I know you can't say no."

"Evil woman," I mumbled to myself.

Instead of placing my hand on her belly, she ducked under my arm and pulled me in for a hug. Then she asked the million-dollar question. "How are you doing?"

"Better now that you're here." It was only a semi lie, and I kissed the top of her head so she wouldn't see the longing etched across my face at the reminder.

"You sure you're up to performing tonight? I know it's been a hard week for you."

I sighed. Hard was an understatement. But this was Levee.

"Babe, you've been planning this thing for two years. There is no way a little heartache could keep me from being here."

Her curls tickled my nose as she nuzzled in close. "Yeah, but I appreciate it all the same. You're a real diva, but you sell tickets."

I laughed. "You'd do it for me."

She tipped her head back, and her chocolate-brown eyes shimmered as she looked at me and vowed, "I'd do anything for you."

My heart stopped. I knew exactly how much she meant those words.

"Anything?" I asked around the lump in my throat.

"Anything."

"Does that mean I can finally take Sam for a romp in the sack?" I asked, opting for humor when the emotions had become too much.

Her eyes smiled. "Sure!"

My head fell back as I lost myself in a fit of laughter. "Really? Just like that?"

"Yep." She pushed from my arms and made her way to the mirror, sweeping her fingers under her eyes. "I know I'm not usually fond of the sharing thing, but seeing as you're completely and utterly in love with Evan, I figure you won't even be able to get it up. This might be the safest Sam has ever been around you."

My laughter stopped abruptly at the mention of his name.

Her eyes jumped to mine in the reflection of the mirror. "You okay?"

I nodded entirely too many times. "Yeah. Let's go find Carter so we can get Sam to his seat. I'm up first." I quickly spun, giving her my back as I willed my heart to slow.

Suddenly, I felt Levee's hand on my shoulder.

"I checked your schedule," she said. "You don't have to be anywhere for two weeks. Why is your tour bus out back?"

I straightened and flashed her a tight smile. "I don't fly."

"It's a five-hour drive home. You could ride with me and Sam."

I shook my head and toyed with the collar on my pale-blue button-down. "I'm not going home." Swallowing hard, I pasted on an award-winning smile. "Nothing at home anyway. Robin agreed to finish off the tour with me." I proffered an arm in her direction. "Let's go."

I knew that Levee wouldn't buy my bullshit, but I didn't expect her to call me on it either—at least, not right then.

"Deny it," she ordered, poking my chest with a single finger.

"Deny what?" I poked her back.

"That you love him. And that you're just fighting the inevitable by trying to stay away from him."

I couldn't deny any of it. She was pretty much spot-on.

But leaving had *never* been about how I felt about Evan.

I threw my hands out to my sides and then slapped them against my thighs when they fell. "Jesus Christ, Levee. Please just drop it."

"Not until you deny it." She poked my chest again. "Say you aren't in love with Evan and I'll never mention his name again."

"What is up with you poking me?" I rubbed my pec.

"Don't change the subject."

I shit you not, the crazy woman poked me *again*. I was probably going to have a bruise from her knobby little fingers.

"Stop." I swatted her hand away.

"Deny it!"

I rolled my eyes, but I couldn't force the blatant lie from my tongue, no matter how much I wanted her to drop it. "I can't," I breathed on a resigned sigh.

"What was that? I couldn't hear you."

I lifted my eyes and glowered at her. "Can you just stop? You of all people know I can't deny any of it. But hey, thanks for gutting me ten minutes before I have to go on stage."

Levee hated feeling guilty, and I fully expected an apology when she realized the salt she'd just poured in my wound.

I didn't get it though.

Her smile grew impossibly wide as she cupped my jaw. "I love you, so get your shit together. The last thing I need is to be forced to issue refunds because Henry Alexander sounded like a dying cat."

She sauntered into the hall and then walked away, Linc hot on her Jimmy Choos.

My four-song set went off without a hitch. On stage might have been the only place I was able to forget about the ache in my chest. But, the minute the last note played, my regrets collapsed down on my shoulders again.

I showered and changed while Levee did her set. Then the two of us smiled for the press as we made our way arm in arm to our seats. A fresh gin and tonic and what I assumed was sparkling cider waited for us at our table. I was tired and really just wanted to crawl into bed and sleep for a week. Instead, I plastered a smile on and chatted with the strangers who stopped by our table between sets.

The latest up-and-comer in country music was busy marching around the stage when Levee turned sideways in her chair and leaned back against my side.

"What do you make of that?" she asked, pointing to where Carter was standing in a cove just on the other side of the backstage door.

He was mostly hidden, but Levee, Sam, and I had the only seats in the house with the exact right vantage point to see him. His back faced us, but his shoulders were hunched over and his head bent low.

I shrugged and began clapping with the rest of the crowd as

Bubba Somebody took his final bow.

Fisting the front of my shirt, she dragged me down to her line of sight and pointed at the floor. "No. *Look.*"

I humored her and focused my gaze at his feet, where a pair of black heels came into view. "Oh," I breathed.

"Yeah. Oh," she giggled.

Suddenly, a woman's hand snaked out from in front of him and traveled down to his ass. Levee and I gasped in unison, our hands dramatically flying out to the sides to clutch each other.

"Oh my God, please tell me you saw that?" she exclaimed, tugging on my arm and pointing to where I was already looking.

Lifting a hand to my mouth, I attempted to stifle a laugh. "Holy virgin robot. Carter found another droid."

Levee and I sank low in our chairs and commenced rolling in laughter. We couldn't tear our eyes away as we watched Carter and his mystery woman going at it against the wall.

We gave each other the play-by-play as though we hadn't been watching the same couple.

"I think he just kissed her!"

"Oh, he definitely just kissed her," I confirmed.

"I wonder if he's going to fuck her. I'm oddly aroused. I've never wanted to see Carter's ass before."

"His ass is fantastic. But what he needs to do is pull one of my equilibrium episodes and drag her to the ground. Much better leverage there."

"This is Carter we're talking about. I don't imagine him being a dry-humper."

I took my eyes off his back long enough to give her a teasing side-eye. "Why do you imagine him humping at all?"

She smirked. "Oh, I don't know. How do you know his ass is fantastic?"

"Touché!"

We smiled at each other and went back to watching the best performance of the evening.

I was so enthralled by Carter's make-out session that I was oblivious to the seat on the other side of me being filled.

A hand landed on my thigh, and a set of lips brushed against my cheek. "Hey, babe. Sorry I'm late. Traffic was a bitch," his baritone rumbled in my ear.

"No biggie," I replied absently. "Look." I pointed to Carter.

The scruff on his jaw nuzzled against mine, and my lids fell to half-mast as the addictive high surged through my veins. Instantly relaxing, I sucked in a content breath as the world slowed.

"I've missed you so fucking much," he whispered, grazing his teeth over the soft flesh below my ear.

The hairs on the back of my neck stood on end and chills traveled up my spine—unfortunately awakening me from my fog.

"What the fuck?" I jumped, knocking the table with my knees and sloshing drinks everywhere.

With no one on stage to drown out my outburst, dozens of eyes landed on me—including Carter, who spun to face me.

And that's when Levee and I exclaimed in unison, "What the fuck?"

My heart was racing, and my head was a spinning wheel of emotions. I couldn't figure out where to focus first.

On Evan, who was sitting next to me in a sexy-as-sin black suit—his hand on my thigh and his lips teasing my ear.

Or on Robin, who was standing on the other side of Carter—her lipstick smeared over both of their mouths.

chapter twenty-four

Evan

The surprise on Henry's face was priceless and well worth the drive to L.A. Though he would have been worth a drive to Zimbabwe.

I'd lied to him. Traffic hadn't been bad. I'd actually been in L.A. since the day before, when I'd left my house about twelve seconds after Levee's car had pulled out of my driveway. I hadn't even packed a bag before I'd gotten on the road.

Levee had left my tickets and a card to Henry's stylist on the countertop. Macy was a godsend. When I'd arrived at the hotel, she'd had a designer suit and a tailor waiting for me. By the next day, after a quick trip through the mall for some toiletries, I'd been ready to attend my very first celebrity affair with the one and only Henry Alexander.

I'd been more excited to see Henry Gilchrist though.

I'd actually been standing in the hall as Levee had confronted him in his dressing room. My heart had been in my throat, fire taking its place in my chest as I'd waited for him to deny her accusations of how he felt for me.

I never could have been prepared for the way his confirmation filled me. While he didn't pour his heart out with professions of undying love, I was still reborn in his acceptance of it all.

Levee's leaving was my cue to surprise him, but I bitched out.

Big time.

I had one shot to get him back. And, if I was going to put the few remaining pieces of my heart on the line for this man, I wanted to do it right. I figured calming my nerves so I didn't throw up on him approximately ten minutes before he entertained thousands wasn't a bad idea. So I tucked tail, headed to a bar in the VIP section, and tried to get my head together.

Carter retrieved me just before Henry went on. I hid in the shadows at the side of the stage to watch, and just like the first time I'd seen him perform, he captivated me completely. I feared at one point that he'd seen me, but when he breezed past me as he exited, I knew my secret was safe. I also knew that I didn't want to waste another minute without him as a permanent fixture in my life.

Pride be damned, Henry was mine.

I knew it.

He knew it.

And, as he pushed to his feet with surprise covering every plane of his handsome face, the entire world would learn it too.

"What are you doing here?" he gasped, slinging his eyes from me to Carter, who was furiously striding toward us. "And what the fucking hell are you doing?" he snapped in his direction.

I glanced around the large venue at the numerous cameramen lining the gating to the VIP area—all cameras poised and aimed directly at us.

Clutching his hand, I gave him a tug. "Let's take this somewhere else."

His eyes bulged and he snatched his hand away. "Don't touch me."

My head snapped back at the rejection. I'd expected surprise, but the anxiety growing in his eyes pained me. I shifted in front of him in order to get a better read on the situation—and to prevent him from running again.

"Stop," I urged.

"Are you fucking kidding me?" he barked, but it was aimed over my shoulder.

"Not here," Carter growled under his breath as he marched past us like a man on a mission.

Robin's tiny body sidled between us. "Cookie, stop. Everyone's watching."

And, upon further review, she wasn't wrong. Our little reunion was currently being projected on the huge screens at either side of the stage.

Well, that is until Carter reached the man with the video camera and snatched it from his hands—along with the press credentials hanging around his neck. Levee's head of security, Linc, joined him just in time to escort the guy from the building.

Okay. So. Not the best start to getting my man back.

Let's try this again.

Stepping around Robin, I looped an arm around his hips and pulled his side to my front. "Let's go somewhere and talk," I ordered, touching my lips to his temple.

His face turned red, and I feared his head would explode as he scrambled away.

"Have you lost your mind?" he hissed, straightening his shirt and glancing around the arena. "Do you want the entire fucking world to see you kissing me? Christ, Evan." He jutted his chin toward the row of cameras.

My dejection quickly morphed into what could only be described as elation as he scanned the crowd to see if anyone was watching.

They were.

But he was protecting me.

And, if that didn't heal the scars covering my heart, nothing ever would.

Staring at that gorgeous man, I felt myself become whole again.

I dropped my voice and said, "I see your point." And then, without a single second of hesitation, I palmed each side of his face and planted a deep, life-altering kiss to his lips.

Keeping my eyes open, I watched his flare wide before he lost the battle with my mouth and they fluttered shut. A second later, his body melted into mine and his lips parted in an invitation I eagerly accepted. Our tongues tangled indecently, and I slid a hand up the back of his neck and into his hair, using it to hold him to my mouth.

His hands traveled up my lats, sliding under my arms until he was gripping the back of my shoulders impossibly tight.

I was vaguely aware of the wolf whistles and cheers in the backgrounds, but I couldn't have cared less. It was Henry. Nothing else mattered.

"Ehm…" Levee cleared her throat. "You two should probably take this back to—"

I peeked open an eye to see why she'd stopped so abruptly when I saw Henry's hand palming her face and gently pushing her away, all the while drawing me closer.

Chuckling, I broke the kiss. "She's right."

"No. She'd definitely wrong." He groaned, reluctantly releasing me to scowl at her.

She smiled smugly and tossed me a wink.

My chuckle transformed into a full-blown belly laugh, which earned me a scowl as well.

"Fine. Let's go." He huffed, intertwining our fingers then dragging me toward the backstage entrance, smiling for the cameras like our public display of affection was the most natural thing in the world.

I mean, it was to us. But they didn't know that. But I fucking loved that they were finding out. We'd probably be trending on social media by the morning. And then the whole world would know once and for all that Henry was off the market and one hundred percent mine. Now, if only I could get him on the same page.

"Did you drive here?" he asked when we passed through security.

"No. Levee sent a car for me. I'm parked at the hotel."

"Of course she did," he mumbled.

I laughed and released his hand but only so I could drape my arm around his waist. "Complaining?"

His arm followed suit and wrapped around my hips as we continued to walk down the long hallway toward his dressing room. "I don't know yet. I'll let you know when I get you back to the hotel and naked."

I abruptly stilled, pulling him up short with me. Arching an eyebrow, I asked, "Am I to assume that means you're okay with me being bisexual now?"

His full lips hardened in a grimace. "I…"

I went back to walking, pulling him with me, and said, "Then you won't be getting anyone naked."

Though it was a fan-fucking-tastic idea, I wasn't risking him flipping out on me and taking off again until we'd talked. And I mean *really* talked, not the kind of talking Henry and I did best—with our bodies.

He released a suffering sigh and dropped his head back to stare at the ceiling. "And…now I'm complaining."

I stopped again and turned to face him, backing him against the wall. "Oh yeah? Well, I'm officially complaining too. Mainly because we could have spent the last week naked, but instead, I've spent it alone, trying to forget about..." Our noses brushed as I leaned in toward his face, caging him in with my hands on either side of his head, and breathed softly, "*You.*"

His blue eyes darkened in an odd combination of guilt and arousal as he stood frozen against the wall. Another act had taken the stage, and the music poured in from the mouth of the hallway. But I heard him loud and clear as he timidly whispered, "Did you figure out how?"

My lips twitched when his cheeks stained pink and his eyes flashed down the hall to avoid contact.

"Nope." I popped the P in his ear and then swept my lips down to his neck.

His breath hitched, and his hands came up to my hips, pulling me close. It took every bit of willpower I possessed not to roll my hips against his. If I had to feel his cock thickening against my own, Henry was going to get his wish of naked but we weren't going to make it back to the hotel. I pivoted, resting my thigh between his legs, and his hands fell to clutch my ass.

"We're talking about jerking off, right?" he asked, turning his head to offer me better access.

"Nope," I breathed, trailing my tongue down his neck. "We're talking about a week of tortured pining and self-loathing over a devastating rejection from the man I'm falling in love with."

He had already been pinned against the wall, but before the word *love* had even cleared my mouth, his entire body turned rock solid.

I smiled, knowing I'd hit my mark. Now, all I had to do was wait and see what he was going to do with it. The hallway wasn't the ideal place for this conversation, but maybe catching him off guard would be worth the gamble.

"Evan..." he breathed just the way that he knew lit me ablaze.

But, with the last week still separating us, it felt more like a knife trailing fire across my heart.

With a growl, I fisted the back of his neck and turned his head so our mouths were close but agonizingly out of reach. "Don't you dare taint my name like that."

His eyes searched mine as he replied in a shaky voice, "I...I don't know what to say."

"I'm sorry," I prompted. "Say it."

"I'm sorry," he repeated, but it was the moisture that pooled in his eyes that issued his real apology.

Now, *that* I could accept.

"We need to talk, but I want your word that you will stop with the games and actually listen to me."

He agreed immediately. "Okay."

"I'm serious, Henry. The chase is over, and that bullshit over me being bisexual is done too. We both have bigger mountains here than our sexuality." I roughly gripped his hard-on as I declared, "You want me." Then I removed one of his hands from my ass and brought it to rest over my pounding heart. "And *I* want you."

He bit his bottom lip and turned his head to look away, unable to lie anymore.

"I have a fuck-ton of issues I need to work through, and I know you do too. So I'm proposing that we both stop trying to escape and face them head on." I cupped his jaw and forced his gaze back to mine. "Together."

He swallowed hard. "I'm not sure how."

"Then I'll help. But, Goddammit, Henry, you have to give me a fucking chance. I can make you feel loved. I can do it—I swear on my life I can. You *are* my exception. Never in my entire life have I been so sure about something." I paused then corrected myself. "*Someone.*" Dropping my forehead to his, I whispered, "I'll be the best damn King Kong you've ever seen."

A strangled laugh escaped his throat even as the tear rolled down his cheek.

Using my thumb to wipe it away, I pleaded, "Just let me try."

His eyes drifted back to mine, and the slightest of smiles pulled at the side of his mouth. "Okay."

"Okay," I repeated, relief washing over me.

"I see Levee's been running her mouth. But that was a good speech."

I grinned proudly. "It was, wasn't it?"

His upturned lips brushed across mine. "It would have been better naked."

"Obviously." I winked, and his entire face lit.

chapter twenty-five

Henry

"**O**h, hell no!" I said as Carter attempted to close the door to my limo after he had escorted Evan and me out the back door of the arena. "You're riding back here this time, big man. We have shit to discuss."

His lips pursed, but that was the only objection he gave before unbuttoning his suit coat and folding inside. He slid around the L until he was adjacent to Evan and me. Then he threw an arm up on the back of the seat and turned his full attention my way.

And I pounced. "What exactly are your intentions with my daughter?"

I can't lie—I had been shocked and upset when I'd discovered that Robin was what made his little robot heart swell. But it was Carter—I trusted him implicitly. I was predominantly worried about Robin. She was fresh off a relapse. The last thing she needed was to jump into bed with someone. Even if it was a good guy like Carter. Hell, maybe especially because it was a good guy like him.

He pinned me with a disgruntled glare. Then he shook his head and peered out the window as the limo eased away from the mass of paparazzi snapping pictures through the glass.

"It shouldn't have happened again," he grumbled.

"Again?" I exclaimed in shock and confusion.

Evan's hand landed on my thigh, shooting sparks that collected two hundred dollars as they passed my groin before traveling up my spine. Covering his hand, I turned to see if he'd heard the same thing, and clearly, he had, because his face was turning red as he attempted to fight back a great deal of mirth.

"King Kong doesn't laugh," I snapped.

Apparently, he did though, because that was when Evan lost it.

"I'm sorry," he laughed. "I just can't believe you didn't realize this. I've met them *once* and I knew something was up."

If he hadn't been so fucking sexy while losing himself in humor—even if it was aimed at me—I would have been pissed. As it stood, he was unbelievably sexy, so I was just mildly annoyed as I refocused on Carter.

"Again? How long have you two been…" I would have finished if the words hadn't made me want to dry-heave.

He uncomfortably scrubbed his palms over his knees and then asked frankly, "Do I need to be job-hunting?"

I jerked my chin in surprise. "What? No!"

"Give me your fucking word," he pressed.

I curled my lip. "Seriously? You know I'll just lie."

Evan cut in. "Excuse me?"

"Oh, no. Not to you, honey." I drew an X over my heart then flashed him a teasing grin.

He pinched the inside of my thigh, but out of the corner of my eye, I saw his lips twitch.

So. Fucking. Sexy.

Doing my best to focus on the situation at hand and not climb into Evan's lap, I impatiently tilted my head at Carter.

He grumbled. "She was eighteen the first time."

"Eighteen!" I shouted, and Evan's hand spasmed.

"It's not what you think," he defended.

"Says every pedophile ever arrested! You're, like, forty!"

He suddenly sat forward, his bodying appearing to grow as he loomed menacingly.

It would have been intimidating if Carter hadn't given me way scarier looks over the years. Like the time I'd bought him a lap dance at the fully-nude male strip club. I was only trying to be generous because I was making him work so late on a Saturday night. But the look on that man's face as he came storming out of the back room with baby oil spread over his pants had me braving the paparazzi and escorting myself out to my car.

But it was the way Evan scooted to the edge of the seat—his posture equally as threatening—that really caught my attention.

I'd never been so turned on as I was when he barked, "Calm the fuck down," at Carter.

"I'm thirty-eight," he seethed at me, not sparing Evan a glance. "And she was completely legal, so if you even think about calling me a pedophile again, I *will* be job-hunting."

I rolled my eyes. "You know, the dramatics are usually my specialty."

His jaw ticked as he continued to glare, but his shoulders relaxed a fraction.

Tugging on Evan's sleeve, I urged him to slide back into his seat and give up the angry-Rottweiler routine.

He stared daggers at Carter as he obliged.

"Perhaps we should start over?" I arched an eyebrow at Carter, his body sagging as he nodded in agreement. "Okay. First off, while I'm not thrilled about you dipping into the family panty drawer, I'm not exactly mad, either. I was just...shocked. You should have told me."

"Agreed," he said immediately. "You know Robin though. She's stubborn as hell and was adamant that you not find out. And then it kinda fizzled out, so I let it go."

"And it's fizzling again?"

He shrugged noncommittally. "Apparently."

"You do remember I caught her using again…like, a week ago. This probably isn't the right time to rekindle anything."

He groaned and shifted awkwardly in his seat. "Yeah. I know. I really thought she was done with that crap. Shit, Henry. This is not something I planned. We have a whole history together that would take me a century to explain, and even then, I'm not sure I'd have all the pieces to the Robin Clark puzzle. I can't make her settle down, but I can sure as hell protect her. Even if it kills me. Christ." He raked a hand through his short, black hair. "That woman is doing my head in."

Poor guy looked so defeated. I knew that feeling all too well when it came to Robin. She was beautiful, smart, and so fucking witty. It was easy to see how he'd developed feelings for her. But, while she was easy to love, she was virtually impossible to hold on to.

But I guessed the same could be said about me. I wasn't into drugs. However, I had enough unresolved issues to fill a…

"Holiday Stay?" I questioned with more than a little disgust as the limo came to a stop at the front doors. "Nope. Keep driving to the Plaza!" I shouted at the driver.

"Uh…this is where I'm staying," Evan said, shoving the door open.

I dove over him and pulled it shut. "No, this is where the bed bugs, semen-stained comforters, and athlete's-foot-infested bathtubs are staying. Your new room is the presidential suite at the Plaza."

"My car is here!"

"And we'll get it disinfected in the morning," I replied curtly.

"Henry, this place is—"

"Shit," Carter filled in. "The security is unacceptable. I'd have to find two guys to sit outside all night, and I really don't have time for that. He can't stay here."

My mouth split in triumph, but I masked it with an exaggerated pout before turning back to Evan. "Bummer. I would have totally stayed here if it were up to me."

"You're ridiculous," he grumbled, but his eyes danced with humor. "Can I at least grab my shit and check out, your highness?"

"Mmm," I purred, rubbing my shoulder with his. "I approve of the new pet name. But sorry. Your request is denied." I grinned then yelled to the driver, "Sally forth, noble steed."

"Wow," Evan deadpanned as we pulled away.

"Trust me. He gets worse," Carter added.

I jutted my chin at Carter then said to Evan, "So does he. You're lucky you don't have any teenage sisters."

Evan chuckled, and surprisingly, so did Carter, all of the tension evaporating for the rest of the ride.

When we pulled up in front of the Plaza, Carter started for the door, but I stopped him.

"Look, you're both adults. What the two of you do behind closed doors isn't up to me. But don't break her heart. She's had a shit life and isn't exactly doing the best job at managing the present. Please don't add any more stress to that equation." I extended my hand to him.

"I'll keep her safe," he replied, gripping my palm for a quick shake.

It wasn't a promise. It was a vow.

As much as I wanted to be mad about them sneaking around behind my back for the last three years, I couldn't find it in me. Knowing I was no longer solely responsible for protecting Robin lifted an enormous weight from my shoulders.

And, as Evan and I were ushered up to our suite, his arm possessively locked around my hips as I signed autographs and smiled for selfies in the lobby, I prayed that, by the end of the evening, the weight of my insecurities would be gone as well.

I wasn't holding my breath though.

chapter twenty-six

Henry

"**Fine. It's nicer** than the Holiday Stay," Evan relented, sprawling out on the down comforter I'd specially requested. "But I'm betting it's not less than two hundred bucks a night."

"No." I bent over the bed and kissed his upturned lips. "But I'm loaded, so get used to it."

"Yeah, I kinda knew that, but after seeing the price tag on the suit Macy dropped off for me, I'm thinking I underestimated you."

I chuckled and flipped through the pages of the room service menu. "I'll have her put it on my account."

"I want to argue that I'm a man and don't need you buying me suits, but you sign my paychecks. You're paying for pretty much everything I own at this point."

I sat down on the bed next to him and swept the dark-brown hair off his forehead. "I thought you quit."

He rolled toward me and looped an arm around my hips. Then

he dragged me to the bed. His heavy chest settled on top of mine, and his blue eyes smiled down. "Consider this me rescinding my resignation." He sealed his decree with his mouth, my lips instantly parting to take it deeper, but it wasn't enough.

For either of us.

He swung a leg over to straddle me as our tongues glided together. He'd discarded his jacket and his tie when we'd gotten back to the room, but he was still wearing the crisp, white shirt that clung to the hard lines of his chest and his back, taunting me. Not to mention the black pants that hugged his ass so perfectly I almost felt guilty about removing them.

Almost.

But not really.

My hands went for his belt.

"Wait," he mumbled, but I swallowed it and pretended that it hadn't happened. "Henry, wait."

"You're mispronouncing 'fuck me.'" I continued trying to undo his belt with one hand while shifting my other down to his erection, which was straining in the front of his pants.

He hissed his approval and momentarily gave up the struggle—not that there was much of one.

"I want you so fucking bad." I lifted my hips so our still-covered cocks ground together, and when he cursed, dropping his face to my neck, I went for the kill. "*Evan.*"

Only it wasn't the kill I wanted.

I'd never seen a man fly away faster. He didn't stop backing up until his ass was against the wall on the opposite side of the room.

While his chest heaved, his eyes held a feral intensity laced with a large dose of fear. "We need to talk."

And, if that was the effect I had on him just by saying his name, I was starting to agree with him.

I knew the panic.

And I knew I loathed it covering *his* face.

"Okay. Let's talk," I said, sitting up and fisting the edge of the bed to keep from reaching for him.

Placing his hands on his hips, he sucked in a deep breath, his chest swelling as he held it.

"Evan…" I was careful not to put any emphasis on it so as not to risk setting him off again.

He watched me with notable unease, but as the muscles in his neck flexed and he rolled his shoulders back, staggering confidence appeared, banishing the anxiety. "Why did you leave me last week?"

I held his stare, "You know why. You talked to Levee."

"I did. And she told me about your little King Kong fetish and how you don't let anyone close. And she told me that it was a big fucking deal that you dropped your guard and opened up to me about your past. I could go on, but you know what? I'm not dating Levee. So I'd really like to hear this from you."

I diverted my eyes to the floor and scoffed. "What else do you want me to say? I'm fucked up. End of story."

"Fine. End of story. Get out."

My head snapped up and I found an inferno blazing in his eyes. "What?" I asked.

"You're still playing games, so I said get out." Cool, calm, casual… Definitive.

"How the fuck am I playing games?"

His jaw hardened as he tipped his head. "Holy shit. You don't see it."

I searched the room as if someone would magically appear and fill me in on what the hell he was talking about. His angry glower burned into me as I avoided his gaze.

"Clearly, I don't," I replied with a heavy sarcasm.

"Get out!" he erupted, swinging an arm to the door.

And, because sarcasm had worked so well the first time, my

dumb ass decided to give it another go. "Uh…this is *my* room."

He barked a laugh, but when I slowly lifted my head, I noticed that it held negative amounts of humor.

"You are absolutely right." He stomped to the chair in the corner, grabbed his coat, and draped it over his arm before heading to the door.

Dread filled my stomach, and my mind screamed at me to stop him. I knew what was on the other side of that door—I'd been living it for the last week. And the panic that built at that reality was the only thing that got my mouth moving.

"I don't know what you want me to say!" I pushed from the bed and folded my hands in prayer. "Tell me what you need to hear and I'll say it every day for the rest of my life. I'm not playing games. I just don't know what you need to hear."

He stopped, but he didn't give me his eyes. The muscles on his jaw jumped and his bicep flexed. Meanwhile, I held my breath for a miracle.

"Why did you leave?" he gritted out.

"Because I suck at letting people in."

His gaze remained on the door as he imperceptivity shook his head. "Last chance."

My heart lurched, and I stumbled several steps toward him. "This isn't a game to me, Evan. I swear."

His hollow eyes swung to mine, and I instantly wished they hadn't, because if I had thought the panic on his face was bad, the anguish was tenfold worse.

"Why. Did. You. Leave?"

Finally, when I feared my heart would explode, my mouth opened and the truth came tumbling out. "Because I was terrified of this moment, right here."

His shoulders fell as a loud exhale raced from his mouth, and if I could believe my eyes, he smiled. "What moment, Henry?"

I blinked. Then the strangest thing happened: I actually answered him...with another truth.

"This one...where you leave. And I'll be left gutted because there will be no one to blame but myself. I won't be able to delude myself that you're walking away because you don't like men. I'll have to accept that you're leaving because, just like everyone else in my life...you don't want *me*." I threw my hand up to cover my mouth, desperate to stop my secrets from escaping, but given the way Evan's eyes became tender, they were already leaking from my every pore.

"Come here, Henry."

I shook my head and rolled my bottom lip between my fingers. "Whether it's now or years from now, you'll leave."

He dropped his jacket to the ground and curled his finger in the air. "Come. Here. Henry."

"I have millions of fans. But it's the people who get to know me who leave. It always happens. Trust me."

"Not always."

"Always!" I hissed.

"Henry," he snapped, his eyes crinkling at the corners as they narrowed. "Come. Here."

"Maybe you should go."

He was terrible at following orders, because his long legs strode forward, not stopping until our bodies collided and I was in his arms.

His lips met my ear, and I swayed against him, desperately needing his comfort and reassurance more than ever.

Evan took a different approach.

"I dated a man for two years," he whispered, and I went rock solid.

'Kay. Not exactly the reassurance I was expecting.

"Umm..."

"Shh... Listen." He walked us backwards until the bed hit the back of my knees. Then he shifted me off-balance until I was flat, his weight heavy on top of me. "We met the first day at the Academy. I figured out in high school that I was attracted to men as well as women, but the moment I saw Shannon, I was done for. I wanted him more than any woman I'd ever been with. But what I never expected was for him to be interested in me too."

I tried to wiggle up the bed and out of his grasp. After my semi breakdown and the confessions I'd never told anyone, his ex-boyfriend was the very last thing I wanted to be discussing.

"I don't want to hear this."

He inched up the bed with me, refusing to release me. "And I don't want to be telling it. But I *need* you to listen."

Just as I was about to object again, he lifted his fingers and pinched my lips shut.

I rolled my eyes then bulged them in a fine-fucking-tell-me way.

"He was a year older than I was, which already made our relationship forbidden. But, also, 'Don't Ask Don't Tell' was in effect for the military back then. We did some serious sneaking around to keep our relationship a secret from not just our instructors and cadre, but also our friends. Until one day at the end of my second year, we got caught making out in the back of a tiny restaurant thirty miles from post. It was a classmate of mine, Dave Bass, and he gave us two options. Either we could go to our chain of command and admit that we were *gay*—thus getting us kicked out—or he'd do it for us."

"Nosy asshole," I mumbled around his fingers.

He lifted his shoulder in a half shrug. "Rules are rules. And we had an honor code. He could've been kicked out for *not* reporting it."

I slapped his hand away from my mouth. "Christ, what the hell kind of bigots run this place?"

"They're good men. Slightly misguided, but it was a decade ago and the country was just starting to catch up on homosexual equality."

"That's no excuse. You shouldn't be punished for being with a man. It's not like you get to choose who you're attracted to."

Pursing his lips, he fought back a smile all while leveling me with a pointed glare.

I sighed, pressing my head into the bed and staring blankly at the ceiling. "Shit. I'm such a fucking hypocrite."

His lips brushed mine. "A little. But we'll figure it out."

I folded my hands around him to return his embrace, hoping that we would do just that.

Shifting to the side, he propped himself up on an elbow, his head cradled in his hand, his other resting on my hip.

I mirrored his position. "So'd you get the boot?"

"Shannon and I thought about it for two days. We were in love."

I winced and shifted my attention down between us, staring at nothing in particular in order to avoid his gaze. That was definitely not fun to hear. But he gave me a squeeze and then slid his hand up my side until he reached my chin, where he tipped my head, forcing me to meet his eyes.

"It was a long time ago. And, if you want the truth, over the last few weeks with you, I've started to feel like love isn't even the right word for it."

Oh yeah. He said *that*. To me.

I bit my lip, suddenly very interested in the rest of the story. Mainly because I wanted it to hurry up and end so he could get back to what he'd learned over the last few weeks with me.

Evan continued. "We'd talked about a future together and made plans for after we graduated. Separation from the Academy was definitely going to change things, but we had each other. I really wasn't all that upset about it. I was a dumb kid with white picket fences and dreams of not having to hide clouding my vision." He grinned, but it never met his eyes. "You have to understand something about me. I've never considered myself gay."

My lips thinned as I arched an eyebrow. "Well, this must be awkward as hell for you, then."

He ignored my joke. "I like men. I like women. But, at the end of the day, I am not defined by my sexuality. I just want to find someone who makes me happy. That's all I've ever wanted. I don't care if you're a man or a woman. I have no preference. When I'm with someone, it's because of the person they are, not the genitalia they were born with."

And it was official. I was a dick. But not the good kind. I was the huge, hot-pink dildo of men. I found my dates based on their sexuality alone. The person they were didn't even factor in my relationships—if you could call them that. All they needed was a cock and a penchant for woman and they were automatically my type.

However, as I realized what a terrible person I was and saw the figurative golden halo forming over Evan's head, part of me still celebrated.

He was with me.

Which meant, if what he was telling me was true, he was with me…for *me*.

It was a simple concept that should have been assumed, but for a man like me, it was overwhelming, and my throat began to close in response.

His strong hands cupped my jaw while his thumb lazily stroked my cheek. "I see you're starting to understand."

Not trusting my voice, I nodded in response.

"Good. Now, let me finish story time so I can make you understand everything a hell of a lot better."

I nodded again.

"I was allowed to leave the Academy after my second year, no penalty. But, once you start your third year, you're expected to sign a contract, much like an enlistment. Shannon had already signed, so if he got the boot and was unable to serve out his time in the Air Force—say, if he were gay—he would have been stuck repaying a ton of money. So Shannon devised a plan. We were only a few weeks from the end of the year, so he told me to transfer out and he'd cheat on a final exam in order to get kicked out without that nasty little *gay* word being added to his file. With promises of him working off his contract and supporting us while I finished college somewhere else, I was completely on board. We approached Dave, the guy who'd caught us, with our plan and he agreed not to out us as long as we left the Academy. I was so fucking blinded by Shannon that I never even wondered how this guy who'd been ready to throw us under the bus because it was his duty had changed his tune in a matter of days to the point that he was okay with lying as long as we left the Academy."

I drew in a sharp breath as my stomach started to churn. As much as I wanted him to get to the part where he kicked Shannon to the curb because, deep down, he knew I was out there waiting on him, I had a sneaking suspicion that that wasn't how it was going to end. And, as pain and regret sifted through Evan's features, I hated being right.

Giving his hip a comforting squeeze, I silently encouraged him to continue.

"It was Shannon's idea to call my mom and John that night and tell them I was leaving school because I was gay. God." He paused, closing his eyes for a long, agonizing moment. When they popped open, the pain was gone, but there was a storm brewing more prominently than ever. "It was the only time in my life I'd actually said the word. But I was in love and Shannon was gay. I wanted to be whatever he was."

I stretched my arm out and pulled his head down on top of it. His large body curled into mine as the memories ravaged him.

"I hate when people call me gay now," he whispered then kissed my arm. "Not because there's anything wrong with it, but because it's not who I am. It's who *he* was."

I lazily drew a circle on his shoulder. "What did your parents say?"

"They were shocked but accepting. It wasn't as bad as I'd thought it was going to be. Shannon sat with me through it all."

At least there was that. I'd heard horror stories about telling the parents. It might have been the only positive about not having a family—I hadn't had a closet to come out of.

"Anyway…I left school a few weeks later. He kissed me in his car at the airport, told me he loved me, and I've never heard from him again."

My.

Heart.

Stopped.

"I'm sorry. What?"

"He cut me out of his life the very next day. Sound familiar?"

I cursed under my breath as guilt consumed me.

"I inadvertently heard the specifics from my friends who kept in touch. You remember my buddy Scott, right?"

"Unless this ends with he killed Shannon, I'm not sure that is a pertinent question at this juncture," I snapped, horrified by what I'd just heard.

He chuckled and kissed my shoulder. "No. The Air Force is a small world. Shannon is a civilian contractor now. He and Scott work together these days."

My body jerked. "Okay…now, unless this ends with you killing Scott since the last time I saw him in your fucking house, I'm really not sure this is a pertinent question."

He laughed loudly, but I saw not one thing funny. I had to have been missing something.

"Scott doesn't ask questions," Evan continued. "And I was so embarrassed that I never told him the whole truth about what happened. He knew that Shannon and I were seeing each other. He knew after I left school that we broke up. And he has gathered over the years that it was nasty. He does his best to never even mention that Shannon exists. But he doesn't know the details."

"Neither do I!" I sat up in outrage on his behalf. "What actually happened? Talk faster."

The side of his mouth hiked up and his eyes warmed. "It was no secret that I didn't give a shit about school. I just wanted to fly. My parents were the only reason I was at the Academy. I would have been just as happy at a community college as long as I could fly when I was done. So, from what I can piece together, Shannon had been cheating on me with Dave, and they were both afraid that, when I found out, I'd flip and leave, taking them down with me. So the real plan Shannon devised was to get me out of the picture before I had the chance."

"Holy motherfucking shit. That asshole!"

"Pretty much," Evan replied nonchalantly, rolling as he pulled me back down, this time with my head resting on his arm.

"Please tell me you got both of their asses kicked out."

"Nope. I did absolutely nothing. And that included living my life. I swore off men. Started dating women exclusively, and for the first time, I started seeing people for their gender and not the person inside." He peered down at me, his eyes sparkling with some unidentifiable emotion. Or, at least, one I wasn't willing to acknowledge yet. "Fast forward ten years and cue Henry Alexander."

A rush of heat washed over me. "I hear that guy's a real prick."

"Nah. He's crazy though. But he also made me laugh. And he was so fucking sexy. And, despite the fact that he was a man who happened to be incredibly famous"—he motioned a hand around the room—"and loaded, he still awakened a fire inside me that had been dormant for so long I'd forgotten it existed."

"*Evan…*" I breathed as my chest tightened.

"Mmm… There it is," he moaned, pressing our foreheads to-gether. "Now, *that's* how you say my name. Not in question, but in prayer."

I wanted to crawl down the bed, strip him naked, and then bury myself so deep inside him neither of us would ever resurface, but my damn curiosity was killing me. "Why didn't you go back and tell them he was gay? Get him and that other guy kicked out for the shit they pulled?"

"Henry, Shannon was a dick and he fucking destroyed me. But I wasn't going to out him. Karma did that for me when a year later when he and Dave got caught and ultimately forced out. Scott enjoyed the hell out of 'slipping up' and mentioning that one." He half smiled before getting serious again. "The point is, he didn't cheat on me and then get rid of me because he wanted Dave. He did it because he didn't want...*me*."

My mouth gaped as it dawned on me why he was telling me about this.

Evan was just as broken as I was, and the eerie similarities were probably what had drawn us together—and then torn us apart.

Reality slashed through me.

"I'm scared too," he whispered, his breath flittering across my lips. "And, in the beginning, I ran, throwing up every barrier I could think of to keep myself from being hurt again. But it was because of me and my demons. *Not* you. If I'd known you left last week because of yours...there isn't a force in the world that could have kept me away."

I slung a leg over his hip and buried my face in his neck. "I'm sorry. I've been so worried about the moment you left that I never even considered that maybe your spiral down could be a good thing."

"I won't leave you," he promised in my ear.

And, for the first time in all the thirty-one years of my life, I allowed myself to believe that someone might actually mean it.

And it was Evan.

That was the highest high I would ever experience.

chapter twenty-seven

Evan

His body coiled around me so tight I could barely breathe.

"Say it again," he urged, but the desperation made his voice crack.

Leaning away, I forced his eyes to mine. "I won't leave you. I'm crazy about Henry Gilchrist. And, honestly, I have very little interest in Henry Alexander—except for the fact that he comes with the package."

He sucked in a deep breath and bit his lip to fight back the emotion that was trying to war its way out.

"I mean it. No more running. No more hiding. It's a leap of faith. I get that. But we can jump together."

He nodded, but I needed more.

"Say it," I ordered.

His chest shuddered, but the words finally breezed from between his perfect lips. "I can do that."

"Evan," I prompted.

A slow smile turned the corners of his lips up. "I can do that, *Evan*."

I growled seconds before sealing my mouth over his in a searing kiss that I prayed would brand us both.

His moan vibrated in my mouth as he rolled, covering me completely from head to toe. My hips lifted on their own accord, grinding against his in a search-and-rescue mission for friction. Never one to disappoint, Henry shifted until our hard-ons found each other. It was a union of beauty, and it sent sparks of overwhelming need through not only my shaft, but directly to my heart.

"This time, I'm taking you," I announced, moving my attention to his neck.

His body tensed, but the subtle circle of his hips continued to torment me.

"This is it, Henry. This is where we start. No games. No fears. No bullshit. This is where you give yourself to me, completely."

"And what about you? Will you be giving yourself to *me*?" he asked seductively.

"No," I answered.

His head snapped back, those bright, blue eyes dimming. "No?"

"I have nothing left to give. You own me. And I'm not just talking about sexually. You've been a whirlwind who has stripped me bare and brought me to my knees more than once. I'm not naïve enough to believe that it will be smooth skies from here on out. The only thing I can do is swear I'll weather any storm as long as you're on the other side, waiting for me."

His breath hitched and he melted on top of me. His naturally hard planes softened until we were flush.

"Jesus, Evan."

"This—tonight—is the moment where you cease to exist and *we* truly begin. Tell me you trust me." With his body still limp, I made a quick move to flip us over, but I didn't land on top of him. Immediately shifting directions, I moved off the bed, his startled eyes tracking me. I stood to my full height and stared down at him. "Say it."

His chest was rising and falling at an increased speed, but there wasn't an ounce of nerves or hesitation in his voice. "I trust you, Evan."

My world as I knew it flipped upside down with only one sentence, but for once, my heart and my soul remained firmly anchored in place—past, present, and forever.

My knees hit the floor in record speed, and I began tugging at the button on his slacks.

He didn't delay in sitting up to join me in my frenzy.

His hands went to the top of my shirt, tearing at it until the material gave way and buttons flew across the room. Then my undershirt was peeled over my head and his open mouth landed on my shoulder while I fought with his pants.

Soon enough, we were both naked and his mouth kissed its way to mine as I knelt on the ground at his feet, one hand working his length from base to tip.

Holding his eyes, I made my intentions clear as I slowly leaned down.

His pupils dilated and his lips parted as he watched my decent with rapt attention.

"Hey, Henry," I said and then laved the head of his cock, the taste of his arousal exploding on my tongue.

"Hmm," he hummed down at me, gripping the side of the bed for dear life.

I licked my lips and winked. "You can consider this your spiral down." And then I gave him the final piece of me and slid him between my lips.

"Fuck," he groaned, his torso falling back against the bed as his hands flew into my hair.

His sizable length bottomed out in the back of my throat before

I was able take him all, so I added my hand to his base until I covered him. Then I worked his cock thoroughly, his abs rippled making for an outstanding view.

While my tongue teased his slit, I trailed my damp fingers between his legs to the tight ring, teasing and taunting his rim as his body writhed.

There was no denying I was out of practice, but if Henry noticed at all, he didn't let on. A symphony of curse words and my name filled the air around us as I pressed a single finger into him, his hips bucking in response. My tongue circled his tip, lapping at the bead of precome that continuously formed, while his fists twisted in the covers until his knuckles turned white.

"More," he begged, arching his back and tipping his hips up.

I needed lube, but that would have required tracking my pants down on the floor for my wallet. And no way I was stopping. Releasing him from my mouth, I glided my tongue down the underside of his cock, feeling it twitch in my hand as I reached his balls and then below. As he realized my final destination, he lifted a leg to the bed in a silent plea.

A guttural moan rumbled in his throat as I removed my finger and drove my tongue into the sensitive flesh.

"Oh, God, Evan," he cried.

My erection was aching between my legs, needy for a taste of what my mouth was devouring.

"I want to fuck you so bad," I mumbled, dropping my free hand to offer my throbbing cock a few strokes of relief.

"Then do it." He moaned. "There's a condom and lube in my bag."

He did not have to tell me twice. I was on my feet, searching the front pocket of his bag, in a matter of seconds. However, I only carried the lube back to the bed.

"Have you been with anyone else since we first hooked up?" I asked, drizzling lube into my palm.

"No," he replied with an adamant shake of his head.

I dropped my wet hand between his legs and circled his entrance. "Do you trust me?"

His hips rose off the bed and he impaled himself on my finger. "Completely."

"No condom," I declared, adding another finger to stretch him.

He licked his lips. "No condom," he agreed breathily.

My cock jumped at the thought of taking him bare. I'd never been with a man without a barrier, and the idea of feeling Henry flesh on flesh was almost more than I could take. A growl tore from my throat as I snatched up the lube with my other hand and liberally poured it over my cock.

After discarding the bottle on the bed beside him, I continued to work his ass while I slicked myself. "Scoot back," I ordered.

He quickly obeyed, moving up the bed until his feet were both flat on the mattress and his knees were bent.

I was forced to remove my fingers as I followed him forward, crawling onto the bed and then settling on my knees between his legs. His lust-filled eyes darkened as I teased my cock up and down his crack, and his body tensed as I poised myself at his entrance.

"Grip yourself," I demanded, pressing in a fraction of an inch.

"Oh...fuck," he gasped, throwing his head back, his face contorting in pure ecstasy. "Evan, please."

I smiled to myself and pressed only the slightest bit deeper, but it was more than enough to make us both groan. As much as I was enjoying his reaction, I was equally torturing myself.

Dropping to an elbow by his head, I sank an inch deeper but still refused to move. "Give me your mouth."

His parted lips instantly found mine, and I swallowed his whimper as I pressed in farther. Our tongues danced as pleasure coursed through me.

"Fuck me," he pleaded into my mouth.

It was a sentiment I shared, but right then, I was basking in the overwhelming feelings of it all. It was better than anything I could have imagined, but that had nothing to do with being bare and everything to do with Henry.

I turned my head and whispered in his ear, "Do you feel that?"

He nodded, the stubble on his jaw scrubbing with mine.

Remembering his words from over a week earlier, I thrust forward, planting myself to the hilt. "This doesn't make you gay, Henry." I roughly bit the lobe of his ear. "It just makes you mine."

His arms folded around my neck, and a loud moan hissed from his mouth. "Yours."

Slowly withdrawing, I corrected him. "*Evan.*"

His muscles clenched around me as he confirmed, "Yours, *Evan.*"

No truer words had ever been spoken. I didn't know what the future held for us, but no matter what happened from that moment on, Henry Alexander Gilchrist would always be mine.

For nearly a half hour, I worked him with my cock and my hands. By the end, we were both covered in sweat with our releases mingling in the ridges on his stomach.

We collapsed, sated, on the bed and then spent the next hour talking and laughing, curled into each other's sides—the way it should have been.

Our first time together might not have gone the way I wanted, but I could live with the memories of that night and the searing pain that had followed if I was lucky enough to keep him.

It was suddenly clear that I'd been right when I'd met Henry. He was a storm of epic proportions. But maybe he was the only one capable of tearing my walls down.

And then to find that my broken pieces actually made him whole?

Well, that was nothing short of perfection.

My sore, sexed-out muscles protested as I awoke to the blaring of my phone on the nightstand. Henry's naked body was draped across me, his even breaths tickling my chest. I did my best contortionist act to silence the noise without jostling him.

Once I got my phone, I saw my stepfather's name blinking on the screen.

I glanced back down at Henry before lifting it to my ear. If my parents were calling so early, something had to be up.

"Hey, John," I whispered, smoothing down the top of Henry's sleep-mussed blond hair.

"So your mother and I just got back from breakfast at The Sunrise," he informed me.

The Sunrise had been a weekend ritual for them for as long as I could remember. Sometimes, they went on Saturday. Sometimes on Sunday. But, regardless of the day, it happened every weekend. And, up until that moment, I'd never thought too much about their predictable routine. However, now, my mind drifted with a sense of excitement as I considered the kind of rituals Henry and I would create together over the next...oh, lifetime.

A huge smile split my lips.

"How was the southwest omelet this morning?" I asked before kissing the top Henry's head.

"I wouldn't know. Didn't get to eat. Your mother dragged me out of there before I could even finish my first cup of joe. See, Sally Walters brought it to our attention that you seem to have forgotten to tell us something."

I tensed as guilt pooled in my stomach. "Um...like what?"

"Um..." he mocked. "Like the fact that you're dating Henry Alexander."

My head fell back against the pillows. "Shit. John, I—"

"Yeah, shit is right. Someone else is eating my omelet right now. Meanwhile, your mom is swirling around this house, snapping at me, and polishing the silver with a toothbrush because, obviously, if you're serious enough about this guy to be swallowing his face in public, you're serious enough to be bringing him home for dinner. Evan, I swear on my life the woman is acting like The Pope himself will be blessing us with his presence."

I chuckled because I knew he wasn't exaggerating. My mom was a little, well, enthusiastic when it came to entertaining. And, considering John had mentioned Sally Walters, the biggest gossip in San Francisco—or, at least, in my parents' circle—I'd guessed that Mom had heard Henry was famous.

"I see the pictures from last night leaked to the press," I said.

"Leaked? From the way everyone at The Sunrise was talking… there was a fucking flood. I thought your mother was going to need CPR when Sally produced a photo of you and Henry going into a hotel *two months ago*. Son, if you need me to paint a picture for you here, she was so upset she didn't even touch her Diet Coke."

That was really bad. My mom did not mess around when it came to her morning Diet Coke.

"She's really flipping out, huh?"

"Evan, you have a boyfriend who is famous enough for Sally Walters to know he's your boyfriend before your own mother, I'd say she's more than flipping out. She's hurt."

I flinched. I hated that she'd found out that way, but there hadn't exactly been a good time for me to sit her down and tell her about Henry. Things had been so tumultuous with us from the start—mentioning him to the parents had felt a tad premature. Hell, I'd spent most of those two months trying to find reasons why we couldn't be together.

"It's not like that, John. Shit. This thing… It just kinda happened."

"I'm calling horseshit. I've met Henry Alexander. Nothing just happens with him. Did he mention that he was on that AirUSA flight of mine? He begged me to be his personal pilot for months after the accident. I swear to you I was retired and had no interest in a new job, but he was so convincing I nearly agreed."

I smiled. Yep. That was my Henry.

"You know how I feel, then. Tell Mom that I fell victim to his persistent charm and didn't have a chance to call and tell her."

He barked a laugh in my ear just as I felt Henry's head tip back.

"Victim to my persistent charm?" he accused softly, the skin between his eyes pinching together in pain.

Last night, I would have apologized profusely that he'd gotten the wrong idea about my conversation. Today, after the promises we'd made to each other both verbally and physically last night, I was almost frustrated that there could be any doubt in his mind.

I twisted my lips and glowered.

Lifting my phone in the air, I pressed the speaker button and John's voice came through midsentence.

"...you serious about this one, or do I need to stop your mom from redecorating the living room?"

Henry began worrying his lip as he waited anxiously for my answer.

I couldn't fight the grin as I replied, "He's the one, John. And I'd honestly say that even if he weren't sitting here, staring at me like I was about to kick his puppy." I held Henry's gaze as I lifted my hand in a Vulcan V.

He smiled, and the breath he was holding rushed from his mouth.

"Oh, hell! Didn't mean to put you on the spot."

"No problem. You're on speakerphone too." I motioned for Henry to say something.

His eyes flashed between me and the phone as though I'd asked him to sacrifice himself to the parental gods. Finally, he timidly said, "Hi, John."

Forget the grin. I outright laughed.

"Mr. Alexander. So we meet again."

"Yeah, but this time, I'm sleeping with your son." His face flashed red as he slapped his hand over his mouth, turning apologetic eyes my way.

Stunned, I cocked my head in silent question. Henry entertained thousands on a daily basis, yet one conversation with my dad turned him into a bumbling wreck.

"I'm going to pretend I didn't hear that and just keep talking, if that's all right with you," John said with more than a hint of humor. "I have to say, when Jackson told me you hired Evan, I wasn't surprised. He's the best pilot I've ever met, and I took the liberty of including myself in that pool."

I smiled huge. Praise from a man I respected never got old. Neither did the way Henry's eyes lit as he looked up at me.

"However, I have to say, you dating my boy is taking stalking to a whole new level."

Henry finally laughed, and his arms tightened around my midsection. "I wouldn't have been stalking you at all if I'd known Evan back then."

"Well, excuse me for not introducing you sooner."

I chuckled, secretly enjoying the ease with which John was accepting Henry. While my parents knew I'd been with a man, Shannon and I had been done before they'd ever had to deal with it. This would definitely be a first for all of us.

"Anyway…I'll let you two go. I didn't mean to…uh, interrupt."

I grinned. "Sorry about the omelet, John."

"Don't worry about it. There's always next weekend. I'm going to try to get a Diet Coke in your mom and see if I can calm her down. Give her a call in a little while and tell her when you can bring Henry home for dinner."

I glanced at Henry, one eyebrow raised in question. His only response was a megawatt grin.

"I can do that," I replied.

"Love ya, son."

"Love you too." I hung up, dropped the phone beside me, and then aimed a scowl at Henry.

He sighed. "I'm sorry."

"For?" I gave not a single damn that he had talked about us sleeping together in front of John. I did care that he'd started to panic when he'd first overheard my conversation.

"You know why," he replied, pushing up on his arms and then prowling up until his lips were on mine.

"I do know why, but I love hearing you tell me anyway."

He nipped at my bottom lip and tugged back the covers between us. After slinging his leg over my hips, he settled in my lap, both of our cocks growing hard when they made contact.

He huffed when I didn't react to his blatant advance. "Fine, because I assumed you were saying something else and, instead of trusting you, I let it bother me."

I gripped his ass, gently pulling his cheeks apart as I ground him against me. "You have to trust me, Henry."

"I didn't freak," he defended, taking both of our erections in one of his hands. "I can't change overnight. I only *assumed*. You can't be mad at that. Actually, I'd say that's a huge step for me. And, if you want my opinion, I think you should reward me for such a great effort by rolling over and offering me that sexy ass."

My eyebrows hit my hairline just as my phone started ringing again.

"Here. Turn it off," he said, nabbing it off the bed and passing it my way.

Scott's name flashed on the caller ID. He must have seen the pictures of Henry and me too and was calling to pretend he hadn't while still covertly conveying his congratulations in a series of coded comments that would require a legend to decipher.

I could call him back.

Powering it down, I asked, "Why isn't your phone blowing up? The pictures of us, including the ones from a few months ago, are all over the place, apparently. Don't you have an agent or someone who should be yelling at you right about now?" I asked, swapping my phone for the bottle of lube on the nightstand.

Henry's smile split his face like a kid's on Christmas morning. Snatching the lube from my hand, he replied, "Because I know better than to leave my cell phone on when shit is about to hit the fan. And also because it was my publicist who released the pictures of us from two months ago in the first place. They've probably been working all night."

My head jerked in surprise. "What?"

Pushing up on his knees, he swirled his finger in the air, motioning for me to roll over. I wasn't about to argue.

Careful to tuck my straining hard-on for fear of breaking it, I flipped beneath him.

"Jesus, this fucking ass," he murmured, gliding his lubed fingers down my crack. "This is going to be so much better than the first time I was inside you. You're still okay with bare, right?"

"Yes. But first get to the part about your publicist," I demanded.

He folded over and dragged his tongue up the valley between my shoulder blades. "I paid a ton of money to buy the pictures off the paparazzi from that first night you came to my rescue and guided me inside the hotel. I didn't want to risk you freaking out and running off after our first night together, but also because I can only imagine how terrible I looked in the throes of a panic attack."

"You bought *all* of them?" I asked in a mixture of surprise and awe. The fact that he'd gone to such lengths to ensure he didn't lose me made my chest warm.

"I did," he mumbled, hooking an arm under my hips to pull me up to my knees. Then he began massaging the lube over my ass. "And I gave permission for the good ones to be released this morning along with your name, age, occupation, and new relationship status of"—he paused, his hand dipping between my legs to find my cock—"taken."

I wanted to be annoyed that he hadn't discussed this with me first, but the possessive way in which he spoke turned me on more than his hand stroking my shaft.

"My phone will probably stay off for a while too," he added, gliding his hand back up my ass. "The media is going to be hounding us both. Let me take you somewhere quiet for a while. I have two weeks off—three if I rearrange my schedule."

My body rocked forward as his finger sank inside, forcing a deep moan from my throat. "Where?" I asked—not that it mattered. I'd have gone anywhere with him.

"Wherever you want. I own a house on Lake Tahoe though. We could be there by lunch." He added another finger, but that wasn't why my chin snapped to my shoulder so I could see him.

It would have taken at least eight hours to drive to Tahoe. We'd have been lucky to be there by dinner. However, a flight would take less than ninety minutes.

He smiled sheepishly. "I know a pilot who could probably take us on short notice."

"You're going to let me fly you?"

He shrugged and then curled his finger inside me. "I trust you, *Evan.*"

I would have kissed him, something deep and reverent that could convey how much it meant that he was willing to face his fears with me. But, on my knees, with his fingers inside me, I was in no position to take his mouth.

I thought he got the message though, because seconds later, he was inside me.

Minutes later, I was crying his name as I came.

And, hours later, Henry had a drink in his hand as I gave him a kiss and then climbed into my cockpit in order to fly my man to Nevada.

chapter twenty-eight

Henry

"**F**uck," I cursed, staring down at Evan between my knees, taking my cock deep to the back of his throat.

Tahoe had been our quiet retreat for over a week, and if people were still all aflutter with Henry and Evan—or Heaven, as we'd been so creatively dubbed—I hadn't been sure. Our TVs, telephones, and laptops had remained off since we'd landed—which, by the way, had been incredibly smooth.

My fear of flying was still firmly intact, but my faith in Evan kept the panic at bay.

One hand massaged my balls as he drove me closer to release with every swirl of his tongue. While it had taken some time for Evan to finally go down on me, it'd quickly become his favorite pastime. I'd woken up with his mouth around my cock more often than not over the last week. This morning being no exception.

I was so damn close to coming when the jarring sound of tiny fists on the door distracted me. "Cookie? Are you awake yet?"

Awake and halfway to my first orgasm of the day if she would back away from the fucking door.

I gritted my teeth, trying to keep from flying off the bed, snatching open the door, and tossing her my credit card to stay at one of the nearby hotels. I loved Robin more than life itself, but a family vacation wasn't exactly what I'd had in mind when I'd suggested this trip to Evan. And this kind of interruption was the prime example of why. However, I needed Carter to accompany me in case Evan and I wanted to leave the house. And, after Robin's latest incident, I couldn't chance leaving her alone again.

On the plane ride over, Carter and I had broached the topic with her of doing another thirty-day inpatient program at a new rehab facility up in Chicago. When she reluctantly agreed, I was elated. Even Carter looked visibly relieved, his face softening as he took her hand in his paw.

Carter and Robin were interesting—and surprisingly not gross—together. They weren't lovey-dovey, thank the Lord Baby Jesus. Really, they just seemed to quietly fight all the time. I had no idea how they liked each other with that much bickering, but every night, Carter's bed remained empty and Robin's door—thankfully on the other side of the house—remained locked. Clearly, it worked for them.

"I'm up," I ground out.

"Oh good! What time do you guys want to eat dinner tonight? Carter and I are going to hit up the grocery store so I can get a few things."

"Five is good!" Evan called out before going back to work on my cock.

"Five?" she shouted. "The meat has to marinate for at least eight hours. I can't have it ready any sooner than six."

"Then six!" Evan and I yelled in unison, his jaw ticking in frustration, matching my own.

"Next time, we're coming alone," I said, pulling at his shoulders until he pressed to his feet.

He kissed me briefly then nudged my arm to signal for me to roll over. As much as I loved seeing Evan's ass in the air with my cock disappearing inside him, I was equally in love with the feeling of his powerful body covering mine as he took me. Actually, there wasn't much I didn't love with Evan. And that included him.

While Evan had been open that we were together and we'd both admitted to *falling* in love, no further declarations had been made. I didn't need them though. His actions spoke louder than words. And trust me—Evan's body wasn't quiet about his feelings for me. I still struggled on a daily basis with believing him and not allowing my pessimism to taint our relationship, but as I fell asleep each night with his arms securely wrapped around me, it was easier to convince myself that this was forever.

"We're almost out of lube," he said, pouring it over my ass, and not just where it was needed. I'm talking about the entire thing, cheeks and all.

"Then stop using so much," I retorted, pressing back into him.

His hands found my hips and lifted me, forcing my ass to slide up and down his stomach. "No way. I fucking love the way you feel fucking me from the bottom with your slick ass grinding against me."

Damn. Now that he mentioned it, I loved that too.

"We'll buy more," I replied promptly.

He chuckled, gliding a damp hand up my back until it wrapped around the base of my neck. Then he slowly glided inside, a gasp escaping my mouth as he filled me.

"*Evan*," I breathed, rolling my hips in a circle as he folded over to reach around and grip my cock.

"Be fast. I'm not risking another interruption," he rasped in a voice that said, "*Be fast because I'm not going to last long.*"

I could definitely do fast.

I fucked him from the bottom while he stroked my cock until neither of us could take it any longer. He pulled out just in time to pump warm ropes of his release on my back as I filled his hand.

As he fell to the side, dragging me down with him, I teased, "Fast enough for you?"

Laughing, he nabbed a towel off the nightstand and wiped my back. "We'll go longer tonight."

"We definitely will." I rolled to face him and found him looking like the cat that ate the canary. "What are you smiling about?"

He discarded the rag and then cupped my jaw before gently touching his lips to mine. "You. Us. This."

I felt the heat rush to my face.

"You," he repeated, trailing his thumb over my pink cheek.

My smile grew to match his. "I'm happy too. But you know, in a few weeks, we'll have to go back to reality. I'll be on the road a lot. And the world has now seen the sexy beast who shares my bed, so men and women alike will be beating down your door, trying to take you away from me."

"Let 'em try." He smirked confidently. "And I'll go on the road with you if you want. I'm pretty sure my boss will be understanding." He winked.

The high swirled in my veins. "You will?"

"Of course." he pressed a lingering kiss to my lips. "I'm not fond of driving, but I'm pretty fond of *you*."

"Well, that's definitely a positive thing considering the things I'm going to do to you."

He pulled me against his chest so my head rested on his shoulder. "I'm looking forward to it. I vote we skip dinner. I'll make us some sandwiches, and you send Carter and Robin out on a date."

I sucked in an eager breath, realizing Evan was a straight-up genius. Then the landline started ringing on the nightstand. I groaned, rolling from his arms to retrieve it from the charging base.

Very limited people had the number to my lake house, considering I'd changed it the day we'd arrived so no one could interrupt us. And, by limited, I meant: Levee.

"Hello, beautiful," I crooned.

"Nope. It's me," Sam said.

"Oh, hey, Sam. I was just about to call you." I winked at Evan. "We were naked in bed and having the age-old debate about whether you're a boxers or briefs kind of guy. See, I say—"

"I'm at the hospital. Levee's water broke."

Ice flooded my veins as I shot straight up in bed. "Is she okay? I didn't think she was due until next month!"

"She hit thirty-seven weeks yesterday. Looks like Bree will be here tonight. I'm gonna need you to get your ass back here *STAT*."

My heart was thundering in my chest as I felt Evan's hand land on my back. Concern painted his face as he moved in front of me.

"Sam, answer me. Is she okay?"

Evan instantly pulled me against his chest, his arms wrapping around my shoulders so snugly I couldn't have fallen apart if I'd needed to.

"She's fine," Sam assured, but it did little to slow my pulse. "She was in a lot of pain on the way here, but she's getting an epidural now. Just hurry up. She'll want you here."

I smiled weakly. "Then I'm on my way."

"It's going to be fine," Evan promised, squatting beside my seat on the plane. "I'll get you there safe and sound. It's a short flight back to San Francisco."

I glanced out the window at the rain pouring down around us. My hands trembled in my lap as he kissed my shoulder. His eyes flashed around at Robin and Carter as though he had been pleading for help.

I tried to put my game face on for him, but it was a worthless effort. It was raining. My terror level had peaked.

"Ready when you are," Javier, Evan's short-notice copilot, called from the cockpit.

Evan had vouched for his experience, but I wasn't all that convinced. However, we didn't have time to wait for Baez if I wanted to get to Levee in time.

"Coming," Evan replied. Then he grabbed the back of my neck and pressed his forehead to mine. "I will get you there safely. I swear."

I swallowed hard and nodded. I was going to flip the fuck out—no way around it. But, if it meant I would be there for Levee, I'd suck it up and do what I had to.

"Let's go," I mumbled.

It was his turn to nod unconvincingly.

But, minutes later, he was gone and the door to the cockpit was shut behind him.

"It'll be okay, Cookie," Robin soothed, dropping her hand into my lap and intertwining our fingers.

She was probably right, but try telling that to my tweaked-out nerves.

When I felt the plane begin to accelerate down the runway, I closed my eyes and did my best to envision Evan in his element.

His rough hands wrapped around the controls the same way they held my jaw when he'd kissed me the first time. "Five."

Those captivating blue eyes that owned my soul gazing out the windshield as the rain pelted down. "Four."

His confident grin he would no doubt be sporting the same way he did every time he so much as talked about flying. "Three."

His heart racing in his chest for no other reason than he knew I was in the back, scared without him. "Two."

My stomach lurched into my throat when the wheels lifted off the ground.

"You okay?" Robin whispered.

Prying a single eye open, I looked at her. "I screwed up the countdown."

She grinned and shrugged. "Or maybe he knew you'd freak out at one."

It was impossible. Evan couldn't have predicted when I would have started counting. But a laugh slipped from my throat because she was right. That was exactly what he would have done.

And it was exactly why my heart slowed well before the plane had leveled out.

I trusted Evan. And, while I could sit there and fret over an act of God sending us crashing to the ground, I couldn't help but remember him saying that my act of God had been having John Wyatt as my pilot on that fateful night.

In that moment, I realized he was wrong.

The true act of God had been finding him because of that horrible night.

If I hadn't been on that flight, I never would have met his dad.

And, if I hadn't met his dad, I never would have been using Jackson to find my pilots.

And, if I hadn't been using Jackson, I never would have had Evan step in to take my flight.

That was my act of God.

And, suddenly, flying wasn't so scary anymore.

Well...until all hell broke lose.

Robin gasped as the plane suddenly jerked, giving us all that dreaded feeling of our stomachs dropping.

My hand convulsed around hers, my other slamming down on the armrest.

"What the fuck is he doing up there?" Carter snapped.

"It's okay," I forced out in a shaky voice. "I'm sure it's nothing," I lied, trying the power of positive thinking for once.

The plane once again bounced, catching only momentarily before dipping again. My stomach threatened to revolt, but I did my best not to lose my lunch—or my mind.

I must have looked like hell, because Carter suddenly reached over Robin and pressed me down so I folded over my knees.

"It's fine," he growled. Only, for the first time, Carter didn't sound completely convinced.

"Son of a bitch!" I heard Evan's voice over the intercom as the plane took another sharp drop.

My eyes jumped to Carter, who was nervously staring at the speaker on the ceiling.

"Okay, so everything is fine." Evan said, clearly frazzled. "Things are just messy up here. Henry, things are going to get bumpy for a few minutes. But please don't panic. I swear it's okay. I'm right here, babe. I love you, and I'll keep you safe no matter what."

The plane suddenly dropped again, but that's not what made my heart lurch.

"Did you say you love me?" I asked, knowing he couldn't hear me.

Evan kept talking. "I might not be King Kong, but I'd find a way to sprout wings and carry us both down safely before I let anything happen to you."

"Did you say you love me?" I repeated louder at the ceiling.

"Just hang tight back there, Henry. It's only a storm. This is completely normal."

"Did you just say you loved me?" I shouted as loud as I could, losing my patience with his inability to hear me.

He continued. "Well, not completely normal, considering I'm professing my love for the first time over an intercom with only Javier locked in the cockpit beside me, but the turbulence you are feeling is *normal*. Henry, I love you, and I'm gonna take care of you up here.

And as soon as I get us back on the ground, I'll say it to your face. Just hang tight for me, babe. It's all going to be okay."

The speaker cut off when he severed the connection, but I could do nothing but sit frozen, blinking at the ceiling.

I was vaguely aware of the plane dipping and shaking, but a wide smile covered my face.

"He did." I leaned back in my seat. "He said he loves me," I whispered to myself.

Robin's hand squeezed mine to catch my attention, "If he has to sprout those wings, you better take me with you." Her green face turned to Carter just in time for him to shake a puke bag out and pass it her way.

But I couldn't focus on the movement long enough to think about being airsick. I'm not positive I remembered I was on a plane.

He loves me.

It wasn't a novel concept. There was plenty of proof that he did. But the way I felt to have heard those words come from his mouth was indescribable. No matter if it had come over the intercom of a plane that could very well have been falling from the sky.

Evan loved me.

I'd go down with a smile on my face.

chapter twenty-nine

Evan

was out of my seat and barreling to the back of the plane before we made it to the gate. Javier was more than capable of taxiing us in.

The weather had been shit the whole flight. I'd managed to avoid the worst of it, but the air had been choppy as hell. Normally, it was nothing I'd be concerned about. You know, unless my boyfriend, who was already terrified of the normal bumps in the sky, happened to be with me. And then, in that case, the alarm bells might as well have been screaming like sirens in my head.

I'd told Henry that I loved him not because I'd feared something was wrong, but rather because it was a fact I knew with every fiber of my being. I'd been searching for the right way to tell him over the last week, but nothing I'd come up with had come close to doing my feelings justice.

I loved him. Wholly. Utterly. Permanently.

And, knowing he was in the back, losing his shit, I hoped that my words could offer him the comfort I was physically unable to provide him from inside the cockpit.

God knows telling him soothed my soul.

I could only pray that it had the same effect on him.

After I pushed through the door, I came to a screeching halt when he came into view.

I'd expected bad.

I'd expected panicked.

I'd even prepared for pissed off.

However, I'd never considered he'd be damn near giddy.

"Hey," I said, cautiously taking in his wide smile and his sparkling, blue eyes.

"Hey," he replied softly.

My feet started moving again. His gaze locked on me as I closed the distance.

"Are you okay?" I asked, dropping to my knees beside him. I smoothed my hands over his shoulders before tracing up his neck to frame his face as though I had been searching for a physical injury.

He silently held my stare, his eyes glistening as they searched mine. Just when his reaction began to unnerve me, he blurted, "I love you too."

A laugh sprang from my throat before I corrected him. "Evan."

His smile grew, and he threw his arms around my shoulders, pulling me off-balance until I was hanging over the leather armrest. "I love you too, *Evan*."

I closed my eyes and allowed his voice to wash over me, soothing me from the outside in. Or maybe it was inside out. Regardless, it reconstructed my heart.

Henry had made me whole again when he'd come into my life.

But, right then, he rearranged the pieces in a way that erased the past.

He still hadn't released me when the plane came to a stop.

Nor did he release me when the cabin door was opened.

And, as Carter and Robin made their way out, I was still tightly wrapped in his arms.

"I love you," I whispered into his ear. "And I'll tell you that every day for the rest of my life, but unfortunately, I have to remind you that we need to get to the hospital to see Levee."

His back shot straight and his arms fell away. "Shit. That's right." He unbuckled his seat belt and dug his phone from his pocket. "I'll text Sam and let him know we'll be there soon."

"I'll grab my stuff," I replied, backing toward the cockpit to retrieve my phone and my ball cap from the storage compartment.

"Hey, Evan?" Henry called. "Sam said she's crowning. What's that mean? He's sending me a picture."

I stopped at the door and waited for him to join me. "That's part of the birth, isn't it? I think it's when the baby's head first pops out."

His eyes flashed impossibly wide as he stopped in front of me. "Oh my God! He's going to send me a picture of her vagina!" He threw his phone at me as though it had been a bomb set to explode at any second. "You have to look at it. You liked that kind of thing once, right?"

I curled my lip and threw it back at him. "Fuck no! I liked pussy. Not childbirth."

He threw it back. "That's just semantics. Take one for the team!"

I pressed my lips together but finally gave in and lifted the phone into my line of sight.

My chest seized.

I didn't know Levee well. But she'd helped me get Henry back. That was one debt I'd never be able to repay. However, even without knowing anything else about her, like how much Henry loved her and she loved him, my smile still would have been unrivaled.

Sidling up beside him, I draped an arm around his waist and turned the phone his way.

On the screen was a picture of a beautiful baby girl with thick, brown hair feathering out from beneath a tiny, golden tiara while she blissfully slept in her mother's arms.

The caption at the bottom read *Hurry up, Uncle Henry. The princess needs a diaper change.*

"Oh my God," he breathed, pulling the phone from my hand to inspect the picture closer. "She's gorgeous."

I rubbed his back. "She really is."

"I'm an uncle." He lifted his eyes to mine, tears of joy sparkling in the sea of blue.

Pressing my lips to his temple, I murmured, "You ready to go meet her?"

"I just flew on a plane. And no offense to the pilot, but it was horrible," he announced randomly.

I tipped my head and smirked. "Well, no offense to the spoiled rock star, but it wasn't my fault."

His hand landed on my chest, and his thumb traced the ridge of my pec. "It was the best flight I've ever been on. I couldn't stop smiling. And laughing. I'm pretty sure Carter thought I'd lost my mind."

I swayed my head from side to side in consideration. "You told me you love me too. There's a strong possibility you did."

His gaze turned serious, and he leaned forward and nipped at my bottom lip. "I'll fly with you again."

"Good to know," I mumbled against his mouth.

He swept his tongue with mine before saying, "And, in the words of Optimus Prime, knowing is half the battle."

I leaned away, shooting him a frown. "Optimus Prime? Still?" I feigned injury, clenching my heart. "You're going to kill me." Using my other hand, I gripped the back of his neck and guided him out the plane door.

"Not today," he replied over his shoulder. "You promised me longer tonight, though we both know length is my specialty."

I released him when he took his first step down. Then, when he got to the second one, I slapped his ass. "All right, smartass. That's enough out of you."

When he reached the bottom, he turned to face me, his bright smile only outdone by his eyes. "Let's go meet our niece, Maverick."

And just like that, I realized that maybe my home wasn't in the sky anymore.

With Henry, I could soar with both feet on the ground.

epilogue

Henry

Five years later…

"Shawn!" **I called** from my chair behind the soundboard in my studio.

Evan was sitting beside me, his hand firmly planted on my thigh as he nervously spun his wedding ring.

Yep. We'd done it. Evan and I had gotten married in a quaint ceremony with only our immediate family and friends in attendance.

However, judging by his eyes when he saw the wedding plans, he hadn't considered four hundred guests, a horse-drawn carriage, and a castle in Scotland quaint or private. But like a trooper, he said not a single word as he walked away, shaking his head. Really, his only objection to the whole process was when I asked him to wear a kilt. I fully explained the merits of its easy access, but he wasn't buying it. And, as much as I would have enjoyed the kilt, he looked even more edible in a black Armani suit the day we said I do.

Shawn's dark-brown hair peeked around the corner before he slunk back out of sight.

A year after Evan and I had gotten married, I'd stopped touring. He hated being on the road all the time, even though we'd taken to flying a good bit. I loved performing, but I had to admit having a stable home with my husband sounded like the stuff fairytales were made out of.

And it was.

So fucking incredible.

Waking up with him. Wandering out to my private studio in the backyard. Levee coming over so we could write songs together, just like the old days. Then calling it a day and coming home to him.

Indescribable.

But, as the years passed and we watched Sam and Levee fill their bedrooms with two more girls, Evan and I both felt like something was missing from our lives. We thought about the whole surrogate thing. He loved the idea of little blond babies. Meanwhile, I'd have given anything for one with his dark complexion. However, yet another act of God made the decision for us.

Evan and I were huddled together on the couch one night when my manager contacted me about doing some charity work with a local afterschool program specifically for kids in the foster system. Given my upbringing, I jumped at the opportunity. That was the day I first laid eyes on the little boy who would become the rest of my life.

While I played for the group of about twenty-five kids, Dominic, with his dark-brown eyes and short, black hair, ignored me completely. He sat in the back of the room with a notebook in his hand and a pencil in his grip. For the intensity with which he looked at it, I was dying to see what was on that paper, so as soon as I was done with my set, I flipped my guitar over my shoulder and headed his way.

His eyes barely lifted to mine before he pasted on the attitude I immediately recognized as my own when I had been that age. The world had given him nothing, and that was exactly what he was going to give back.

I knew in that moment I was going to give that little boy the world. Whether it was talking to him about the numerous zombies he had scrawled across the page or purchasing him a new pair of shoes to show off to his friends in order to make him feel even an ounce of pride in himself, I was going to do it.

A lengthy discussion with Evan ultimately ended with us filing for the adoption of both Dominic and his five-year-old little brother, Shawn.

It was a long process before it was finalized, but eventually, all of our last names were Alexander-Roth.

Growing up, I had never really pictured myself as a parent, but besides marrying Evan, it was easily the best thing I'd ever done. Those boys expanded our hearts and then filled every possible crevice.

"Come here, buddy. You're not in trouble," I called to Shawn.

Evan's eyes snapped to mine in question, but I waved him off. That one interaction basically summed up our parenting style.

Evan was the hard-ass disciplinarian the boys so desperately needed. Meanwhile, I was, much to Evan's dismay, a little more lax and nurturing. I just didn't have it in me to punish them—and they knew it.

"Henry, he can't beat up other kids. You can't condone this," Evan whisper-yelled.

"His not being in trouble doesn't mean I condone it," I whispered back.

He pursed his lips and glared at me.

The squeak of sneakers against the tile came from around the corner where Shawn remained hidden, but it was Dom who appeared. "What's wrong with him?" he asked, handing me yet another school supply list.

What in the ever-loving hell these schools did with five million pencils and folders, I'd never understand.

"He got in a fight," I replied, passing the list to Evan.

Dom's eyes went huge, and his mouth formed a hard line. "Good. I hope he kicked both of their as—" His eyes jumped to Evan, who was leveling him with a scary—but kind of hot—scowl. "Er...butts," he finished.

"What do you know about this? Your brother won't tell me anything," Evan asked.

Dom sighed and glanced back at his brother, who was once again peeking around the corner at us. "Some kid at school was picking on him yesterday because you guys are gay."

"Oh, shit," Evan mumbled under his breath.

I twisted my lips and pressed a hand to my chest. "Well, technically, *I'm* gay." I flicked a thumb in Evan's direction. "Dad here is—"

Evan's hand flew out and covered my mouth. "You're not in trouble," he called to Shawn. Then he looked back at Dom. "Take your brother and get ready for bed. We'll talk about this later."

Dom smiled mischievously and backed away.

While I usually adored quiet time with Evan, the lasers he was shooting at me had me contemplating asking the boys to stay.

"What?" I finally asked when the heat—and not the good kind—became too much.

"You cannot tell our kids that I'm bisexual."

I spun my chair to face him and leaned forward, resting my hands on his thighs. "It's true though. Just because you abandoned the opposite sex doesn't change anything."

He shook his head and placed his hands on mine to stop them from sliding any higher. "Shawn blacked the kid's eye. And, if you'd seen him, you'd see his lip was split wide open."

My breath hitched and my stomach rolled. "He's in second

grade! Don't they still pull hair?"

"No. They don't," he said frankly. "This is serious, Henry."

Suddenly, I was starting to agree. "So, what do we do? Do they make a book for this? I'm willing to read some non-erotica if I need to."

He frowned, but the side of his mouth twitched. At least he still found me humorous.

He lifted my hand and gave it a tug until our rolling chairs collided; our mouths quickly followed. When we came up for air, he tipped his forehead to mind and said, "We need to call the school and let them know what happened. I won't stand for him being bullied by some little shit who's probably learning this crap from his homophobic parents."

My eyebrows shot up in surprise, and I chewed on the inside of my cheek to stifle a laugh. "Did you just call a kid a little shit?"

"He put his hands on my son!" he defended.

I patted his leg. "All right. Calm down there, papa bear. We'll hit up the principal first thing in the morning."

"Good, but in the meantime, we need to get in there and teach them that you can't cure ignorance with violence. They need to understand that love is love. Between a man and a woman, a man and a man, or a woman and a woman. And, babe, I know you consider yourself gay, but you know how I feel about labels. I sure as hell don't want the boys growing up thinking it's okay to cast them on others. This is our opportunity to teach them tolerance and acceptance."

Yeah. I'd lucked out big time with Evan.

I smiled. "You're incredible, you know that?"

He nodded, punctuating it with a kiss. "So you've mentioned."

"Sooo..." I drawled. "Just so we're clear, after we give the boys this talk and they go to sleep, we can still be gay in bed, right?"

He glared.

"It's a valid question! This sexy, protective side of you is doing some seriously dirty things to me."

Maintaining his stoic expression, he released me and stood from his chair.

I ogled his ass as he walked away.

Just before he rounded the corner, he paused and looked over his shoulder, his eyes filled with heat—the good kind. "If you hurry up and get your ass in the house and take my back on this, I'll do some seriously dirty things to you tonight."

I smiled impossibly wide and made a show of scrambling from my chair.

He laughed with wild abandon as I jogged in his direction. When I got close enough, he tossed his arm around my shoulders and kissed my temple.

"I love you."

Smiling, I shoved my hand in his back pocket and gratuitously groped his ass. "I love you too."

the end

Sam and Levee's story.

the fall up
Available Now

acknowledgements

Over the last eleven books, we have learned it takes a village for me to press publish. I feel like I've thanked the same people over and over again, and it's because I *have*. I'm one of the lucky few who has kept the same betas since I started writing. I've said thank you in a million different ways, but they deserve a million more. None of this would be possible without my team.

The brilliant betas: Ashley, Bianca, Bianca, Natasha, Megan, Amie, Miranda, Lakrysa, Mara, and Tracey.

The M/M experts: Abbey, Allison, and Taryn.

The proofreaders: Stacy, MJ, and Gina.

The editors: Erin Noelle and Mickey Reed.

The formatter: Stacey Blake.

The bloggers: All of you.

The readers: Yes, that means you.

See? That's a lot of people. And there are so many more it would take me another book just to thank them all.

So, in closing, I'd like to say ***thank you*** to the whole freaking village who make this career possible. I love you all!

about the author

Born and raised in Savannah, Georgia, Aly Martinez is a stay-at-home mom to four crazy kids under the age of five, including a set of twins. Currently living in South Carolina, she passes what little free time she has reading anything and everything she can get her hands on, preferably with a glass of wine at her side.

After some encouragement from her friends, Aly decided to add "Author" to her ever-growing list of job titles. So grab a glass of Chardonnay, or a bottle if you're hanging out with Aly, and join her aboard the crazy train she calls life.

Facebook: www.facebook.com/AuthorAlyMartinez

Twitter: twitter.com/AlyMartinezAuth

Goodreads: www.goodreads.com/AlyMartinez

Printed in the USA
CPSIA information can be obtained
at www.ICGtesting.com
LVHW022342291024
795187LV00032B/850

9 781533 171801